Other books by Kim Yesis:

Side by Side Tales from Behind the Canvas, a memoir

Artist in the Allagash, a wilderness journal

Coming Soon:

Brush with Fire
Book 2 of the Mayenne Bay Series Novels

Artifice

Book 1 of the Mayenne Bay Series Novels

KIM YESIS

Artifice
Copyright © 2025 Kim Yesis

ISBN: 979-8-9904549-1-0

Cover design by Charity Munoz, *www.charitymunoz. com*

Printed in the United States of America

For Peter

Map of Mayenne Bay

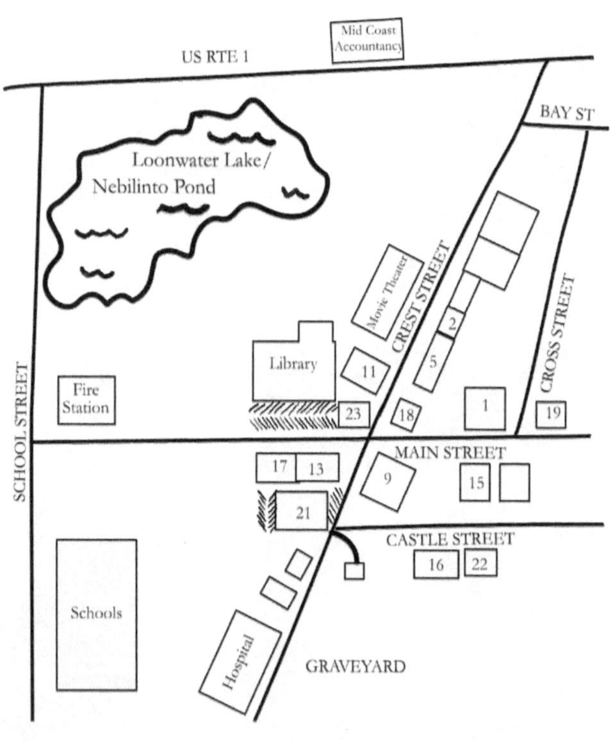

1-Bank
2- Bobby Tripp
3-Chamber of Commerce
4-Claire's Apartment
5-Consignment Shop
6-Creative Agenda
7-Fish House
8-Free Choice Hair Salon
9-Grace Grocery
10-Hardware Store
11-Historical Society
12-Main Street Coffee Bar
13-Mainsail Wine & Cheese
14-Mayor's House
15-Peabody Shoes
16-Police Station
17-Roxie's Frames
18-Salty Dog Toys
19-Seafoam Candy
20-Town Office
21-Unitarian Church
22-USPS
23-Vicki's Lingerie
24-Wharf Cafe

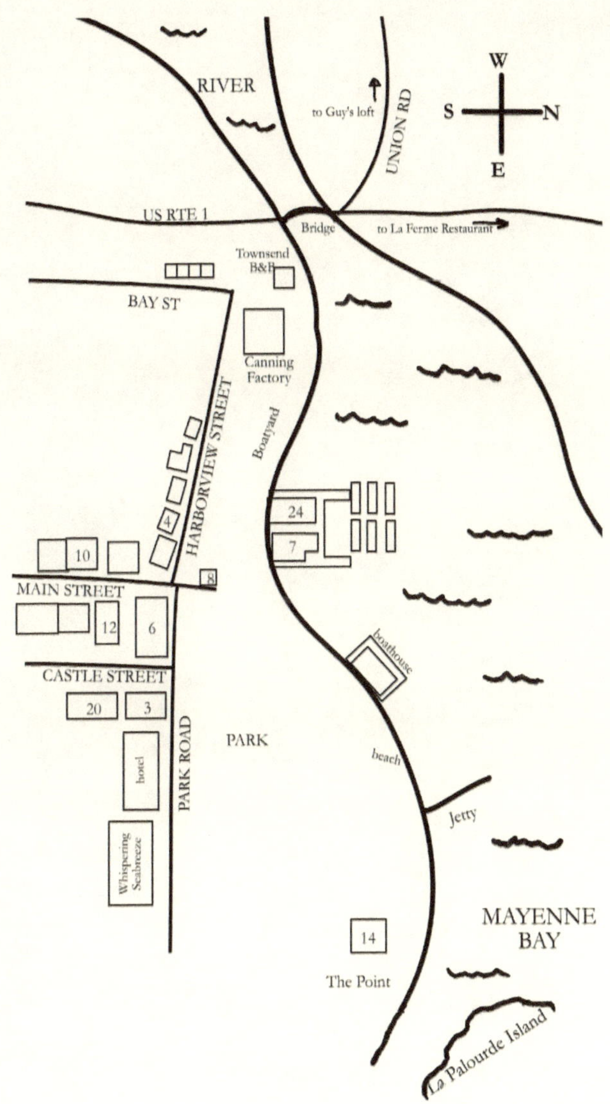

W
S
E
N
RIVER
to Guy's loft
UNION RD
US RTE 1
Bridge
to La Ferme Restaurant
Townsend
B&B
BAY ST
Canning
Factory
Boatyard
HARBORVIEW STREET
24
7
10
4
8
MAIN STREET
12
6
CASTLE STREET
20
3
hotel
PARK ROAD
PARK
boathouse
beach
Jetty
Whispering
Seabreeze
14
MAYENNE
BAY
The Point
La Palourde Island

1

Hungover

Claire Munro dragged the quilt off her body and lay motionless against the sheets. She loved the morning; she just hated starting it with a hangover. She'd had only one glass of wine last night, but her own temperance hadn't saved her from the lingering effects of a phone call from her mother. Her waking sluggishness bore testament to having, once again, indulged her mother's angst. She rose, padded her way into the kitchen and hung over the sink on her elbows where the dirty rag from last night's cleaning purge hung as limp as she felt.

From the time she was a young girl, Claire had been Hannah Munro's confidante. Claire hadn't asked for the job; she'd simply meant to be kind when, one evening after dinner, she'd discovered her mother crying alone in the kitchen. Claire had taken over clean-up while Hannah had poured out her heart. As the years passed, what had begun as an act of sympathy had devolved into a disturbing pattern of dependency. Hannah cried out for solace, and Claire dutifully sopped up her mother's tears like an old towel. Hannah went on her way unburdened, while Claire, drenched in vicarious emotion, was left to wring herself out.

The year Claire had turned thirteen, her father, Gerald Munro, had left the household, only to be replaced by a revolving door of Hannah's hopeless boyfriends. The most recent was a controlling freeloader from God-knew-where who put even Gerald's combative and drunken behavior to shame. Yet, Hannah didn't throw the sponger out. She just wasn't made of that kind of stuff. Instead, she recycled her despair in call after call to Claire. Claire had hoped living at a greater distance from her mother would discourage Hannah's calls. Instead, it had intensified them.

In exasperation, Claire had ended last night's conversation with a curt "Get rid of him, Mom" before jamming her thumb to her phone and slapping the device with a cathartic whack onto the kitchen table. After an interval of pacing and shaking out her limbs, she had snatched a rag and begun cleaning the kitchen cabinets in furious circular motions. The toxic energy had to go somewhere, or she would never sleep. While she worked, Claire spewed her frustration aloud, a habit formed over twenty-nine years of ministering to herself. But this time, her tirade ended in harsh self-reproach: "She's not the only one to blame; you've enabled her all these years."

Spoken plainly for the first time, the veracity of it had struck her like a splash of cold water. She'd stopped scrubbing, slid down to the floor and, not being one to skirt the truth even when it hurt, sat very still for a minute to fully feel the sting. She leaned the back of her head against the cabinet and regulated her breath, agitation finally giving way to fatigue. Then, she rose, tossed the rag into the sink and headed for bed. Sleep would come quickly now that she understood herself, now that she'd finally come to grips with what must be done. But the slumber that overtook her was overshadowed by a dread that still gripped her upon waking.

Through the window over the sink, the early April sunlight struck patches of spring grass and the stubs of early chives, alluring come-hithers into the fresh air. Claire returned to her bedroom to throw on clothes, so easy on a Saturday morning when the day had no set agenda. She gravitated to her favorites, uplifting yellows and blues that felt soft and fell loose over her slender frame. She wasn't a fan of makeup, and her short cut auburn hair took no time at all. Within minutes, she was making her way toward the blue water, mini-backpack over her shoulders.

She walked briskly. At the end of Harborview, she turned left onto Main Street and continued apace down to the boardwalk where the town's two dockside restaurants, the Wharf Café and the Fish House, competed for morning patrons. It was just a quarter past seven, but the harbor was awake from end to end, enlivened by the brilliant sunshine and the tide flowing in from the Gulf of Maine. All the ice formed during the harsh winter months had dissolved into a dazzling blue liquid except for a few spotty remnants still clinging to the shadows. Claire turned right toward the shoreline path in the park and allowed the vitality of the waterfront to work its usual magic on her soul.

Living near a real, working harbor was a new and engrossing experience for Claire. Mayenne Bay Harbor had once been a vital port of call with a huge commercial shipyard. Many deep-water sea captains had hailed from this town. Their handsome houses, each topped with its own style of rooftop lookout, stood up and down the shoreline in varying states of repair. The town center and port had, over a century ago, been decimated by a great fire. Mayenne Bay had risen from the ashes with a resilience Claire detected in its people today. Boatbuilding and commercial fishing survived the devastation, though on a much smaller scale, and though its glory days had come and gone, the town's maritime history endured in the minds and marrow of its native inhabitants.

As a refugee from New Jersey, Claire had only a

second-hand claim to this heritage but, since her arrival in February, just two months ago, she'd fallen in love with Mayenne Bay. It hadn't been love at first sight. With characteristic due diligence, she had scouted out the town the day of her job interview and spotted flaws aplenty. Tired school buildings, old firetrucks and vacant stores. Splintered park benches and a wind-battered boathouse. Economic woes and a housing shortage. The idyllic bay views were not enough to mask the town's struggle to redefine itself, to blend longstanding traditions with continued viability. This state of affairs had kindled a kinship in Claire's heart. She, too, was reinventing herself. That day, she had looked squarely at Mayenne Bay's blessings and blemishes and adopted the town as her own, warts and all.

Claire reached The Point, the tip of land that jutted farthest out into Mayenne Bay, and circled back through the now fully awakened park. A sweaty jogger with dreadlocks huffed by. A gray-haired man in a faded, green cardigan shuffled past clutching an old paperback tightly to his chest. A group of gangly teenagers kicked a soccer ball around the grass. Over on the wharf, small-boat owners slid their timeworn craft into the bay at the public ramp. Lobstermen made their way to and from the dock to load their traps. Further down, at the boatyard, she could see workers pulling huge pleasure craft from dry storage and hustling to restore them to their slips. Several seaworthy vessels were poised in front of a great cradle lift waiting to be conveyed back into the water. Others, the worse for wear, waited in the yard to be made fit for duty. The operation was impressive, even if it was only a remnant of what it once had been.

Claire's footsteps slowed to take in all the people who materialized around her. She'd never been able to curb her curiosity—her "flânerie" ("people-watching" sounded much more refined in French). It was one of her favorite pastimes. Others might call it prying or eavesdropping, but to Claire, human behavior was a captivating study, and she never tired of guessing what people's stories might be.

Sometimes, she didn't have to guess.

Strangers often approached her when she least expected it. She couldn't explain the reason. Did she look like a safe bet? The offspring of Fred Rogers? Did she secrete a special pheromone? She'd never found an adequate explanation but had long ago accepted this magnetism as one of her lots in life. Some people asked for directions or information and went on their way. Others sought a little company or a sympathetic ear. Still others carried a burden, a real problem to solve. Claire could never tell right off how things would go. On any given day, an encounter could prove a gift or a curse. She didn't have all the answers but did her best and met people with the same impulse of kindness that had first spurred her to listen to her mother.

After an hour of walking the park, her lassitude had fully lifted, but last night's underlying lesson held fast. Hannah would cling to her housemate and defend his parasitic presence with the same breath she drew to condemn him. And she would persist in unloading on Claire…unless and until Claire put an end to it. A fleeting hope arose in Claire's chest that an ultimatum might stir her mother to change. More likely, she knew, it would shred the tie spun of two decades of mother-daughter confidences. Tears of sadness filled Claire's eyes as she stared out at the bay, and a wave of resentment passed through her frame that a once gratifying bond had degenerated into an unfiltered free-for-all.

Was it any wonder her own life plan no longer included a partner? Twenty years of marriage had reduced Gerald to a drunken womanizer and Hannah to an emotional beggar who clung to every man she met. Not one marriage within the Munro family had lasted, except Claire's maternal grandparents, who were miserable. Claire's own attempts to find a mate had ended in utter flops, the first a user, the last a controller. Fearing she was headed for the same hamster wheel as her mother, she had simply stopped dating. It wasn't misandry; it was just high time to stop chasing a statistically improbable life and accept the one she had. The decision had determined her move north.

She had scoured online employment sites, spied "Accountant Needed – Mayenne Bay, Maine", and looked no further. The new job had been a lateral move but a personal declaration of independence. It sounded cliché—a woman escaping to a small town for a fantasy future—but Claire had no illusions. The miles that distanced her from her suffocating ex and her tumultuous childhood home—with the maddening exception of her mother's calls—afforded her a new, no-frills beginning. It was enough.

"Excuse me, Miss!"

Claire started in surprise and spun toward the voice. A tiny, well-dressed, white-haired woman approached. She bore a large, leather shoulder bag that made her gait a bit lopsided. Her eyes shone with intelligence, and her smile was broad.

"I'm sorry to intrude," the woman said pleasantly.

Claire dropped her eyes to her toes, an instant reaction to strangers learned over the years. She'd trained herself to gather her composure before responding to people. Though she believed in openness and honesty, unfiltered, they could be a tricky business. And she'd matured enough to allow that, though her insights were often right, they just might be wrong. A measured approach was best. She arranged her face into a welcoming smile and looked up at the old woman.

"Not at all. Can I help?"

"I haven't been back here for years," the woman told her with an admiring glance around the park. "I'm looking for a place to eat. Could you recommend a restaurant?"

"Of course," Claire answered readily. "Both the Wharf Café and the Fish House, on the dock, are very good." She pointed in their direction. "And there's a coffee shop up Main Street." She swung her arm the other way. "You really can't go wrong at any of them."

The old woman nodded her thanks and went on her way, torso waddling left and right with the unbalanced weight of the bag.

You really can't go wrong.

These parting words echoed in Claire's head, making her almost giddy. They were true for herself as well, here in Mayenne Bay, at least, so far.

2

Off the Hook

Guy Gardiner never relied on chance. His luck just wasn't that good. Every Saturday since his first glimpse of her in early March, he'd arrived precisely as the Fish House had opened and planted himself strategically with a view of the door. Maybe, just maybe, she would show up today. The approach was a little old school in a world of speed-dating and web hook-ups, but Guy was all for the intimacy and pace of up-close and personal.

The tiny, old fish-shack-turned-restaurant, aptly called the "Fish House", didn't exactly scream contemporary meet-up. Sitting inside was like breathing history. It had housed fishermen's gear for more than a century and afterward had served locals as a bait shop. The original shack, now severely weather-beaten, extended over the water on aged pilings. An addition had been constructed on the dock itself when the shack had been repurposed but even this could hardly be called new. Inside, the building had tired beams, worn floorboards and walls that were strung with old fishing nets and the chipped and faded buoys of retired lobstermen.

Guy traced his fingernail along a timeworn crack in

the stained wooden table and glanced around. The character of the place appealed to him. It had done the same for her, too, at least once. She had been leaving her booth just as he had been choosing his. He felt a bit foolish sitting here on this—his third—attempt to encounter an apparition that might never re-materialize but he clung to his plan like bait on a hook. What other choice did he have? He didn't even know her name.

He sat alone at this early hour, but the banging and clinking in the kitchen signaled the restaurant's anticipation of a full house. A flicker of reflective sunlight caught his eye as the door swung open. An attractive, thirty-something man in a fitted sport jacket stepped in, pen and notebook in hand. His crisp shirt and pants were incongruent with the usual informality of Mayenne Bay, especially on a Saturday morning. Guy instinctively looked down at his own attire: well-worn jeans, a soft, green flannel shirt and his favorite loafers—stripes he had no desire to change. He was uncomfortable enough in his own skin this morning without adding stiff clothing.

Not two minutes later, another flash of light signaled the entrance of a slight figure, about five-and-a-half foot tall. She wore jeans, sneakers and a pale, yellow sweater that offset a light olive complexion and auburn hair. Guy inhaled and straightened his back. *It's her.* He blinked a few times to be sure he could believe his eyes. The woman's unpretentious style grabbed his attention as fully as it had the first time he'd spotted her. She paused to adjust to the indoor light. Her large eyes—they were hazel—shone as they cast about the place and landed on a clean booth by the window, the same she had chosen last time.

Guy thrilled with his own shrewdness, having anticipated her table choice and seated himself nearby. He watched Hazel Eyes make her way to the booth, then slide her lithe form neatly onto the bench with her back to the door, oblivious to his fixation. She brushed back her chin-length hair with her fingers, closed her eyes, breathed deeply in, then out, and shook her shoulders, as if relieving tension. Eyes open again, she pulled a book from her backpack and opened it to a marked page. Finally, she reached for a menu, sat up straight and looked around expectantly for the wait staff.

Guy didn't have much experience with blazing concentration before breakfast, but the usual fog evaporated from his brain like water from a hot frying pan. This morning, right here, right now, was the very moment he'd sought, the kind everyone has from time to time if they're paying attention to life at all. His whole body warmed to it, and his heart pounded in his ears. But at the mere thought of speech, his jaw locked, his throat constricted, and his tongue swelled into an over-sized slug. Verbal paralysis was an affliction Guy had known all his life. Silence was his default position, and it unsettled him to no end when life demanded more, even if that "more" was his own doing.

Say something. Another man would.

He rolled his eyes at this, his own instinctive invocation of masculinity, as if just manning up and summoning testosterone would free his vocal cords. He dropped his eyes to the floor, drew in several gulps of air and endeavored to gather his nerve.

"Ready to order?"

Celeste Baptiste, the young Fish House waitress, interrupted Guy's concentration with her usual Pollyanna-like voice and rapid-fire litany of breakfast specials spouted in a single breath. Normally, Guy enjoyed chatting with Celeste. Today, his frustration choked his throat, and her ample bosom, which threatened to burst from the confines of her snug polo shirt, blocked his line of sight.

"Tea," he uttered hoarsely and randomly jammed his finger at the menu.

Celeste nodded, took the cue and whisked away to the kitchen.

His eyes again sought the floor where he hoped to find order for his jumbled thoughts. When he finally drew breath to speak and sat up intently to use it, the air gushed wordlessly from his lungs. A white-haired woman was making her way to Hazel Eyes' booth.

"Hello, again," called the woman as she neared.

Hazel Eyes swung her gaze from the window to the approaching visitor. Her hair followed obediently in a gentle arc, sparkling with shimmers of rusts, browns and golds in the morning light. Guy instinctively reached for his sketchbook, though what he really needed were a canvas and brushes. He caught the corner of a welcoming smile on her mouth and knew intuitively that the same welcome lit her eyes.

The old woman reached the booth and obstructed his view for the second time, but he heard Hazel Eyes speak.

"Why don't you join me?"

"How very kind," the visitor said and slid into the opposite bench. Her gaze roved over Hazel Eyes like a soft caress. "I noticed your hair in the park. Mine was the same color when I met my husband." She breathed audibly. "He died last year."

The silence that followed was broken only by faint clatter from the kitchen and the sport-coat guy on his cell phone.

Slumped in his seat, Guy groaned inwardly. The widow reminded him of those irritating people who dump their problems to the captive audience in the grocery line. He leaned in, straining to hear Hazel Eyes' response. *You're eavesdropping!* he reproved himself quickly and reached out to dunk his tea bag for cover. When had that cup arrived? God, he was a fool. Celeste was probably laughing her head off in the kitchen right now, but Guy couldn't help himself. He tightened his grip on his pencil and applied himself to the feeble subterfuge of sketching with one ear bent toward the two women.

"I'm very sorry," replied Hazel Eyes with a tilt of her head. "What was his name?"

"Robert. And I'm Georgia Wilson."

"Claire Munro," returned Hazel Eyes.

Claire. Guy let the name sink in.

Only as Georgia was winding up a half hour later did Guy jerk awake to the platter of crab omelet, hash browns and toast Celeste had deftly slipped onto his table. Heat collected around his face and ears for…he stopped counting how many times. He carelessly threw on some ketchup and dove into the tepid meal. By the time he wiped the last bit off his plate, his cheeks had cooled and he could hear Georgia tenderly thanking Claire.

Claire absent-mindedly fingered the corner of her book while she watched Georgia exit. Her expression vacillated between the bitter and the sweet of what she had just heard. Guy felt chastened for his earlier cynicism and even more fascinated. What kind of person welcomes a total stranger to her breakfast table? Now more than ever, he had to know.

Claire looked around as if finally awakened to the place and was startled to meet Guy's blue eyes. She acknowledged him with a self-collected nod. He nodded back, a brilliant scarlet again burning through his fair complexion from his neck up to the roots of his blond hair. He'd never been able to control this mortifying response and steeled himself to endure nature's little theater without losing eye contact. Had he been equipped with social graces, Claire's nod would have triggered words of charm, wit or intelligence. Guy was not such a man. His first move was always a crap shoot.

Why did you come here if not to meet her? rose his urgent, inner desire.

He threw the dice.

"I'll bet that doesn't happen often."

He leaned toward Claire to be heard over the growing noise in the room and forced a smile to cover the crack in his voice.

"What?" she asked, eyebrows raised.

"Hearing the life story of a complete stranger."

"Oh." She dazedly waved one hand. "People often stop to tell me their stories."

Her eyes dropped to the cup in her hands. From experience, Guy knew that silence was better than speech at this critical moment. Predictably, words failed him anyway. All he could do in his impotence was await his fate. He didn't look away from her, just in case.

All at once, she lifted her head. Something—perhaps his obvious embarrassment?—seemed to raise her confidence because she began to speak about her experiences with soul-baring strangers. Relieved from the pressure of speech, Guy really took her in—her expressive face, melodic voice and the graceful movement of her hands as she spoke. He perceived that she was taking him in, too, with a penetration that belied her ease of manner. First captivated by her appearance, he was now taken by her warmth with a second perfect stranger in the same morning. He listened without interruption until Claire abruptly stopped herself, twisted around fully on the bench and faced him, contrition on her face.

"I'm so sorry. I tend to run on when I'm given an opening." She followed these words with a wince.

"N-no," Guy stuttered in protest. "I find it interesting. I like the talking."

Claire threw him a doubtful look.

"Really," Guy persisted. "When someone else has

the floor, I'm off the hook." His mouth twisted into a wry smile. "I've been linguistically challenged since birth. I think I've got the listening part down, though." He followed this uncharacteristically wordy confession with a shrug.

Claire laughed.

"We're a sad combination, then."

"Or maybe a complement," Guy suggested, his tone intentionally playful. "I'm Guy Gardiner, by the way."

"Claire Munro."

And the ice was broken.

They chatted across the space between their tables. The conversation was disjointed at first and interrupted by passing diners and visits from Celeste but, after a time, it began to flow. As the tables filled up around them, it became difficult to hear. In a do-or-die maneuver, Guy grabbed his tea mug and art pack and slid onto the bench where Georgia had sat. His eyes searched Claire's for approval. They answered with hesitant consent.

The two resumed their conversation and drank tea and coffee for some time. Fellow diners came and went around them, but Guy and Claire lingered in the booth by the sunny window, calling Celeste over for refills.

"I think it's time to go," Claire whispered. "Poor Celeste is looking a little harassed."

"That's because she is." His tone was sharp, and he jerked his head toward the well-dressed man with the cell phone. "It's the outlander over there—'la-ROY', I heard Celeste call him, which I presume is just a fancy way of saying 'LEE-roy'. You've had your back to him. He's been hitting on her all morning."

Claire turned and frowned toward the man.

"Is that the investor everyone's talking about?"

"Think so."

She sunk one arm deep into her backpack as Guy raised his mug to drain the last swallow.

"Do you have the time? I can't find my phone."

He twisted his wrist toward his chest to look at his watch, forgetting the liquid in his mug. Cool, green tea spread unmercifully onto his shirt. He looked down at himself and shook with the frisson that traveled across his chest. His face turned white, then red again. He peeked up. Claire was giggling uncontrollably and reaching over to hand him a spare napkin.

"I'm sorry," she apologized sheepishly. "I don't think a comic could have timed that better. Good thing it wasn't hot."

In his haste to blot the wet spot, Guy rose and stepped back from the booth. He bumped into Celeste, who was just passing with a tray of dirty dishes on her shoulder, giving her a blind spot where he stood. An ear-shattering clatter drew the attention of every patron in the place. Patty Libby, the Fish House owner, and the dishwasher poked their heads out the kitchen door to find the source of all the commotion.

Now, in addition to the tea stain, Guy's shoulder and sleeve were smeared with pancake remains, cold scrambled eggs and syrup. He bent down to rub a toe struck by a fallen mug, then dropped to his hands and knees to pick up the mess alongside Celeste, who was struggling to maintain self-control. Wisps of dark brown hair stuck to her sweaty face, and hot tears formed in her eyes.

To add insult to injury, one plate—one single, tortuous, relentless plate—rolled under the nearest table and spun in a recurring rhythm against the dead silence the crash had induced. Wock, wock, wock, wock, the plate repeated mockingly. The two diners at the table sat stiffly as Guy reached past their legs to stop it. SLAP! The plate ended its dance, and the chaos was over—for the restaurant, that is. Guy was all turmoil.

He stood up again to the full five-feet, eleven inches

of his wiry height, just as the hum of conversation resumed, clearly fueled, judging from the many pairs of mirthful eyes on him, by derision. He brushed food from his shirt—nothing could be done about the syrup—but succeeded only in smearing. There was grease on his pant leg, dirt at the knees, and pancake bits stuck to his loafers. His face and neck were now the color of a beet. He choked for breath.

Claire, throughout this episode, had shaken in silent laughter to the point of tears in her eyes and an ache in her side. She had at first risen from her seat to help but, seeing Guy and Celeste had things well in hand, had sat back down to the role of spectator and given way to hilarity. She doubled over when Guy slapped the rogue plate into submission. But by the time he'd risen from the floor covered in dirt and breakfast, she'd disciplined herself back to sobriety. One look into his face, in fact, and all hint of amusement dissolved.

Guy lowered himself awkwardly into the booth and ever so slowly made eye contact.

"I'd better…" he faltered.

"Yeah," she answered.

Lips pursed and brow furrowed, her gaze dropped for the second time to the cup in her hands. Guy watched her and waited in silence for the inevitable. Two for the Guinness World Records today—shortest relationship…ever…and the only one ended by cold eggs and pancakes. After what felt like an eternity, Claire raised her head.

"My place is just around the corner. If you'd like, you can get cleaned up there," she offered in a single breath.

Guy's mouth dropped open, but no sound followed.

They rose and made their way to the door, ignoring the still gawking crowd. At the cashier's desk, Claire paid, then stood aside while Guy did the same. He mumbled an apology to Patty for the mess and left a huge tip for the beleaguered Celeste. They stepped out onto the boardwalk in awkward silence and turned up Main Street.

Along the way, Guy repeatedly cast sideways glances at Claire. The little experience he had with women told him they dared more with him because they sensed they were safe. This had to account for Claire's invitation. How threatening could a man be covered head to toe in food? Incredible as it was, after the fumble in the restaurant, he was still in the game. He took heart in this. After all, a man had to play to his strengths.

3

As the Crow Flies

Leroy Hood pocketed his phone and slipped out of
the Fish House, not bothering to disguise his annoyance at
the din caused by the clumsy man and busty waitress. He
headed for the park where he paused to withdraw a small
notebook and pen from the inside pocket of his sport coat
and began to scribble down observations. Leroy had first
arrived on the scene in early March, before the air had
shaken off its persistent chill. He had since wandered the
town at all times, day and night, observing and jotting notes,
even in blowing snow. Not for the first time, his pen dwelled
overlong on the no-frills, public boat ramp and the worn
structures and overall plebeian aura of the park.

A soccer ball streaked past his ear, immediately
followed by a pack of unkempt adolescents. "Sorry, Mister",
called a blonde girl with a ponytail. She was echoed by the
tall, dark-skinned boy at her heels. The rest ran by in silence,
casting uneasy peeks at Leroy, whose upper lip had raised in
a sneer. He turned his back to the kids, smoothed his jet-
black hair and straightened his jacket, as if to disassociate
himself from something unclean. Then, he returned to his
examination of the park.

Like almost every other small town along the coast

19

of Maine, Mayenne Bay struggled for a sustainable economy. Long-standing, traditional industries like fishing and boat-building were insufficient to gainfully employ all the town's inhabitants. Tourism provided a seasonal boost but was both competitive and fickle. Most new businesses that had ventured to gain a foothold had not lasted. In their wake, the failures had left a landscape dotted with empty buildings and a disappointed populace with little trust in outside investment.

Many inhabitants were descendants of generations of Mainers, working for modest wages. Others were newcomers who brought with them elevated employment and lifestyle expectations. The latter tended to land higher-paying, professional jobs. They swooped in, bought up old houses at inflated prices and remodeled—often embellished—them. On one hand, it was hard to resent the influx of money and the facelifts to worn out structures. On the flip side, improved properties raised values and triggered tax increases, making homeownership more expensive and even elusive for some. While the town council celebrated augmented revenues, many residents strained to hold onto their homes.

The prevailing feeling of insecurity had catapulted thirty-five-year-old Sandra Edgecomb into the mayor's office on a platform of economic development and improved housing. Sandra had all the right credentials—those that mattered to Mayenne Bay voters, anyway. Born and raised in town, she had graduated from Mayenne Bay High School and earned her business degree from the University of Maine. After ten years in business management at a Massachusetts firm, she had returned to the waterfront home she'd inherited from her parents. Sandra was a known entity, homegrown and rooted enough to give her a personal stake in the town's future. Her affection for her hometown had been amplified, not weakened, by a decade spent living out of state. It didn't hurt, too, that she outshone her uninspired predecessor and contender in both imagination and energy. Sandra, the voters had agreed, would find the answers.

As she did on most Saturdays, Mayor Edgecomb spent the morning in her office. From her window looking over the park, the sight of Leroy Hood in the course of his daily ritual curved her painted lips into a smile. She doubted he was aware his close scrutiny of the town populace was a two-way street. Beneath the veneer of small-town complacency, the natives were alert to his presence. Hardly a person in town had not seen or spoken of the handsome, well-dressed businessman with the southern drawl energetically courting town leaders with a plan for their future. Not all had equal faith, but some, like Sandra, predicted Leroy would be the town's salvation.

She looked down at the April 4th town council meeting minutes grasped in her hand. The council had, after heated debate, consented to grant Leroy a confidential executive session to present his real estate development proposal. It was a win worth savoring. With the council's support assured, Leroy would soon have a free hand on the rudder, and the mayor's promises would become reality. The May 2nd executive session couldn't come fast enough.

Four members of the public had strenuously objected to taking Leroy's scheme behind closed doors. Old Jay Brown put forth his usual argument that taxpayers had a right to know all of Mayenne Bay's municipal affairs. He delivered a similar citizen rights message at every meeting, so Sandra and the council had listened more out of courtesy than for substance. The statements of Meilin Li, owner of the Creative Agenda art supply store, flanked as she had been by Roxanne Nadeau, owner of Roxie's Frames and Peggy Cyr, town librarian, had been more difficult to dismiss. The three women held the respect of the community and spoke eloquently in favor of measured development fitted to the town as well as open deliberations over Leroy's…or any… proposed project.

Leroy had countered that a private session was necessary to protect his bargaining position once his proposal was disclosed. His charismatic self-defense and carefully reasoned argument combined to make a strong case and cast him in a very favorable light. Though the detractors spoke well—so well that Sandra had felt compelled to openly throw her backing to Leroy—the motion in favor of the executive session had cleared by a unanimous vote. Now she and the town council alike eagerly awaited the intimate details of Mayenne Bay's path to deliverance. Sandra's mouth curved mischievously. She wouldn't object to some intimacy with Leroy in the process.

Sandra hadn't thrown her political weight lightly. She'd caught wind, through her able assistant, Sally Eaton, who kept her ear close to the ground, of street talk antipathetic to Leroy. Leroy was an unknown, an outsider, and Mayenne Bay was slow to embrace new people. Yet, to Sandra, he was exactly what they needed at this critical juncture. With the town's coffers dangerously low and the ever-present threat of unemployment and homelessness, there was no time to smooth ruffled feathers and staunch bleeding hearts. Meaningful development would not be wrought by soft-pedaling and capitulation; it required cold calculation and real daring. There would inevitably be mistakes and possibly casualties, but the pains and sacrifices would all be for the long-term good of the community at large. Leroy seemed to apprehend this as fully as Sandra.

Property owners like herself had been Sandra's fiercest supporters in the election and were Leroy's champions now. Solidifying the town's finances to bolster infrastructure and attract business was essential to its— their—future well-being. The mere rumor of a potential investor had brought many to Sandra's door. If the town council stalled for general approbation from the townspeople, the opportunity might be lost altogether. The voters had elected Sandra to do the job and would simply have to trust her. Anyway, she reasoned, they wouldn't be able to argue with success.

Leroy turned and looked in the direction of Sandra's office window. Her heart jumped. His good looks and virility were unmistakable even at this distance. The mere memory of his cologne intoxicated her. She tossed the minutes onto her desk and moved to the mirror hanging behind her office door. She was a pretty woman, generally attentive to her appearance. Leroy gave her additional motivation. A shiver ran through her thin frame as she checked her lipstick and brown, upswept hair. Leroy was, without a doubt, bewitchingly manly and attractive, but the real draws were his intelligence and drive. Sandra sensed he was the kind of man who succeeded.

She left her office hoping to cross his path, as she sometimes did. She traversed Castle Street, took the alleyway between the Main Street Coffee Bar and Creative Agenda, and made her way toward the waterfront, taking in the town. As she strained her neck for Leroy, Sandra was waylaid by Jay Brown, still spewing the same blather against the closed-door executive session he had begun at the town council meeting. Jay visited the mayor's office frequently and had recently begun buttonholing her in public places as well, where he calculated her response would be more measured and accommodating.

"Jay, the thing is done," she said flatly.

He grunted and drew breath to renew his pitch.

Sandra managed to escape just in time by latching onto Police Chief Manning as he passed by, on the pretext of hearing the latest police reports. She threw the chief a conspiratorial, sideways glance, took his arm and forcibly accelerated his pace. The chief, both amused and sympathetic, compliantly gave way. Jay had no choice but to withdraw arms, but Sandra knew she'd bought herself only a temporary reprieve. The persistent old-timer streamed only one channel, seven days a week.

At the bay end of Main Street, Sandra waved off the chief and continued onto the boardwalk, searching. No Leroy. She climbed the steps to the Fish House where Leroy was a frequent patron due more, Sandra suspected, to its shapely waitress than anything else. Through the window, she spied a few lingering diners and Celeste, tired and disheveled from a hectic morning shift, furiously wiping tables. Most likely, she had once again served the entire dining room single-handedly.

Celeste was the poster child for Sandra's economic development initiative. Like most businesses in town, the Fish House ran on a chronically strained, skeletal staff, its ineffectual "Now Hiring" sign in the front window worn and faded by time. Patty treated her employees well and often rolled up her sleeves to work alongside them. It was not always enough. Many residents, especially the young, were leaving town for more fertile ground and the promise of a more certain future. Citizens needed more than a stunning shoreline; they needed an economic reason to stay. This was exactly why Leroy's project deserved support. If she had it in her power, Sandra would call the executive session this very day.

But where was Leroy?

She dropped down the Fish House steps and scanned the boatyard area. There! Conspicuous in his sport jacket, Leroy checked his Rolex, then greeted…who was that? It looked like Jack Wayne, the town manager. On a Saturday? Leroy exuberantly shook hands with Jack, who seemed subdued by comparison, even self-conscious. *As well he might be*, Sandra thought soberly. A weekend meeting with a prospective contractor was unusual by itself, and she hadn't been informed, which Jack knew was protocol.

At that moment, Meilin Li exited the park path onto the wharf, stopped and squinted toward Leroy and Jack, now in close conversation, then headed up Main Street toward her store. Sandra winced, apprehending the optics. The very last thing she needed was to have the project mired down in false impressions or unfounded misgivings. Meilin had leveraged her credibility well before the town council last week. Sandra couldn't help respecting both the woman and her business acumen, regardless of their present political differences, but nor could she allow Jack's and Leroy's indiscretion to strengthen such an influential adversary. She would follow up with both men on Monday.

She turned for home just as a masked figure, dressed all in black, his arms encircling a potted plant, whisked by. He dashed up Main Street and made a right onto Harborview. Sophie, Mayenne Bay's florist, followed on the runner's heels in hot, though far less speedy, pursuit. At the sight of the mayor, she stopped in surrender and leaned over at the waist to recover, arms braced against her knees. Her breath came in labored puffs as she tried to speak, half laughing, half exasperated.

"Are you alright, Sophie?" Sandra asked, approaching.

"Yes, I'm fine," Sophie gasped. "The little devil. It was stupid to chase him. I reacted without thinking when he grabbed the plant. Left the store completely unattended."

She glanced back toward her florist shop, threw up her hands and laughed out loud.

"Do you want to call the police?"

Sandra reached into her pocket for her cell phone.

"No, thanks," Sophie answered, holding up her hands. "He's just a prankster. He's struck a few times around town, taking stuff—for the dare, I guess—but it always turns up somewhere. There's a contest going to see who catches him first. Doesn't look like I'm going to win, does it?" She laughed again. "The Fish House is taking bets to benefit the restorative justice program. I put ten dollars on the new rookie, Ben Tripp."

Sandra stared at her with a mixture of concern and wonder at her complacency.

"I had no idea," she said, embarrassed. A mayor should know what was going on in her town. "I'll make sure Chief Manning is aware."

Sophie stretched her back, shook her head and gave a dismissive wave.

"Oh, the chief knows. He placed a bet on Ben, too. The bandit is harmless. That plant will turn up unharmed if he's true to form. Anyway, I'm sure you've got more pressing matters with the executive session coming up and all."

Sandra recognized the thinly veiled appeal for information but simply nodded.

Sophie's voice dropped to a conspiratorial whisper, and she jerked her head toward Main Street.

"Just so you know, Jay is headed this way."

Sandra's head turned. There he was, marching toward her, a man on a mission. The threat of being cornered again refocused her. She moved quickly along the wharf toward the boatyard to put as much distance as she could between herself and Jay…and to find Leroy and Jack. She wasn't about to have anything else going on in her town without her knowledge.

4

Deck's Watch

Meilin unlocked the door to Creative Agenda and flipped on the overhead lights. She stuffed her purse behind the counter and headed directly for the coffee machine to brew a pot. As the machine gurgled, she returned to the storefront to re-fasten the drooping Mayenne Bay Art Show poster and to check the overall window display. Then she poured her first mug of coffee—the only one she would drink in peace all day—and began her daily ritual of wandering the aisles, restoring out-of-place items to their rightful shelves and scrutinizing the work of last night's cleaning service.

Meilin liked starting the day by putting the store in shipshape condition, a remnant of her days as an art gallery owner when her livelihood depended heavily on visual appeal. She had to admit that, in a retail store, showcasing and even simple orderliness proved far more elusive, but she had grown used to the challenge by now. She ended her tour at the counter where she leaned over onto her elbows and sipped leisurely from her mug.

The store was soothingly quiet in the morning hours before the hectic Saturday rush. She usually took advantage of this interval of solitude to clear her head and reflect in a sort of abstract meditation. Today, her thoughts were closer to earth. Her sighting of Leroy Hood and Jack Wayne conferring on the wharf was foremost in her mind. It was odd that they would conduct town business on a Saturday, but the men's talk had appeared anything but casual. She had perceived the mayor's discomfort, first over the men's rendezvous and then over Meilin as witness to it. Perhaps the meeting hadn't been officially sanctioned. She and Sandra were on opposite sides of the Hood development scheme but, this morning, they had shared a feeling of disquiet. What did it mean?

Leroy was keen, sophisticated and articulate, clearly intent on success, but otherwise a stranger. Jack was a native and, as town manager, had a lot of say when it came to Leroy's project. He was not, in Meilin's estimation, a man of unassailable principles, judging from his past pattern of capitulation to the overriding influence of the moment. Nor was he a match for the persuasive powers of a man like Leroy. The combination of Jack's limitations and Leroy's ambition gave Meilin pause. Was she overreacting? Perhaps, but these, commingled with the conspiracy of silence within the town's government, did not engender confidence.

She was fully conscious of her own bias; she was heavily invested in the town's future and would rise and fall with its fortunes. All of the proceeds from the sale of her urban-Connecticut art gallery—offloaded in the nick of time before the 2008 economic downturn dealt the art world a serious blow—had been put to work on her Mayenne Bay home and store. Now, Creative Agenda was thriving, and the renovated apartments above were full. As much as any other business or property owner, Meilin was counting on the mayor's economic initiative to secure and grow her investment.

But not at any cost.

She loved her new home. At first a standout due to

her Chinese-American features, she had been met with overt curiosity and a guarded welcome. She'd expected as much in a place so unused to diversity but had simply pressed on with her business and, later, her activism. Gradually, she had earned respect, and hearts had warmed—not all, but enough that Meilin now felt she belonged to this town. She couldn't pinpoint the precise moment her assimilation had been achieved but knew herself now to be accepted as a regular citizen. As the only person of Asian descent among 4000 inhabitants, she constituted .00025 of the town demography—not much of a statistical presence, but it was enough for getting on. Anyway, Meilin knew how to make herself heard.

Long before Leroy's arrival, she had discerned what the town's leaders either overlooked or minimized: Mayenne Bay's idyllic maritime setting and small-town atmosphere were intrinsically valuable to its economy. These assets, qualities they all saw and felt every single day, had not surfaced at all in the council's recent public discussions about development, so focused were the mayor and council on Leroy's grandiose ideas. Meilin held that economic development should not require the sacrifice of what made Mayenne Bay attractive in the first place. It was in the town's long-term interest to preserve and capitalize on its present attributes and not to blindly or ham-fistedly snuff out their allure. Small, sustainable enterprises, Meilin had argued to the council, were a more viable solution for Mayenne Bay's recovery. Her own thriving store was just such an example. In this sentiment, she was joined by Roxie, Peggy and many others, but the mayor and council had turned a deaf ear.

In January, well before Leroy's arrival two months later, Meilin, Peggy and Roxie had formed a committee to collaborate on the launch of the town's first annual art show. They had meant this undertaking to model the economic potential of small ventures. Their pitch to the town council claimed an art show would draw visitors and increase traffic to businesses in town without detrimental effect to Mayenne Bay's character or charm. It would generate good press and improve, possibly define, the town's brand. Despite all these advantages, winning the argument for this "penny-ante endeavor", as one of the councilors coined it, had been an uphill climb.

One aspect of the proposal had drawn the council's particular censure. Fearing low turnout for the show's inaugural year, the committee proposed an easy registration process with no pre-entry judging. Even obscure artists with scant bios, whose only credentials were their sample works, could participate. The council had pounced on these indiscriminate standards and predicted embarrassment for the town. In the end, the mayor had swayed the vote in the committee's favor. The inclusion of amateur art, she had argued, would be far less embarrassing than a dearth of submissions. Besides, there was value in all economic stimulus for the town, regardless of size. It had been a weak win for the art show committee, but a win nonetheless.

In the wake of that battle, just as the committee got the art show underway, Leroy had arrived on the scene. Even before the April 4th town meeting, the rumor mill had rumbled about a possible construction plan at the present site of the old fish canning factory, a tantalizing, double silver bullet to uplift the economy and discard an old relic at the same time. Concerned about putting all the town's eggs in the proverbial single basket, Meilin had delved into the Mayenne Bay Area Chamber of Commerce records about earlier initiatives of similar size. Not one had survived. Bigger had not proved inherently better. Smaller endeavors, like Grace Grocery, Creative Agenda, Roxie's Frames and the art show, tended to have greater staying power. And they didn't compromise the waterfront. Meilin chafed, having watched Leroy steamroll ahead without impediment and, now, prepare to slip behind closed doors with a council predisposed in his favor.

She rocked back on her heels and allowed herself a moment to gloat. The art show committee's predictions looked likely to be validated. The June 1st submission deadline was weeks away, and they were already flooded with artist registrations—so many that the committee had to scramble to secure additional exhibit space. There was some amateur work, but the greater percentage involved seasoned talent. Mayenne Bay's own art club was abuzz with activity. Bookings at the local B&B and hotel were up for the weeks covering the exhibition. Artists from all around were suddenly painting in the park and along the boardwalk. And the media's interest had been warm and constant since the idea was first made public. Meilin sniffed her indignation. She wouldn't hold her breath for a pat on the back from the council.

Her phone jingled a sea shanty tune, signaling it was ten o'clock, time to face the public. She flipped the door sign over from CLOSED to OPEN and went to refill her coffee mug. The bell over the door chimed behind her. Rhonda Grace, a senior at Mayenne Bay High School famed for her colorful paintings of cats, stepped in. Rhonda had been the first member of the art club to register for the show and often assisted Meilin in the store.

"Good morning," Rhonda called. "I wasn't sure if you needed help today, so I thought I'd swing by."

"I swear you're psychic," joked Meilin. "We got a truckload of new stock yesterday. It's in boxes out back. Want to get started on that?"

Rhonda headed for the storage room as the doorbell sounded a second time and a third. It didn't stop ringing until four o'clock when the stream of shoppers finally trickled to an end. Creative Agenda was so well patronized, Meilin had to wonder how Mid Coast craftspeople and artists had survived before it opened. After Rhonda's exit, Meilin flipped the door sign back to CLOSED, turned the latch until it released its distinctive click and watched Rhonda beeline for Grace Grocery, her parents' store at the corner of Main and Crest.

Main Street was almost empty now. How quickly Mayenne Bay settled down on a Saturday evening before the tourist season. Its people weren't indolent; they just knew when to quit, an aspect of the town's life that had drawn Meilin to it. She wasn't one to pine for a city that never slept. She had lived that life and found it exhausting in ways her long retail hours could not equal. Mayenne Bay's off-season schedule had a rhythm fitted to the place, like the coming and going of the tide. In a few weeks, when Memorial Day arrived and "the Season" was again upon them, there would be no end to the activities deemed necessary to entertain tourists well into the evening. It made her wonder why they came if their coming meant transforming this place into the very thing they left behind.

She lingered at the door window for a while longer to watch the waning activity outside. From the direction of Harborview Street, she saw Guy Gardiner approach his car. They traded waves. Oddly, among art show registrants, a few local artists were missing. Guy was one. Meilin couldn't understand his reticence. He'd done the graphics work for the striking art show poster, so he'd known about the event longer than most, and he was exactly the caliber artist that would boost the show's prestige. Meilin made up her mind to corner him about it.

While she closed out the register and cleaned the coffee pot, her thoughts returned to her morning sighting on the wharf and the mayor. Sandra's public endorsement of Leroy Hood had heavily influenced the council's vote for a confidential executive session. This had been quite a blow to the opposition, but Meilin felt she should have seen it coming. Sandra Edgecomb was a capable, intelligent woman with the town's interests very much at heart. Meilin could even say she liked her and agreed with her on most matters. But Sandra turned to a jellyfish in Leroy's company. With the mayor in Leroy's thrall, regardless of the woman's sharp brains and good intentions, Meilin sensed vulnerability and feared the consequences. In her estimation, the combination of a conflicted mayor, a compromised town manager and an ambitious investor, operating under cover, threatened to end in shipwreck.

She felt her skin crawl. Haste. Secrecy. Impaired judgment. The town citizenry had been waiting a long time for revitalization and had endured a great deal of privation in the process. Some simply left. Most stayed and squeaked through, year after year, determined not to abandon the town. They deserved, at a bare minimum, forthrightness and clear-thinking from their leaders. For this reason, Meilin, alone and unsanctioned, anointed herself officer of the deck on permanent watch. As a business and property owner and a chamber of commerce member, she had the advantage of being close to the inner circle. She would keep her eyes and ears open and make her watchfulness known, much as she had done this morning when Leroy had met with Jack. She would monitor the progress of Leroy's plan and continue to argue in favor of transparency. She would enlist everyone she could into the same cause.

She tucked her dark hair behind her ears, raised herself up fully to her five-foot two-inch height and squared her small shoulders. "...though she be but little, she is fierce," she said aloud, quoting Shakespeare, then laughed. There was no one else present to witness her pledge or share in the joke, but then she had chosen a solitary duty. So much rode on the outcome of Leroy's proposal. She just had to make sure his project was something Mayenne Bay could undertake without sacrificing its very best.

5

Catch of the Day

It was late afternoon by the time Guy left Claire's apartment and returned to his car on Main Street. Once he was out of sight, he leapt and punched the air, looked around self-consciously, then covered the remaining distance with more restraint. He spied Meilin at the door window of Creative Agenda and waved, hoping she hadn't witnessed his boyish outburst.

He had followed Claire to her place, the lower level of a Federal-style house on Harborview Street, and entered through the front foyer. He'd parked his backpack by the door and followed Claire to a hallway bathroom. The tea blotches on his shirt clung uncomfortably to his body, and his sticky loafers made a tacky sound with each step. When Claire flicked the bathroom switch, the light almost blinded him. The walls and fixtures were bright white, unchecked except by a daisy shower curtain, a spring-green rug and towels to match. It was the cleanest bathroom Guy had ever seen. He stepped inside and removed his soiled shirt, feeling a bit guilty dropping it into the pristine sink. Claire disappeared, then reappeared thirty seconds later with a large, navy-blue T-shirt, a washcloth and a towel. He

35

accepted them wordlessly and closed the door, only now realizing how strongly he smelled of bacon.

Guy's knees twitched as he scrubbed. He'd come to Claire's place under the lame excuse of sullied clothes. Entering a woman's home—for any reason—after only a few hours of chat had not, up until this point in his life, ever happened. Not even once. Yet, here he was, staring at his half-naked image in Claire's glimmering bathroom mirror. The whole morning had been a bit surreal.

Ten minutes later, his shirt was rinsed, his pants clear of food and his loafers ready to resume their soundless tread. Guy stretched his washed shirt over the shower rod next to the damp cloth and towel and checked that everything looked as clean as when he had entered. He stepped out and headed hesitantly toward the noise down the hall. He had sensed a growing uneasiness in Claire as they had made their way here, as though she regretted her invitation. He held his breath now, uncertain of her next move.

Claire's weak smile as he entered her kitchen was confirmation enough that she had acted impulsively at the Fish House. Guy was surprised and a bit confused to see she had nonetheless cobbled together a respectable lunch and spread it on the table. Hospitality had overridden disquiet, for the time being. He checked his watch. It was already noon. Even his body clock was having trouble keeping up today. At Claire's gesture, he lowered himself onto a chair, one of four around a small round table covered with a plaid cloth, while she turned to the whistling tea kettle.

Guy took in the room. It was clean and unpretentious but extraordinary in its effect. The polished wood floor positively shone. Sunlight poured through the ample windows, illuminating pale yellow walls and bright white cabinets and trim. A brick-red door warmed the room with reflective light. Salty bay breezes seeped in through the partially opened windows, gently ruffling white curtains and the leaves of several vibrant houseplants before passing over to cool his heated face. Cobalt-blue accents dotted the room in startling contrast to its soft backdrop. Guy couldn't detect a dark or dusty corner anywhere, nor did a single item appear to be out of place. There was a quiet orderliness to Claire's kitchen and an atmosphere that radiated something like honesty.

He snuck a sideways glance and was relieved to find himself safe from her penetrating regard. He recalled an article he had seen about how, over time, a home takes on the personality of its owner. He'd dismissed the notion as a psychological fiction and the work of an overactive imagination. Now, as he surveyed this kitchen, he found himself wondering at the wisdom of it. Open. Soothing. Bright. Was he describing the room or Claire? Both, he concluded. He winced at the stories his own kitchen would tell and made a mental note to find and read that article…and to clean his apartment.

Claire set a mug in front of him. The revitalizing fragrance of steeped peppermint wafted into Guy's nostrils. In his nervousness, he sipped too soon, but the tongue-searing served to restore his attention fully to his present company. She sat down and motioned to him to help himself. There was an awkward silence while they filled their plates.

"Can I see your sketchbook?" Claire asked abruptly.

"What?"

He dropped a pad of butter onto his pant leg—he seemed destined to wear more food than he ate in Claire's company—then scooped it back onto his plate before silently rising to retrieve the book from his pack in the entryway. Claire brushed some crumbs aside, laid the book down on the clean surface and slowly began to turn the pages.

"Is this me? And Georgia Wilson?"

"Uh, yeah." Guy shifted awkwardly and colored. "Just for practice."

"Practice?" she repeated and resumed her page-turning. "These don't look like practice. It must feel great to be able to do this. I don't have hobbies…unless you count reading and herb-gardening."

Guy looked into a face so artless it was both intimidating and sweet at the same time.

"Why wouldn't they count?"

"They're not creative. They don't involve talent."

"Not everybody has a green thumb. And what about your talent with people? You made Georgia feel good. I saw it on her face."

It was Claire's turn to blush.

"Listening to a sad, old widow isn't a talent. Her heart just spilled over…though not the way you did this morning." She barely suppressed a giggle.

"Very funny," he retorted, relieved to be able to enjoy the joke with her now.

"That was slapstick comedy."

"It's all in the timing," he answered sportingly, then quickly changed the subject.

"So, you're a counselor, of sorts?"

Claire shook her head.

"I studied counseling alongside accounting, but nothing came of it. I've always been fascinated by people and lend an ear to the occasional stranger."

"But you do more than listen. I heard you with Georgia." Guy froze, instantly regretting this admission. "It was…hard not to," he mumbled the fib, remembering his conspicuous eavesdropping.

Claire seemed not to notice.

"Sometimes I think of something useful, but most

people do the lion's share themselves once they have a safe zone to talk freely."

It was Claire's turn to change the subject.

"What about you? What made you start drawing?"

Guy choked. No woman, other than his mother and sisters—and they didn't count—had ever before invited him to talk open-endedly about himself.

"I've drawn as long as I can remember. It's the only thing that has ever motivated me. Lately, I've been thinking I'd like to paint professionally, so I've been working more sketching and painting practice into my schedule."

"You paint, too?"

"Yes, in between projects. I do graphic design from home."

Claire tilted her head.

"That's solitary work."

"Yeah, but I don't mind. I struggle with conversation."

Her eyebrows rose.

"You've been talking all morning."

"I have, but believe me, this is not my norm. I've never met anyone as easy to talk to as you."

He ended breathlessly. The woman seemed to draw everything out of him. Was this what strangers experienced? Guy stared down at the peppermint dregs in his cup. Here he was, a tongue-tied, thirty-year-old man, still trying to figure out what he wanted to do when he grew up. A social maladroit with no articulable future. Across from him sat an eloquent woman of humanity and caliber—a double-major, no less—with a promising career, who would fit the pitiful pieces of his existence together at any moment. He braced himself for the fiction that would serve as her polite request for him to leave.

It never came.

Later that evening, as Guy stepped into the solitude

of his own apartment, the events of the day flooded over him. He and Claire had talked well into the afternoon. Words of real sense had flowed from his mouth. Something about Claire transformed him from awkward school boy to eloquent companion. Well, maybe eloquent was an exaggeration, but at least he'd sounded more like English was his native language. It didn't seem possible to him that they had only just met. A "moment", he had called it. It felt more like a hyperlink. Neither had shown any sign of wanting to stop until Guy had remembered he had to pay his rent by five o'clock. He simply had to go.

At home, Guy removed the borrowed T-shirt, only now reading the quote printed across the front: "Silence is better than unmeaning words—Pythagoras". He interpreted this to mean that Claire understood his slow tongue—that bedeviling slug that stoppled his speech.

He stepped under the hot water and let it run over his spinning head. The realization that he, not his companion, had chosen the time to part this afternoon warmed him far more than the shower.

***

Claire watched through the kitchen window until Guy disappeared around the corner, then turned and stood perfectly still. What a day! She was awestruck by her own behavior. Her defenses against entanglement had been completely disabled. This handsome artist had ensnared her with his humor, his humility and his deep blue eyes. He had blurred her firmness of purpose and revealed her armor to be made of mere clay. Her skin tingled at the vulnerability she had exhibited in his company.

"It was you who invited him…in a fit of…what was it?" she asked herself aloud.

At the Fish House, Claire had judged Guy to be

smart, interesting, even funny, but it was the mishap with the teacup and breakfast tray that had tipped the scale in his favor. To his credit, he had stood before her at the restaurant in undisguised mortification and had risen bravely from the ashes. Courage like that merited moral support.

"Who are you kidding?" her voice returned with elucidating honesty. "That wasn't moral support. It was a full-scale rescue attempt…mixed with real attraction. Ugh."

Mortification overtook her. She dropped her head into her hands. Experience had taught her to be cautious with men. Yet, today, she had completely disregarded its hard-won lessons. In the course of just a few hours, she had allowed a total stranger to hold sway over her attention, derange her plans and even enter her house.

The moment Guy had accepted her invitation, she had apprehended her impetuosity, but the deed was done, and she hadn't had the heart to recant. In short, she had lost the struggle for self-possession. Nothing terrified Claire more than to think she was in control of herself and to find out she wasn't. Nothing vexed her more than to have her lack of self-command exposed.

She began to pace the living room.

"You opened your home to a perfect stranger and spilled intimate details of your life. And that critical eye of yours? It didn't even blink! Impulse drove you today. Or was it libido? Totally out of character and even foolish. You behaved like a schoolgirl."

An involuntary thrill ran through her as she remembered the day had ended well.

She moved to the cupboard for a wine glass and filled it almost to the brim with rioja. She gulped quickly, then grabbed cheese, crackers and an apple and headed for the couch with the open bottle. It was going to be a two-glass night. She lowered herself onto the cushion and sat back to coax her body and her breathing back to normal.

Her refuge in times of inner conflict was often a book or the outdoors, but she couldn't concentrate, nor was she fit for public exposure. She would have to find release another way. She set down her glass and rose to clean the already pristine bathroom.

An hour later, emotions mollified, bathroom gleaming, Claire returned to resume her wine and cheese supper on the couch, ready for an hour or two of quiet reflection.

She almost got her wish.

The call came just as she drained the last drops from her first glass. She eyed the caller ID and recoiled. It was her mother…again. Not even twenty-four hours had passed since the last agonizing vitriol. Claire's stomach squeezed tight as a sailor's knot, and the tenuous calm she had achieved was eclipsed by renewed exasperation. She poured more wine and stared at the phone. "Mom", it read simply, with a photo of Hannah smiling broadly in a floppy beach hat. Claire was sure a very different version of her mother was on the other end.

She debated whether to answer the call at a time when her head was so muddled and her nerves so strained. Two rings. Three rings. If she took the call, she feared she wouldn't be able to suppress the truth this time. Five rings. Her own feelings were too raw to withstand another bellyful of whining. The day with Guy had unsettled her. She felt edgy, impatient, reckless. She slid her backside to the edge of the couch and sat up stiffly. Like it or not, her reckoning with Hannah was upon her. She drew a deep breath, accepted the call, and spoke with undisguised pique into the device.

"Hi, Mom. Perfect timing as ever,"

"I thought you'd never pick up!" her mother chided.

Predictably, this comment was followed by an emotional diatribe that ranged from ear-splitting cries to pained undertones and back again, all centered on the man-of-the moment in Hannah's life and his offenses of the day. Claire knew she must allow her mother to fully run out of steam before Claire would have a chance to speak. She put the phone on speaker and propped it on the coffee table against her book-of-the-moment, then leaned back to sip from her glass, hoping to maintain a degree of detachment while she awaited her opening.

When Hannah finally drew breath, Claire cut in and delivered her message in one continuous stream so her mother could not interrupt.

"Mom, I love you, but you've been repeating the same complaints in call after call, about guy after guy, since I can remember. I end up carrying your emotional garbage. It's gut-wrenching for me. I'm losing sleep. You have to get hold of yourself. If you're not willing to commit to a change—to get rid of the guy or see a counselor or life coach or something else to improve your circumstances—I'm going to have to stop taking your calls for a while."

There was dead silence on the other end. Claire didn't break it. After a few excruciating seconds, her phone screen went dark. Her arrow had hit the mark. Maybe it would jolt Hannah into action. The hope was folly but one Claire couldn't fully suppress. One thing was sure: Hannah would not call again for some time. Mission accomplished.

Sadness, not triumph, overtook Claire in the wake of the call, arising as much from the break with her mother as from Claire's own inability to resolve the situation in a way that kept their bond intact. Tears trickled down her face. Until this moment, she hadn't appreciated that her mother's calls, however unwelcome and galling, had buffered her own loneliness in this new place. She sank even lower in spirit at the irony of it and curled up on the couch cushions. There was no point to the rioja now. With a muffled sob, she reached up for the afghan on the back of the couch, drew it over her body and sought the solace of sleep, her anxiety about Guy entirely eclipsed by grief.

6

Oyster Cove

A week to the day after he met Claire, Guy positioned his easel on the waterfront park path to face The Point. Before him was a storybook scene—a range of choppy blues dotted with whitecaps and featuring a few intrepid sailboats leaning into the brisk April wind. To the right, stood the mayor's historic house overlooking the waters. He held up his hands, index fingers and thumbs extended, to form a makeshift frame around his intended composition. Through this, he spotted Claire walking by.

"Claire!"

She stopped, looked over and reddened.

"Guy," she said simply, her tone irresolute.

Guy watched her waver about what to do. Courtesy and, he guessed, curiosity won out.

"Mind if I take a closer look?"

Without waiting for an answer, she walked around to the front of the easel.

Guy stared at her back. Tempted though he had been, he had not sought her out this past week, not even for something as innocent as returning the borrowed T-shirt. Though their parting last Saturday had been upbeat, he had sensed in her an undercurrent of vacillation. Without fully understanding, he'd stifled his own impatience to see her again. Now, here she was, polite and interested, but strained. Disappointment flooded over him until he remembered that, just a week ago, he hadn't even known her name.

"I've never watched someone paint live," she said.

Guy took the hint and picked up his brush. It was far easier than thinking how to reply. He began to slap paint around in confusion—this was all he could manage with Claire spectating—until rescued by another familiar voice.

"Good morning," called Meilin as she walked up to the canvas. "That's going to be stunning, Guy. Are you tentative about putting in the mayor's house? Definitely keep it in." She turned to Claire. "Hi, I'm Meilin Li. I run Creative Agenda. I've seen you walking a lot and should have introduced myself before now."

"Claire Munro. I guess I could say the same."

Meilin turned back to the artist.

"Guy, this painting would be perfect for the art show. Why haven't you registered?"

"You haven't registered?" Claire repeated incredulously.

Two intent pairs of eyes were trained on Guy. He shifted his feet and mumbled something about not being ready. Really, how could he deliver an intelligible answer before such daunting stares?

"You're more than ready," Meilin countered. "You can enter up to three paintings. I'll bet you have way more than that in your studio already."

Claire's expression spoke her full agreement with Meilin.

"There's still time, right?" he hedged nervously.

"Yes," Meilin answered, "but it's filling up fast. Hurry before we have to cut off applicants."

Guy nodded, wondering if the threat was truth or fiction. He had to admit the show would be a convenient opportunity to exhibit but he was apprehensive about his fitness for public scrutiny. Meilin, with all her experience, clearly disagreed, judgment he should not take lightly.

And then, there was Claire.

Behind him, Meilin gushed to Claire about the quantity of registrations. She explained the economic impetus for the event, too, which provided a convenient segue into Leroy's project.

"I'm admittedly one-sided when it comes to the waterfront," Meilin said. "I want to preserve it. I'm concerned the council will allow overdevelopment that will detract from its natural beauty and curtail access by the public."

"But we're talking about the canning factory site, right?" Claire asked and looked in that direction. "It's derelict and ugly. If the town allows an investor to revitalize it, then, with proper oversight, this could be a good thing."

"You're right, but the council is very hungry for revenue, enough to compromise that oversight, in my opinion. The likelihood of cutting corners is high."

"Shouldn't we hear the man out first?"

"We can't. He'll lay out the project behind closed doors to a very exclusive audience."

While Guy peeled off his latex gloves and began to pack up, he watched Claire digest this information, consternation on her face.

"I'm going to withhold judgment until after the executive session," she replied. "If the outcome is as you say, I'll be as concerned as you."

That was enough for Meilin.

"You ladies up for breakfast?" Guy interrupted. "I'm headed for the Fish House. My treat." There was safety, he calculated, in asking both, knowing Meilin would decline.

"Sorry, I can't," she said. "The store opens in an

hour. I've got a bunch of stock to unload, and Rhonda can't help today. I'll be looking for your show application, Guy." She threw him an imperious look, then turned to Claire. "Want to get involved? I could use some help with registration."

"Love to."

"Sold!" called Meilin as if wielding a gavel. "Stop by the store so we can get you started."

She turned and marched up Main Street.

Guy repeated, this time only to Claire, "Breakfast?"

She flexed her jaw. Hesitation, again.

"Okay."

Despite her lack of enthusiasm, Guy bent over his pack to hide his pleasure.

"Great. Just two stops to make on the way."

Claire followed him to his car, where he stuffed his gear onto the back seat. Then, they circled over to Sophie's Florist Shop.

"I'll be right out."

Guy emerged from the shop with a generous bouquet of spring flowers.

"For Celeste, to make amends."

They walked to the Fish House and sat at the booth by the window. Celeste arrived to serve them, and Guy immediately handed her the blooms.

"This is really sweet," she told him.

She set the coffee pot on the booth table and stuck her nose into the bouquet.

"It's the least I could do," Guy answered earnestly, "after that fiasco last week. I promise not to jump up suddenly this morning unless I know exactly where you are."

"The funniest part," Celeste said, "when I look back, was that spinning plate." She broke into a nervous giggle, then cupped her hand over her mouth. "Sorry, but it was really comical the way you crawled under the table and just slammed it to the floor. You should have seen those people's faces. If I hadn't had such a bad morning, I'd have collapsed in laughter instead of fighting back tears."

Guy shrugged impishly, then, picking up on her reference to the "bad morning", looked past her around the dining room.

"I see today you're spared the antics of 'la-ROY'."

"Not entirely. He was here earlier." She jammed one hand on her hip. "He comes in a lot. First, he just flirted but, lately, he's begun hitting on me." She jerked her head toward Patty at the cash register. "Patty's keeping her eye out now. She'll take care of him next time he tries."

"Good plan."

"Does he really call himself 'la-ROY' instead of 'LEE-roy'?" Claire asked.

"Yeah, and makes a pretty big deal about it, too, if you get it wrong." Celeste smirked and added over her shoulder as she headed for the kitchen, "So, I make sure I do."

"You made her day with those flowers," Claire said to Guy, then uttered, "Oh!" and pointed out the window.

A masked youth, dressed in black, dashed along the wharf with a shiny metal bucket in his arms. Guy and Claire turned their heads in unison toward upper Main Street in anticipation of a hardware store clerk in pursuit. None materialized.

"I heard about the masked bandit at the office, but this is my first sighting," Claire said, craning her neck. "He's quick."

"I sure couldn't catch him."

By the time they exited the Fish House, a mass of gray clouds had collected overhead, threatening rain and dropping the temperature. Claire pulled her sweater close as they walked again to Guy's car. Guy wrestled for speech. To cover, he handed Claire the borrowed T-shirt, clean and folded. Finally, the words came to him.

"Have you been to Oyster Bay?"

"No."

"There's a cove just outside the village. I'm going there next week to paint and to check out the Books and Blues Festival afterward. It's a great event. Music, books, food. And no black flies. Oyster Bay times it just right."

Spring in Maine is defined less by the calendar than by the interval of muck and insects linking the last of the lingering cold to the summer heat. The Books and Blues Festival was a well-timed entr'acte squeezed between winter's slipping grip and the full onset of those blood-sucking flies.

Guy plunged recklessly ahead.

"If you're interested and don't mind leaving early, we could drive over together. I start painting at first light. Afterward, we could grab lunch at the café—fresh fare right off the dock—or at the festival."

They both studied their shoes during the silence.

"If I come with you, can I watch you paint?" Claire asked without lifting her head.

Guy's heart jumped. Spectators made him tighten up. But this was Claire, he reminded himself, who hadn't made him feel stupid when tongue-tied, soaked in tea or covered in scrambled eggs and syrup. If this was her sole condition to join him…

"Of course. I'll pick you up next Saturday at 4:30 a.m."

"Wow, you were serious about first light. I'll be ready."

Guy fumbled with his keys, positively giddy. Just seven days ago, he had begun to believe Claire was a figment of his imagination. Now, they had plans for a third meeting, an entire day together. His euphoria was dampened only by his self-consciousness painting in her presence. He had one week to steel his nerve.

In the days leading up to the Books and Blues Festival, Mayenne Bay transformed. The spring rains gave way to sunshine and turned the park from shades of brown to pale green with dots of yellow. Forsythia budded, pansies blossomed and daffodil shoots reached for the sky. The harbor teemed with newly alighted boats. Stores displayed summer wares in expectation of "the Season". The uptick in energy was palpable as the little town prepared for its population to double or even triple almost overnight.

Slogging away at work, Guy was numb to everything except his projects and the prospect of another day with Claire.

Claire was a bundle of nerves.

***

At the first hint of dawn on the last Saturday in April, Guy unpacked his art gear onto the sands of Oyster Cove, situated at the very tip of one of Maine's many fingerlike, Down East peninsulas. The cove was invisible from the shoreline road. No street signs advertised the spot, as though locals had determined to keep it to themselves. Judging from its beauty, they could hardly be blamed. Mixed brush, including juniper, bayberry, sumac, beach rose and salt-tolerant grasses insulated the back side of the beach from passing traffic. The shoreline, a sandy crescent curving from a rock cliff to an outcropping of pines, was protected from rough waters by a small barrier island just off shore. The view out to sea was magnificent. Soft breezes blew off the water, and small waves lapped as the tide moved in.

Guy set up his easel, hooked his over-stuffed backpack beneath to serve as anchor and squeezed daubs of color across his palette from dirty, wrinkled paint tubes. Just as enough sun cleared the horizon, he snapped on his protective gloves, pulled his baseball cap low over his brow and pulled out a brush.

Claire's preparations for the morning were worthy of a scout badge. She sat in a folding chair, a blanket on her lap against the cool morning air, a thick book in her hands—something about narcissistic disorder, from what Guy could read of the title. An accountant who read psychology. Not very long ago, that would have surprised him. She leaned over to draw two thermal mugs from her bag, one of steaming coffee, the other of tea. The fragrance of jasmine green reached Guy's nostrils.

"Here."

Claire extended the cup to him, then sat down again and leaned forward, captivated, as Guy blocked out a composition. Her interest was so genuine that any anxiety he'd felt about having a spectator blew out to sea. As he worked, early beachcombers stopped by to gawk, comment or ask questions. Tuning into his irritation, Claire interceded and drew their attention away.

"Thanks," he said when the last had gone. "I'm a slow painter. The interruptions make it worse. I get self-conscious and freeze up."

Several hours passed in silence before Claire snapped her book shut and stood up. She stretched upward in every direction, then dropped easily to touch her toes, palms flat to the ground. Guy winced, feeling pain just watching her.

"I'm going to bring my stuff to the car and walk to the village. Then I'll be ready for lunch, I think," she announced. "I'm getting hungry. Are you?"

"What time is it?"

"What does the clock have to do with it?"

Guy didn't have a ready answer. He always ate lunch at noon. Hunger had nothing to do with it. He tried to explain but fell flat.

"That's the goofiest thing I've ever heard," Claire said and laughed at him outright. "I'll meet you on the wharf, okay?" He nodded. "It's 11:15, by the way," she threw back at him, still laughing.

Guy was sure he'd have an appetite in exactly forty-five minutes.

It was two minutes to noon when he arrived at the café and found Claire already seated along with another woman about the same age. The stranger's dark brown hair was pinned up roughly at the back of her head and flattened on top by a wide head band. She sported faded yoga pants, a baggy sweatshirt and well-used running shoes. Guy stepped hesitantly over to the table, uncertain of his reception. He looked from Claire to her companion and back again.

"Hi. Can I join you?"

"Of course. I've been waiting for you," Claire said with forced politeness.

Something was afoot.

7

Books and Blues

"Renée, this is Guy Gardiner. Guy, this is my co-worker, Renée Pincer, administrative manager at the office," Claire said simply, as if this clarified everything.

It didn't, especially as Renée's face contorted with emotion and Claire's with commiseration.

Guy stoically stowed his disappointment not to have Claire all to himself and nodded deferentially to Renée as if she were the most natural addition to the table. He had no idea what he'd just walked into and had no plans to put his foot in it. He dove into the haddock wrap Claire had ordered for him, glad to fill his mouth to the no-talking point as a way to distance himself from the conversation. In contrast to his gorging, the two women sipped, nibbled and picked in a sort of shared, mechanical cadence. As had been the case with Claire and Georgia Wilson, the meal itself seemed a mere prop to the real event at the table. Food busied the hands while Claire and Renée puzzled out Renée's dilemma.

Renée was in a terrible quandary over a tempting job offer. She loved her present job because, though the pay wasn't optimum, it wasn't stressful. The new position would catapult her career and pad her bank account, but the level of responsibility scared her. It sounded like a simple employment decision to Guy, but as the women worked through Renée's indecision, he sensed Claire suspected more beneath the surface.

Guy could have excused himself from this intimate tête-à-tête but, having grown up in a home of strong females, he'd learned to admire women's talk around the table. Women really work a problem. They stay with it like a potent onion whose flavor they know will be worth the tears, sharing the labor and dabbing their eyes until they get the desired result.

Renée peeled that onion, peeled and cried and peeled and cried some more. The final layer, she revealed, was a sick parent in her care. She felt torn between time for caretaking and money for her own future security.

Guy watched her in pity as she walked away, leaving him and Claire to their tea and coffee.

"Do you think your friend will be okay?"

"I hope so. Funny thing, though. She's actually not a friend. We work in the same office, but I hardly knew her at all until today. She just happened upon me and started…"

"Spilling her guts. I'm seeing a pattern, counselor."

"Please don't call me that. I just seem to be in the right place sometimes."

"Something about you, though, causes strangers to pick you from others in the crowd."

Claire nodded in acknowledgement, then shrugged her lack of explanation. Her face clouded.

"I never know how people will react after they realize how much they've revealed. Strangers who'll never see me again probably don't give it a second thought. I suspect Renée will feel uncomfortable, even embarrassed, in another hour."

"She seemed to feel better by the end."

"Yeah, but a co-worker is too close for my comfort.

She'll have to look me in the eye on Monday. She'll wonder if I'm judging her and if I'll keep her confidences. She may avoid me and even find some way to blame me."

She turned to him with a face full of concern.

"A man would probably just punch you on the shoulder and move on."

"Really?"

"Just a guess."

Guy shrugged, never having studied heartfelt disclosures by men from any particular angle.

"But you didn't approach Renée. It was the other way around. You aren't responsible for how she behaves afterward."

He knew from Claire's face she wasn't buying it.

"Technically, you're right. But you're being rational. Emotions aren't rational."

"Did you just elevate me, a mere man, to the ranks of rationality?"

Claire's face lightened.

"I've always thought of accountants as automatons, human calculators who just follow the rules," Guy said. "Seems to me you're an unusual blend, a touchy-feely people-magnet and a disciplined number-cruncher at the same time. How do you manage to swing between the two?"

Claire sat perfectly still for a moment.

"I have absolutely no idea."

They both laughed, then rose and headed for Oyster Bay's village center.

"Do they actually harvest oysters around here?" Claire asked Guy as they exited the wharf.

"Mostly from farms now. A sign of the times. Oyster Bay was home to Maine's indigenous people for thousands of years before it was settled by Europeans. It has always relied on the sea for sustenance. Today, that means aquaculture."

They crossed the road and wandered aimlessly from one festival display to another like rudderless boats. Around them, people moved to the music or collected around street musicians, book purchase in one hand, lobster roll in the other.

"Claire! Guy!"

The pair swung around to the voice of Peggy Cyr emanating from the crowd.

"Wow," Claire exclaimed, signaling to the bags of books drooping from each of Peggy's arms.

"This year is one of the best," Peggy told them. "I'm off to unload these into the car, then I'll cover the rest of the tents."

She adjusted her grip on the bags and beelined for the parking lot.

"Peggy's one of the first people I connected with up here. She really gets bibliophiles," Claire said.

"What's there to get?"

"The love of a real book in your hands. Pages to turn. The crack of the binding. The smell of paper."

"Let's see what we can find, then."

Guy grabbed her by the elbow and guided her toward the nearest book vendor. Between browsing, they resumed their conversation from lunch.

"Why accounting and not counseling?" Guy asked as he flipped through a biography of Van Gogh. "If you're hearing people out anyway, why not do it for a living?"

"I completed the senior year practicum but never took the license exam. My heart was in it, but I couldn't keep a professional distance. Feelings are like clothing for me; I have to try them on to fully understand them. I can tap in but have trouble shaking them off." She looked up at him with a half-smile. "Not a recipe for success as a therapist."

"Why accounting, then?"

"With accounting, you always know where you are. There's order. Predictability. And no debriefing is required, unless the client is contentious. Tax season is a little trying but I like the challenge." She turned to him. "Okay, your turn. Why drop a perfectly good vocation in graphic design for the uncertainty of fine art?"

This time, Guy didn't flounder for an answer.

"I love creating art. I can't think of anything else I'd rather do long-term. In the meantime, graphic design pays the bills."

"When did you start drawing?"

"At about five years old. I started by copying comics and photos, then shifted to artwork—Rockwell, Rembrandt, Homer, Whistler and Van Gogh."

Their heads jerked as sounds from the R&B stage signaled the first band was setting up.

"Whoa, look at those amplifiers," breathed Claire, eyes wide.

"I do love R&B," Guy said, "but not when it blows out the speakers. Should we head home?"

"Won't you mind missing the music?"

"No. The early start is catching up with me."

They headed for the car and navigated around darting pedestrians and traffic to the main road leading from town. By the time Oyster Bay was visible only through the rearview mirror, the throbbing base of the band began to pump. They both sat back in the silence, relieved to have escaped the ear drubbing.

"This was fun," Guy said when he finally turned onto Harborview Street.

"It was," Claire agreed.

He pulled up to her door and reached behind his seat for a bag. Inside was a pale green sweatshirt that read "The book is better".

"I couldn't resist."

Claire laughed.

"Thanks for the shirt…and the day."

"Why don't we exchange numbers in case something like this comes up again?" Guy proposed.

He'd been practicing the question in his head the whole trip home. He'd aimed for a neutral tone and had fallen a bit short, but the words were out, and he didn't regret them. Claire reached over, pulled his sketchbook from his art pack and jotted her number on the cover. Suddenly, Guy couldn't remember his own. To cover, he dialed Claire's phone.

Within minutes, he was over the bridge onto Union Road, heading west. In a few miles, he turned right and rolled down a long, gravel driveway to a white ranch house with an attached garage. Curtains in the ranch window jerked apart, and the plump face of Mrs. Annabelle Clark, a seventy-eight-year-old widow, peered out and waved. Guy waved back. He and his landlady co-existed quite peaceably, despite his occasional late rent payments. Annabelle, he knew, took comfort in the safety of a trustworthy tenant, not to mention the occasional chores he performed, and would rather he pay late than not at all.

He mounted the stairs to his loft above the garage, opened the door and paused on the threshold, grinning stupidly at Claire's number on his sketchbook. They had spent three days together so far, and this promised a fourth. The slow progress was excruciating for a man smitten in the first minute of the first encounter. Guy felt a nascent recklessness in his chest, a dangerous, damn-the-torpedoes impulse to throw caution to the wind and declare his attraction. He checked the thought. He would have to conceal his high spirits for now. Claire needed time. How much? He didn't know.

***

The morning after the visit to Oyster Bay, Claire awoke at six o'clock and lay in bed caught up in the bunched and twisted blankets of a fitful night. Even before she could rub the sleep from her eyes, her sense of reason was warring with the inexplicable and weak-minded fascination she felt about Guy.

She had no plans at present to pull her heart out of deep freeze for a man she barely knew. Yet, in his company, her strenuous objections to dating, meant to keep her head above water, crumbled like piecrust. Something about this gentle man relaxed her guard, like a warm shower over sore muscles. She crackled with curiosity about him. He was like an unfinished sentence, a thought she couldn't complete, and Claire didn't live well in limbo.

She slid from bed and showered. As she dressed, Claire was taxed by an uncharacteristic and, in her opinion, absurd desire to impress Guy. It was one of those girlish things that welled up instinctually, she supposed, and it felt ridiculous …undignified. What if she bumped into him today? She tried on three different outfits before she decided what to wear, then forced herself out of the bedroom before she was tempted by a fourth.

After breakfast and a vigorous turn around the park, she made her way to see Meilin about helping with art show registrations.

"Good morning, Claire."

Meilin leaned out from a pile of boxes to greet her.

"Hi, Meilin. I came about volunteering. Mind if I look around first?"

"Take your time."

Claire wound her way up and down the aisles and stopped at the journal display, intoxicated by the smell of new paper. She had never been able to resist a fresh notebook, not since grade school. At least a dozen sat unused on her bookshelf. She preferred them that way—unspoiled and full of potential. She pulled a journal off the shelf whose cover read "The unexamined life is not worth living". She listened for the faint crack as she splayed its pages, inhaled their scent, then tucked the book under her arm.

"By the way," Meilin said, poking her head around the journal display at Claire, "did Guy mention he registered for the art show this week?"

"What? No, but I'm glad. I guess you gave him the needed confidence boost the other day."

"It wasn't me."

Meilin threw Claire a meaningful look.

Claire reddened.

"But I haven't known him that long."

"Just long enough."

Meilin moved to the counter to give Claire time to recover. She pulled out her tablet, opened it to the website registration page and gave Claire a tutorial of the process. Just as they finished, they were joined by Roxie Nadeau, a petite, muscular woman with short-cropped, brown hair, multiple ear piercings and intelligent, brown eyes. Meilin made introductions.

"Just got final approval to use the Unitarian Church community room for the show," Roxie beamed.

Meilin threw her hands together in excitement.

"It's been tough bringing them around, but I knew you could do it."

"Congratulations," Claire added.

"Thanks. I'm going to need more hands to get this exhibition organized and hung," Roxie told Meilin.

"Claire is taking over registration, which will free me up some more," Meilin said. "Let's take this up at the next committee meeting."

"Welcome aboard," Roxie said to Claire.

The three shared phone numbers before parting.

Claire returned home happy about these new friends but filled with underlying apprehension. As was her habit when in the throes of uncertainty, she sought clarity through cleaning—this time her bookshelves—hoping for a lightbulb moment. Finally, it came to her. She dropped an armful of books onto the coffee table, sank down hard onto the couch and looked her uneasiness square in the face.

"Admit it. You volunteered to handle the art show registration just to get closer to Guy, and he beat you to it. Disappointing, yes, but what really unsettles you is that you like him that much." She jumped up as if this last admission physically hurt and shook it away. "You have to cut the man off, Claire, and soon, or else give him a decent chance. Fish or cut bait."

She headed for the wine cabinet.

8

Executive Session

On the second of May, to the west of town, in a secluded, rustic cabin far down Union Road, a lone man stared out the window at the pines and birches. He didn't really see them. Even the strong woodsy fragrance that reached his nostrils didn't wake him to their presence. If Leroy Hood smelled anything this morning, it was desperation.

Mayenne Bay was just the kind of town he'd been hunting for. Hungry. Unsophisticated. Picturesque. And its working harbor lent authenticity to the place. It was a location that would draw investors who valued the views from their lofty windows over the rustic charm his contenders argued to preserve. Leroy snorted derisively. Charm was overrated, imaginary. Money, by contrast, was real, tangible, its value clear. Even the mayor and town council saw the raw truth of it—so clearly, in fact, that the vote in favor of tonight's executive session had been unanimous.

The net had been cast.

The town council was scheduled to convene at seven o'clock this evening. Leroy glanced at his Rolex—five o'clock—then looked over at the flimsy table that strained under the bulk of his laptop, printer and the cluttered aftermath of handout preparations. He had handled every detail himself, keeping his cards close to the vest until the last possible moment. He had tested the audio-visual equipment in the meeting room the previous day and rehearsed his entire presentation several times this morning. Nothing was left to chance. He always prepared well beforehand. It allowed time to mull the finer points.

His stomach growled, and a smug expression overspread his face. His habit of fasting at the critical junctures of his projects gave him an edge, a sharpness of mind. Tonight's meeting was crucial, the pivotal point when he would finally be freed of constraint to attract greater investment. Food would only dull his wits. There would be plenty of time to indulge his appetite after the meeting.

He was no novice in the real estate game. He knew how to kick the tires, to draw attention to features that depressed property values. The abandoned canning factory site, a disfigurement on the shoreline and long unproductive, was made-to-order for an exclusive, upscale, waterfront condo complex—a cheap buy and an easy sell. It was on this portion of his scheme that Leroy would be most vocal tonight. He would also cautiously hint at the surrounding public access spaces unfit for a newly fashioned Mayenne Bay. This would sow the early seeds of the project's second phase: a high-end yacht club and marina where the public boathouse now stood. Quietly, he'd already begun to generate interest in this scheme.

Leroy made no apologies for his vilification of Mayenne Bay's common rabble in the name of profitable development. Gentrification, the pundits called it, holding their noses as if rejuvenation was viler than the rot of a dying town. It was the way of the world and music that played well among the privileged. He'd done his homework in town and detected like minds enough. Tonight, behind closed doors, he would work to advantage to secure the inner circle before his detractors caught wind of his full intentions. Timing was everything in this business. Leroy had it down to a science.

He turned his handsome, salon-tanned face to the window again and weighed his position pragmatically. Having assiduously worked to win the trust of the mayor, the town manager, the town council and even the chamber of commerce, he could now, with very few exceptions, identify each party by name and personal interests. He had also discreetly courted area property owners and could count several among his early investors. Discreet, personal, beforehand politicking was the most powerful tool of persuasion in his repertoire. The knowledge it gave him enabled him to subtly and artfully incorporate messages into his pitch, aimed at a well-cultivated audience.

He hadn't silenced all the skeptics. For this reason alone, the grant of a confidential executive session had been a major victory. The eloquent librarian and two store owners who'd threatened to derail him wouldn't be permitted to attend. Leroy was equally glad to have that Jay Brown character excluded. The old man, however coarse and cantankerous, conveyed his everyman-taxpayer-rights message infectiously. Alone in front of the room tonight, Leroy would control the rhetoric and fully expected to breeze past the finish line. He foresaw nothing but smooth sailing on the horizon.

Mayor Edgecomb—Leroy's shoulders shook with derision at the thought of her— had publicly jumped into his corner. If he'd let her, he was sure, she would also have jumped his bones. Time and again, Sandra had caught up with Leroy on his reconnaissance tours around town. He'd made sure of it and had used these encounters to advantage. Last month, after some flirtatious banter to warm her up, he'd informed her that more than one town was under consideration for his plan. His outside investors had granted only a limited timeframe for the location to be settled. Leroy had studied Sandra's face as she'd digested his message. That his plan was not a slam-dunk for Mayenne Bay had clearly startled her. Predictably, she'd urged the town council for a prompt and favorable decision following Leroy's presentation tonight. The skids had been greased.

At six o'clock, Leroy walked over and slipped the handouts, laptop and thumb drive into his briefcase. He made his way to the bedroom for a leisurely shower, then applied a hint of cologne and dressed. His medium-gray suit and a crisp, white shirt, carefully selected and prepared earlier that day, hung ready for him. Soft leather shoes. No tie. This was Maine. He needed the air of credibility without appearing too formal.

After combing the last stray hair into place, he turned to view himself in the mirror. Professional and confident, yet relaxed and affable. God, he was good at this. He slid his trusty notebook and pen into his pocket, drained a tall glass of water and made his way to his car.

At exactly seven o'clock that evening, radiating enthusiasm, Leroy stepped in front of the microphone in the town meeting chamber. The mayor, town manager, city lawyer and town council all looked up at him with eager, receptive expressions. Sandra, impeccably attired in a tight skirt and low-cut blouse, had chosen a seat in the first row directly in front of the podium. She uncrossed her bare legs, leaned in and licked her lips. Leroy had to suppress a smirk. The woman's meaning couldn't be more blatant. He flashed the room a charming smile of bright, white teeth, one that deepened the distinctive dimple on his right cheek, and noted with satisfaction that the group went completely silent in anticipation.

"I want to start," he began in a humble tone, "by saying that I've come through the school of hard knocks in land development, especially during my years in Florida. Be assured that I've learned my lessons and will put them to good use in Mayenne Bay."

As any seasoned entrepreneur would do, he proceeded to paint his design in the best light. He exhibited professional drawings of a brand-new condominium complex in place of the old factory and provided a timeline and budget for demolition and new building construction. Throughout, he skillfully convinced the audience of his knowledge, resources and connections, inside and outside of Maine, while deftly inserting his planned seeds of division. He touted a growing list of investors, dropping names his audience would instantly recognize. The crowning moment was his prediction that his first investors would accrue an early return—a calculated move. It was always best to end with earnings. Money speaks.

After shaking hands cordially with every attendee, Leroy waved and strode from the meeting chamber, leaving the council to its deliberations. He had no doubt about the outcome; it was written on their faces just as it had been on Sandra's the day he had relayed the fiction of competing towns. She hadn't had the self-composure to disguise her anxiety. Leroy had no qualms about misleading such a gullible woman to achieve his ends. In fact, he congratulated himself on his expert cunning. Talent like his didn't just fall off trees.

He slid into the driver's seat of his car and leaned back for a moment in sheer exultation before starting the engine. The right corner of his mouth curved, again deepening his dimple. He was fully aware he could take advantage of Sandra's attraction at will but judged it wiser to hold her in reserve. Besides, he'd already made arrangements for his young and voluptuous woman-of-the-moment to meet him at the cabin. He knew from experience that there was no better outlet for the surfeit of energy he felt tonight.

The hunger in his stomach rose up again, but he would not soon break his fast; hunger would only intensify his pleasure.

***

Sandra stared down at the bloodied rag clenched in her fist and then out the large bay window of her two-story clapboard. Mice. Like she needed this to start her Friday morning. She stepped over to throw the wad into the trash can, reset the trap and slid it back under the stove. Where were the effing cats? Stretched across the floor in a pool of sunshine, a length of fur yawned and flippantly twisted the end of its tail. The other was nowhere to be seen. She scowled. She tolerated the stench of cat litter solely for the cats' role in a vermin-free home and would not suffer freeloaders for long.

She leaned against the sink and flipped on the faucet to scrub her hands. She had no recourse but to handle the infestation herself. She was a public figure now, living conspicuously in a small town. Her reputation for fastidious care of her ancestral house generated expectation of the same in the execution of her office. She couldn't engage a professional exterminator and set the rumor mill grinding over the mayor's revolting rodent problem. Nor could she shake the fear that this morning's bloodied mouse was an inauspicious omen.

More than ever, Sandra needed to project a self-control she didn't feel. The executive session last night had unsettled her, a sensation that had survived the night and resurfaced in her first waking moments. For the first time, she had detected undercurrents in Leroy's message at odds with her intentions. He had, skillfully and audaciously, intimated the unsuitability of the townspeople for their own town. This didn't change Sandra's mind about the condo project, but it did raise questions about her management of its originator. She'd been a strong voice for taking necessary risk, even enduring some pain, all in the name of improving the town. In this, she had judged her mindset and Leroy's to be in sync. Now, she suspected his ambition might be something else, something more. He bore closer scrutiny. She squirmed in her own skin as she realized she was sounding a bit like Meilin.

Later at the office, Sandra got wind, through her right-hand, Sally, of a second development concept circulating in town, an alternative to Leroy's scheme. Sally didn't have much in the way of details, but her connections, Sandra knew, were solid. Sandra spent her morning hours making discreet calls about this rumor but discovered little. She would continue trying. The vote last night had been unanimous in favor of Leroy's proposal. She didn't want to risk delay or disruption for some flaky, grassroots distraction.

She slipped out to grab a coffee from the Main Street Coffee Bar and was confronted at the door by several members of the Mayenne Bay French Club calling for bilingual interpretive signs on Castle Street. There had never been actual castles in town, which begged the question of how the street got its name, a riddle not high on the mayor's list of priorities. The club contended that Castle Street was named for the Castle of Mayenne in the Pays de la Loire region west of Paris, France. "Mayenne", like "Maine", they argued, derived from French provinces.

No one had unearthed hard evidence to tie the town's francophone settlers to the Loire region. Even the Mayenne Bay Historical Society found the club's claim dubious, but the club would not cede this connection to the old country to any other claimant. Castle Street was theirs. The interpretive signs should say so. Sandra listened, hedged and stalled, but they would not relent. Only when she agreed to look into it further did they finally leave her in peace. By then, her coffee was cold.

Back at the office, she received a call from the 45-year-old widower, Louis Mac Rainwater, an Air Force veteran and electronics engineer passionate about his indigenous Wabanaki roots. Louis had settled in Mayenne Bay rather than on designated tribal land because the harbor was reputed to have been a favored fishing spot of his forebears. This history, plus the artifacts that had already been discovered along the shores, he explained to Sandra, had prompted his call to action.

"I wanted to let you know in advance, Mayor, that I'll be coming forward at the next town meeting to call for a site evaluation before any demolition work begins on the old canning factory," Louis told her respectfully.

Sandra's gut tightened. She understood both the significance of the archeological evaluation and the potential delay it posed to starting construction. It could push the project into next season, or worse, into another municipality. She hung up grateful to Louis, at least, for the advance notice.

At four o'clock, Sandra locked her office and headed for Grace Grocery on the corner of Main and Crest. Viewed from the mayor's chair, the place was a beacon of hope and enduring economic success. Thomas and Beatrice Grace had purchased the abandoned, former general store for a very modest sum over nineteen years ago when the premises had been a mid-town eyesore. There had been talk about tearing it down over the years, but the citizenry couldn't stomach the idea of razing a historical icon, no matter how blemished or impractical its presence. The store had unwittingly come to symbolize their spirit—stalwart and resilient—in hard times. Through bankruptcies, layoffs and closures all around, the store had stood, holding its breath, until the Graces had given it new life. Sandra patronized it often if for no other reason than to remind herself of the town's potential.

Bagged purchases in hand, she plodded wearily home, longing only for a quiet meal, a hot shower and a rodent-free evening. Jay accosted her in the park over government transparency and oversight of this year's garden walk. Sandra let him spew this time, hoping she'd glean information about the competing development concept, but tongues had apparently not yet wagged in Jay's direction. She managed to shake him off at her gate and left him standing on the street.

She scrubbed her hands hard before starting supper as if the dead mouse remains still lingered. It occurred to her she was also trying to wash away the residue of a Friday run amok. The development project. Louis. The French club. Jay. God, she could use some personal space, but it was not to be. She had run for the mayorship with her eyes open. Accessibility to constituents, appearance and reputation—these were her currency now, at least until she could achieve some results. Her credibility among the citizenry was key to keeping progress on track, to holding Leroy in check, to managing needed change. She couldn't permit the slightest sign of doubt or weakness right now, not even the size of a mouse. She dried her hands while she gazed out the bayside window at the turbulent, blue water, a fitting metaphor for her own life.

9

Shipshape

On the other end of town, Guy was making use of Claire's number for the first time and chose to text rather than call so she would feel less pressured.

"Plans for supper?"

"It's Friday night. I'm too tired to go out," she thumbed back.

Before disappointment could overtake him, Guy's phone buzzed with a second reply.

"Want to come over?"

Both surprised and pleased, he quickly returned a "yes". There was a knock at Claire's kitchen door at five thirty.

"Come in," she called without looking up from the shopping bag she was emptying. "I was thinking of a cheese and apple plate with bread or crackers," she told Guy and grabbed the cutting board. "I hope that's okay. I'm pretty drained from work."

An involuntary sigh escaped Guy's lips. He was familiar with this "meal". His sisters ate it frequently enough. In his book, it could hardly be classified as supper.

Claire didn't miss his reaction.

"I happen to like cheese and apples," she retorted

sharply, a fist on one hip. "If you want something else, you'll have to cook it yourself."

Guy had momentarily forgotten just how perceptive Claire could be and, in return, was treated to this little flare of defensiveness. From the energy she radiated, he guessed her emotions could intensify into a formidable force but he was unfazed by her outburst. He had, with the help of two hyper-sensitive sisters, spent years perfecting the side-step.

Desirous of a real meal tonight, he accepted Claire's challenge.

"I'll cook."

She was instantly disarmed.

"I'm sorry I snapped at you."

"It's alright. It's my fault. When you accept an invitation to eat, it isn't polite to turn your nose up at the menu."

Claire smiled at his conciliatory answer, opened the pantry and withdrew a navy blue apron from the back of the door that read "I improve with wine" in white embroidery. She pulled it over her head and headed for the refrigerator while her hands worked to tie the strings from behind.

"I originally had a chicken dinner in mind," she told Guy over her shoulder as she pulled out the makings of the meal. "I just didn't feel like cooking it by myself."

"Problem solved."

They spent the next hour working through stove-top chicken in barbecue sauce, herbed rice and coleslaw. When all was said and done, Guy carried the final platter to the table, set it snugly between the other dishes, then joined Claire, who was already seated.

"Don't worry," he said, wincing at the mess in her normally immaculate kitchen. "I've got clean-up."

Claire picked up her knife and fork.

"A hot meal cooked by someone other than me. I

don't get this very often."

"You did half the work. And thank you for feeding me. I had planned to take you out."

"Home-cooking was more fun, don't you think?"

"I do."

He began loading his plate.

"And now I know you can cook."

Guy suspended a chicken thigh in mid-air. There was a subtle message behind Claire's words.

"How about next time at my place?" he invited, guessing this was what she wanted.

She licked homemade barbecue sauce from the corners of her mouth and smiled, waiting for him to make the suggestion a reality.

"Tomorrow night?"

"Yes."

With that single word, Claire conveyed to him her need to force an early reckoning of their relationship.

By eight o'clock, Guy was on Union Road heading home. Despite the cool evening, perspiration collected under his shirt. Dinner with Claire at his place tomorrow evening. The invitation had flown out of his mouth, but he wasn't sorry. Claire was nervous, holding back. Perhaps she felt vulnerable having opened her home to him— twice— and would feel surer after seeing his. Logic told him this was the only way forward, but the closer he got to home, the more he doubted its wisdom. As he shut off the ignition, a telling bead of sweat ran down his left temple.

Since he'd rented the loft from Annabelle five years ago, Guy had been perfectly content there. In a single room, he could shift from computer graphics to oil painting to general living, with an occasional spill outside into the vegetable garden Annabelle allowed him.

But this was all before Claire.

He climbed the stairs, swung open the door and

froze at the threshold, an imaginary Claire at his side. Through her eyes, the loft lay before him in its naked reality. In the far left corner was a closet-sized bathroom with a stall shower barely wide enough to lift his arms. Beside it was an unmade twin bed separated from the rest of the place by a shaky privacy screen. The area in front of the screen served as the no-frills, living-kitchen-work area. The wall to the left formed a minimalist kitchenette—a sink, a small combination range-oven and two overhead shelves. A few feet from the sink stood a wobbly café table Guy had bought at a flea market and steadied with a folded piece of cardboard. Two hard, backless stools flanked the table. Nearby were a faded, saggy loveseat, a floor lamp and a single end table. The remainder of the space housed the combined chaos of his graphics design and painting, which cast a shadow of disorder over the entire place.

The article Guy had re-read after his first visit to Claire's apartment—the one about a home reflecting the personality of its owner—rose again in his mind, this time to chastise. Never before had he so deeply lamented his habits of clutter and procrastination. Never had he felt so acutely that a thirty-year-old business owner should have more to show for himself than the utter mess before him. He released a long breath through clenched teeth. He had less than twenty-four hours to render the place—it could never be impressive—less than repugnant for Claire, plus buy groceries and cook a meal. What had he been thinking?

He changed his clothes and began the purge, scurrying well into the night to reverse months of neglect and be free to focus on dinner tomorrow. It was well after midnight before he finally stood back to survey his efforts and heaved a sigh of resignation. What he had formerly deemed functional was now, at least, clean and orderly, though it would never be a candidate for *Better Homes and Gardens*. *It'll have to do*, he told himself and fell into bed.

By the time Claire arrived next evening, Guy was running on adrenaline reserve, having slept poorly the night before, risen very early and prepared dinner the better part of the day. He held the door open wide in welcome and suggested she wander freely, to the extent one could wander in a six-hundred-square-foot space, while he poured wine and iced tea. Having formulated an opinion of Claire from her apartment, Guy had no doubt she would do the same from his. He watched guardedly as she milled around, feeling no small measure of vulnerability as the discerning Claire took in every inch of his home.

"I can see how this works for you," she said finally.

He laughed.

"That's your polite way of saying you could never live like this."

"It wouldn't be my lifestyle of choice, no, but it's uncomplicated and just right for what you do."

"A ringing endorsement." Beneath the sarcasm, Guy felt he had got off easy. His dread lifted. "Have a look at this lasagna before I pop it in, will you?"

Claire looked it over, inhaled deeply and approved the dish with an eager nod. He slid it into the tiny oven, willing it not to smoke. While the casserole baked, they drank, picked at the antipasto plate he had assembled and sifted through Guy's paintings to a Rossini 33-LP record. With every minute that passed, Guy's worries over the loft's deficiencies diminished, only to be displaced by self-consciousness over his art. He reminded himself that he'd invited Claire expressly to lay bare the man he was. That included his art. To his relief, she seemed impressed. Her enthusiasm brought him back from the brink and restored his equanimity just in time for the buzzer announcing the finished lasagna.

Their shift to the eating area revived Guy's anxiety. The café table groaned under the combined weight of the place settings, salad bowl and steaming casserole dish as if it resented its new burden of hosting two. Claire wordlessly bent over to shift the cardboard under the table base before lowering herself onto the flimsy stool. It held. Guy breathed. Before seating himself, he served her salad, suddenly conscious of his mismatched plates and flatware and the proximity of the table to the heat of the oven. Claire adapted to the arrangement with grace and apparent ease. He took heart in the simple fact that she stayed. Didn't action speak louder than words?

After dinner, Claire cleared plates and ran hot water in the cramped sink to wash dishes. Guy was sure that, by now, people-reader as she was, she could sense the undercurrent of his growing feelings. He was grateful, for once, for his slug-tongue's hold over his speech, knowing a premature declaration could blow his prospects.

"You know," Claire mused aloud as she dried her hands, "I can't believe I invited you to my place having known you only a few hours. That was a first."

The slug held tight—a good thing. Guy was only just beginning to understand her complicated nature, and she was clearly a very cautious person if she was still taken aback by her own daring that first day.

"I didn't see any sign of nervousness."

Claire laughed outright.

"Didn't I talk your ear off? That's a sure sign."

"But you invited me over."

"You'd just doused yourself with tea and covered yourself in breakfast leftovers in a restaurant full of people. Remember? I thought you needed a way out."

To hide his disappointment, Guy fiddled on his laptop for an after-dinner movie. They shifted to the worn sofa where he pulled the two stools over and set a bowl of popcorn plus tea and coffee on one and arranged his laptop on the other. Finally, he lowered himself down beside her.

"It's my turn to confess."

"What?"

"I saw you at the Fish House one Saturday morning. Every Saturday after that, I got there when it opened just in case you showed up again. You, uh, seemed like someone I'd like to meet."

Claire sat perfectly quiet. For Guy, the wait was excruciating.

"I had no idea." Her voice was low. "If I had, I'd probably have thought it was creepy. Now, I can say I'm glad we're becoming friends."

Friends. The word stung Guy's ears. Still, he reasoned, it wasn't the worst way to begin.

"What do you want to watch?"

"Whatever you want."

The music to an old Star Trek movie filled the loft.

Two hours later, Guy closed Claire's car door and watched her drive away, relieved their relationship had survived her first visit to his loft. The fact that she hadn't immediately spun on her heels and left was a significant achievement. It was a low bar, but considering what he had to work with, he could declare the night a success. He ached for more but, first, would need a sign from Claire.

10

We Have Time

The month of May flew by in a blur as Guy raced to complete his paintings for the art show. In the little time he carved out with Claire, he sensed greater ease, due perhaps to their increased familiarity following her visit to his home.

On June 1, the eve of the art show submission deadline, Guy arrived at Claire's place for a private showing of his three finished canvases. From the look and smell of the kitchen, they were set for a quiet evening over homemade pizza and art. The fragrances of garlic and fresh oregano filled the air. He stowed the paintings in the living room and took his place at the table where Claire slid a crisp sourdough crust, covered with crushed tomatoes, gooey mozzarella and mushrooms, onto his plate. Guy savored the pie with one eye on Claire, waiting for her posture to transition from workplace tension to home comfort. He was toying with the idea of telling her how he felt.

The startlingly loud ringtone of John Philip Sousa's Stars and Stripes Forever brought the world back into focus.

"I have it turned up too loud," Claire said apologetically as she hopped up and fished frantically through her bag for her phone. She raised her thumb to reject the call, then hesitated.

NOOOO, moaned the voice in Guy's head.

With a plea-full, I-can't-help-it look, she answered it. "Hi, Daniel."

From across the table, Guy could hear a deep, young voice bursting with excitement … an offer … great salary … new car. He squirmed. Another man in Claire's life?

Claire interrupted him midstream and threw another look of apology to Guy.

"Congratulations! Are you in town?"

Daniel was coming over.

While she explained the invitation, Claire pulled together another pizza and slid it into the oven. Daniel was her cousin, her best friend. He'd been on the hunt for a job in Portland and finally landed a full-time position after a series of part-time, meager-paying gigs. He was, in so many ways, wise and capable, but had ever been a child of optimism and impulsivity when it came to money.

"For Daniel, a full-time salary at almost any level looks like a windfall. You must have overheard. He's spending his first paycheck before it's been earned. I have to slow him down, force his feet to the ground. He'd do the same for me if the shoe were on the other foot."

Daniel arrived in a matter of minutes, which told Guy he'd been in the neighborhood and expecting an invitation, though he clearly hadn't expected Guy. After a quick acknowledgment to the third wheel, Daniel helped himself to wine and pizza as only close family can do, oblivious to the evening's signs of intimacy. Between chews, he told Claire and Guy all about his new job.

Guy rose, signaled to Claire to stay seated and began clearing the table to give the counselor room. A person in need had appeared. A session was inevitable. He set the tea kettle on the stove and turned to watch the cousins in action.

Daniel gushed with the self-confidence of a man who saw the world at his feet. As she listened, Claire reached over, pulled her tablet from her work bag and gently prodded him for specifics. He answered in short soundbites between mouthfuls of food and tangents into his many plans. Claire let him spout. Daniel ran out of steam just as the tea kettle found it, one of those uncanny synchronizations Guy had begun to notice whenever the counselor was at work around food.

At this opportune moment, Claire gave Daniel a penetrating look—it was almost scary, really—and turned the computer screen toward him. On it was an Excel spreadsheet she'd cobbled together during his verbal download. Over the young man's shoulder, Guy could see she'd broken down Daniel's new salary to a monthly figure and deducted the cost of benefits, taxes, college debt and day-to-day living Daniel had quoted, leaving a rather meager allowance for fun and games. There was no new car on the menu, no vacation in Europe, no large screen TV.

Quick-minded Daniel took in the calculation and jumped to his feet.

"I can't believe this!" He flung his arms. "This is crap! My whole salary's gone, and I haven't even started work! They're taking everything!"

With an impassive expression, Claire let her cousin's tantrum exhaust itself, then pulled up her full height into a quelling posture, especially remarkable as she was the shortest person in the room. Daniel leaned back against the cupboard while she stood exuding an absolute strength. Guy stared. The eyes that had glowed with the cool light of detachment now flared with the cobalt blue punch of the kitchen decor.

"Daniel, quit whining, sit down and listen," she said with the bluntness of a near relation. "You aren't thinking clearly. Your expectations are unrealistic."

It was a brief but potent speech. After a moment of residual grumbling, Daniel settled down.

"Okay, then."

Claire walked him through the calculations. Guy listened, too, then drifted into a silent assessment of his own financial practices. Some habits would have to change if he wanted to avoid his own spreadsheet seminar.

When Claire finished, she rose from the table, leaving Daniel to sit in sober silence and stare at the figures. She had not, despite her cousin's maelstrom, lost track of gastronomy's power to assuage the afflicted. She produced a pan of freshly-made custard—Daniel's favorite—from the refrigerator as if it had been waiting there all this time just to sweeten his bitterness. It was an act of prescience that spooked Guy.

The three of them spent the next half hour sipping hot tea and coffee and sliding soothingly cool custard down their throats. Daniel, with Claire's guidance, created a personal budget and got his first lesson in cash management. She shot him a copy of the spreadsheet by email and, before he left, spooned him a supply of custard to take home.

"You're more like a mother to him than a cousin or friend," Guy observed as Daniel pulled the door shut.

"Tonight, it might appear that way, but that's because money is involved. It's his Achilles heel. In so many other ways, Daniel is wise and insightful." She struck her forehead with the heel of her hand. "I'm sorry. I totally forgot the point of the evening. I haven't had a chance to see your paintings."

They moved into the living room to survey Guy's submissions. Claire bent down, bewilderment on her face.

"How can you speak of your work as amateurish? These are beautiful."

Guy was moved. When Claire looked at his

paintings, she saw so much more than paint. It made him feel larger than life. He snuck a sideways glance at her. Though the moment to declare his feelings had come and gone, he would leave tonight with more than he'd brought; he would leave with Claire's unalloyed vote of confidence ringing in his ears. This would make all the difference when he put his work in the hands of the art show committee tomorrow morning.

Just one week later, the Mayenne Bay Art Show opening reception was upon them. Claire brimmed with vicarious excitement. Guy was tight with jitters.

"The reception is in there," directed a young volunteer who blinked fake eyelashes and tugged at a knitted dress at least one size too small. She handed Guy his name tag, then pointed a hot-pink fingernail toward a set of double doors.

Guy pinned on the tag, turned and froze as though the entrance to the library conference room was a portal to the dark side. For him, it was. Conversation about art had never been a problem; it was the small talk at these affairs that threw him. Navigating a crowd of drinking, chit-chatting strangers was his worst nightmare. His tongue threatened a resurgence of the slug in the back of his throat.

Claire took his arm and steered him into the room. He gave her the wheel, feeling cowardly, but grateful, and even envious, as she made her way seamlessly through the crowd, smiling and unabashedly making eye contact as she moved. She brought him to a stop at the drink table where she grabbed two glasses of iced tea, swung around and handed one to Guy.

"Social props," she said matter-of-factly.

"It shows?"

"A bit. You'll be more at ease with this in your hand. You can take a sip while you're thinking what to say."

He made a face at her but recognized the truth of it. They took in the room for a while from the safety of the drink table.

After a few minutes studying the crowd, Claire whispered, "Do you know the man in white?"

There was no mistaking whom she meant. He wore white painter pants and a matching smock shirt with a few paint smudges across the front. A red scarf encircled his neck. His sleeves were rolled up to his elbows as though he were at his easel. The dark blue beret on his head was cocked to one side revealing scraggly strands of overgrown, white hair. His beard was equally unkempt, giving him a scrubby, careless appearance.

"Oh," Guy replied sarcastically. "You mean Pierre Cliché. All he needs is a Gauloises cigarette hanging from the corner of his mouth to perfect the caricature."

Claire lifted her hand to hide an involuntary snigger. They could overhear Monsieur Cliché speaking to another guest in an exaggerated, beatnik-like style.

"I'm sure that name didn't appear among the registrations," Claire said as she eyed Pierre appraisingly. "What a character. He's really worked hard on that persona. This is a man who needs to belong."

"Well, he's failing," Guy snorted. "He's made himself so outlandish, he's in a class by himself."

Pierre detected Claire's gaze and, at the sight of her open expression, beelined in her direction. She stood her ground to receive this oddity while Guy took refuge at the shrimp platter and watched. Pierre talked animatedly and gesticulated wildly. His entire being, in fact, was a study in unbridled motivity. Guy guessed the thread of his conversation was as random as his body movements.

"Well?" he asked Claire once Pierre had latched onto the next passer-by.

"Well, first, you're a coward," she teased in a tone of

mock offense. "You abandoned me." Guy didn't deny it. "Secondly, his name is not Pierre, it's John. John Mills. He doesn't speak a word of French and doesn't smoke, as far as I can tell. And the diagnosis is the same: He's desperate to be a part of something. He's chosen artists. Could be worse." She looked up at Guy. "I know one. He's not so bad."

Before Guy could unravel this left-handed flattery, they were interrupted by the shrill laugh of a striking, young woman in spiked heels posed enticingly in the doubledoor frame as if wanting to attract the most attention possible before making an entrance. She succeeded. She stroked her long red hair and shook it back provocatively, a motion that emphasized her round breasts and lifted her short T-shirt to reveal a diamond-studded navel above her low-cut jeans. Her smile, accentuated with glossy red lipstick, was self-confident, leaving no doubt she was well aware of her good looks. The crowd jostled for a vantage point to watch the exhibition. Claire's eyebrows rose. It was Guy's turn to hide a snigger. He couldn't wait for her analysis of this one.

11

First Impressions

Before Claire had a chance to comment on the enticing redhead, Meilin tapped the mic. The noise in the room lowered to a muffled hum as she gave a brief welcome and acknowledged the show's broad support and many volunteers. Finally, she introduced the art show committee.

"Since the show is to benefit the library, Peggy Cyr was an obvious choice."

The middle-aged, native Mainer stepped up next to Meilin and spoke a few words over half-moon glasses about her hopes for library improvements from the proceeds.

"Next is Roxanne Nadeau, who collected and tagged all the artwork and led the team that arranged the exhibits. We had so many entries that no single premise was large enough to house the entire body of work."

Roxie waved.

After Meilin's rundown of the exhibit locations, she invited the crowd to visit the displays over the next two weeks leading up to the awards presentation. Volunteers spread out through the room handing out art-walk maps.

Many in the crowd lingered at the library to chat and finish their drinks. Guy was not among them. He placed his hand on the small of Claire's back and took his turn steering them through the room, this time toward the exit. It was a beautiful Maine night, and they deep-breathed the cool, salty air in unison as they stepped out beneath a blanket of stars and headed for the first exhibit.

"All abstract work," said Guy as they entered the first venue, Mainsail Wine and Cheese.

"Yup," answered Ken Cross, store owner and self-appointed art docent, from behind the counter. "This is Christy's feature hanging over my head."

Christy Chase, Ken's partner of several years, had divided a large canvas precisely in half from the upper right corner to the lower left, forming two equal triangles separated by a wavy, white boundary. The upper left triangle was painted pale gold, the lower right a medium blue and dotted and dashed with white. The title, "Wave Meets Shore #4", Guy and Claire found, was indispensable to interpret the design. Once they understood, however, they approved, then circled to view the rest of the paintings.

The next stop was the Main Street Coffee Bar where the dining room had been entirely re-arranged to make room in the center for a mélange of media—pottery, sculpture, woodwork, textiles, basketry and glassworks.

"All three-dimensional," Guy said.

Claire bobbed her head in understanding as they slowly took in the exhibit.

The third and final destination was the Unitarian Church community room, the most spacious of the venues, which housed paintings in all media from impressionistic to realistic. Amateur works were interspersed tastefully among professional pieces. Guy's oil paintings hung conspicuously on the back wall facing the main doorway. "Tugboat on the Harbor", a fiery-red tug, "The Point", a view looking out onto the larger bay from shore, and "The Cove", a scene from Oyster Cove, formed an attractive cluster.

"Good location," Claire whispered.

"Yeah."

He pulled Claire to the side, and they both watched the crowd's reaction to his work.

"You don't need to hear the comments. Watch the body language. The unsuspecting viewer gives honest and uninhibited feedback."

When Guy had his fill, they began to wander the exhibit clockwise. Claire peppered him with questions about style, medium, composition and so on. He watched in amusement as she, in her newfound enthusiasm, put her nose right up to the paint. When they finally reached Guy's three seascapes, Leroy Hood was waiting for them. Several other guests encircled the developer.

"Are you the artist?" Leroy asked, reading Guy's name tag to be sure. To Guy's curt nod, he said, "Wait, you're the one who tackled the waitress at the Fish House. Great entertainment." Leroy laughed, which drew in the others. "He tipped a whole breakfast tray onto himself. Classic slapstick."

Stony-faced, Guy began to turn away, but Leroy stepped into his path. Clearly, he hadn't finished his little theatrical and meant to detain Guy a bit longer as a prop. Guy glared and again turned to leave. Leroy stopped him a second time.

"I'm Leroy Hood." He threw Guy a dimpled smile and waited for recognition. Guy said nothing. Leroy proceeded undeterred. "I'm giving our guests here a tour. This tugboat is great. One of the best, I would say." Heads moved up and down in agreement. "I thought you'd appreciate the feedback." He beamed beneficently.

"Right," Guy answered tightly.

Leroy waited for a few more onlookers to collect around him before he delivered the punch line.

"I was the impetus for this show. Development of

the arts in Mayenne Bay is an important part of my overall plan for improvement."

The circle of listeners responded appreciatively. Guy did not. When the group moved on, his eyes followed Leroy's back, indignation rising.

"That was weird," Claire observed with a frown.

"Weird doesn't begin to describe it. Like he's some kind of hero. Who knows if it's even true?"

"I was referring to his comment about your painting. He's apparently oozing with money. He waits around to tell you he loves your work, best in show, et cetera, but not enough to buy it…," she leaned over and looked at the price, "…even for so little, as if his compliment were compensation enough."

She wrinkled her nose.

Guy shrugged it off.

"Frankly, I'd rather not count the man among my collectors. Let's move on before he returns for an encore."

They passed Pierre Cliché—Guy wondered if he would ever be able to call him John Mills—who was holding forth to anyone in the vicinity on the significance and challenges of his work. He gestured so dramatically that he bumped into people and repeatedly had to slide his beret back to the top of his greasy head. Claire watched and listened from the sidelines.

"His paintings suit him," she said quietly into Guy's ear, "like he's trying for something but not quite achieving it. Even his signature is disordered, sprawled differently on each canvas and illegible. Does it say John Mills?"

"Yeah, but Pierre Cliché would be far more fitting."

"Your signature was the same on each canvas, and you placed it discreetly. I almost couldn't find it."

"It's a fine balance. I want people to know it's my work but I don't want my name to interfere with the creation. It's always at the bottom, but the actual placement is determined by the composition."

"Sounds like you've given it a lot of thought, whereas Pierre…" She let the thought dangle.

"You'd be surprised how much thought artists give to their signatures. Signatures have the potential to become trademarks. Everyone recognizes Norman Rockwell's, for example, with or without the painting behind it."

Claire studied Pierre and tilted her head thoughtfully.

"He's a sad character, I think."

Guy looked from Claire to Pierre and back again. Her peeling back of people's onion layers seemed to be an involuntary reflex. He shifted uncomfortably. *I wonder what she makes of me.*

The next artist was eighteen-year-old Rhonda Grace, daughter of Thomas and Beatrice. Rhonda was a local celebrity for her acrylic paintings of plush cats worked in close detail and exaggerated colors. She stood before her display, surrounded by family and well-wishers, in a pale-blue shift dress that beautifully offset her smooth, brown skin. Her tightly curled, black hair was held back by a matching satin hairband. Her dark eyes positively glowed.

"The name 'Grace' fits her," observed Claire. "And look how she signed her canvases. Precise and clean. Same corner each time. I'm beginning to think there's a whole school of psychology to be discovered in artist's signatures."

Guy introduced Claire to Rhonda.

"You've already sold two!" he exclaimed, eyeing the red dots on the painting title cards. "Well done."

The final display consisted of two medium-sized still lifes in distressed frames. Though finer details were lacking, the artist had used bright colors and bold strokes to achieve arresting flower compositions. Claire was very taken by these. She and Guy snaked around several viewers to escape the glare from the overhead lighting and get a better look but they were partially obstructed by a short man in a shabby, green cardigan who stood about twelve inches from the paintings, muttering.

"I saw that man while I was painting on the wharf," Guy whispered with a leftward jerk of his head toward the green cardigan.

"He walked by me in the park," Claire said, then turned back to the flower paintings.

"Impressionistic style, right?" She checked Guy's reaction. "Just look at those lupines. Too bad the light is so poor."

She shifted again, to no avail.

"Mm," murmured the shabby man as if in response.

"That's a bit over-the-top," Claire said discreetly with a nod toward the lower right corner of one canvas. The artist's signature, "M. LaBelle", stretched prominently in garish, neon-orange script across the entire corner and flared brilliantly in the fluorescent light. "Even for a painting this colorful, it's a bit distracting." She moved in closer to read the artist's bio. "I would guess, from that conspicuous signature, that M. LaBelle is one of those extra-large personalities. Looks like 'M' is for Monique. Monique LaBelle."

The man in the cardigan blinked and shifted his weight from one foot to the other. Some commotion arose near the door, and all three craned their necks to find the cause.

"Oh," Claire said, eyes sparkling devilishly. "Do you think this dramatic signature could be the work of our little narcissist?"

"Narcissist?" Guy asked. The book Claire had been reading at Oyster Cove flashed across his mind.

Claire inclined her head almost imperceptibly toward an approaching group at the center of which was the woman whose appearance at the reception had caused such a stir.

"I'm guessing this creature is Monique."

Sure enough, the flashy young woman and Monique LaBelle were one and the same. Monique and her entourage stopped in front of her paintings, crowding out Guy, Claire and the cardigan-man. The artist bestowed a cool, self-assured smile on her fans.

"They're beautiful, Monique," crooned Gloria Townsend, owner of the Town's End Bed-and-Breakfast.

The sentiment reverberated among Monique's other admirers and was echoed lustily by Leroy Hood, who hung to the back, flanked as he was by his business associates and the mayor. Monique flitted and floated before them like an exotic bird but said very little.

By this time, the church community room had become almost too congested to move. Guy and Claire decided it was time to leave.

"Come on, confess," Guy teased when they finally made their way out the door. "You were having more fun analyzing the artists than looking at the art. John-Pierre the Disordered, Rhonda the Sweet and Monique the Narcissist."

"You don't find it fascinating? The signatures alone make a study, but seeing the artists in person next to their work and signatures, I can't help but draw parallels. It's true for you, too. Your personality radiates from your paintings and signature."

"I hope you aren't classing me with Monique or John-Pierre."

"Of course not, but the principle's the same. There's a subtlety to your work that I see in your nature."

"Maybe," answered Guy, not sure how far to commit to her theory.

"All I'm saying is that I don't think you can easily separate the work from the artist. Monique is daring, attention-seeking. Look at her bold colors and neon signature. John-Pierre's canvases and signature, like him, are theatrical and disordered. Rhonda is open, straightforward, like her cats. Don't you think there's a pattern here?" She stopped and turned to him. "Mind going home now? I've had enough people for one night. My head is swimming."

Guy was taken aback.

"I thought you liked people. You mingle so easily."

"I do like people and I do mingle easily, but having the skill doesn't mean I thrive on it. After a few hours in a noisy crowd under bright lights, I need time back in my shell."

She looked up at him after this confession, auburn hair and hazel eyes shining in the moonlight. In an instinctive gesture of empathy, he took her hand and squeezed it. Claire squeezed back and, though Guy loosened his hold to leave her free, she didn't withdraw. Their pace slowed to a stroll as each fell into silent reflection over this new connection. Claire trained her eyes on the ground. Guy, grateful for the cover of darkness, grinned like an idiot. He hadn't needed speech at all. He should have known.

12

Search for Meaning

On Friday evening, a week after the art show opening, Claire met Guy at the church community room after work.

"The "Tugboat on the Harbor" painting sold!" he told her, relief on his face. He had feared none of his paintings would sell.

Claire sped directly to his display to take in the red-dot "SOLD" sticker and beamed her pleasure. She took Guy's arm, and they walked the entire exhibit again looking for red dots.

"The man in the green sweater is back at Monique's work," Guy remarked.

They both stood for some time considering him.

"I see you've discovered Morrie," came a voice from behind.

Guy and Claire jumped and swung around, self-conscious at having been caught openly staring. It was Peggy, whose kind face bore no judgment.

"His name is Morrie?" was all Claire could think of to say.

"Yes. He lives at the Whispering Seabreeze residence and is always about town. Comes into the library at least once a week."

"I've seen him," Guy said in a low voice. "Is he…okay?"

"Some people find him strange, but I don't see it," Peggy answered. "He's a loner but intelligent and a great reader. All topics. Math, science, psychology. I'm helping him now with some art history books inspired by the show. He's visited Monique's flower paintings every day, I think."

They all turned in tandem toward the display where Morrie stood captive.

"I wonder what has him so transfixed," Claire said.

Peggy shrugged.

"Hard to say, though Monique seems to have gathered quite a following. In fact, I was coming over this way to post this."

She proceeded to Morrie's side. Guy and Claire trailed behind her.

"Hi, Morrie. Looks like you're not Monique's only fan. Gloria Townsend went nuts over the 'Lupines'. And now this sale."

Peggy reached out to affix a red dot to the name tag for Monique's painting of blossomed beach roses, then turned and gestured.

"Morrie, this is Guy Gardiner, one of the artists. His work is on the back wall. And this is Claire Munro. Claire and Guy, meet Morrie Appleton."

The three greeted one another then turned back to the art on the wall.

"I really like Monique's pieces. Do you know much about her?" Claire asked Peggy. "She didn't provide much of a bio with her registration."

"I only know what I've seen here. Never laid eyes on her before."

They all slipped into thought and then quickly out again. Peggy returned to the library. Guy and Claire each headed home. Morrie continued his solitary vigil.

Next morning, Guy dressed hurriedly and loaded his art gear into the car. He had agreed to join Claire on her Saturday morning walk along the waterside before breakfast but had overslept. By the time he reached town, it was already swarming with the usual volume of seasonal visitors in June, forcing him to park several blocks from the wharf. With the extra distance to cover, and hindered further by his weighty gear, he arrived late.

Before him, the bay twinkled in the full sun like a field of diamonds. Seagulls circled overhead in anticipation of the incoming catch. A schooner slid gracefully to dock, and several smaller sailboats made their way in the other direction. It was the kind of scene that had first drawn Guy to Mayenne Bay. There was always something to paint.

He spotted Claire seated at an outdoor table at the Wharf Café, sipping coffee, her face turned toward a man just rising from the table. Morrie! Even at a distance, Guy couldn't mistake that green cardigan. Did the man wear nothing else? Guy allowed Morrie to take full leave of Claire before he approached the table with an expression mixed of contrition and incredulity.

"Where did he come from? He wasn't so friendly last night."

He stowed his gear and made his way around the table to his seat.

"No, he wasn't. I was walking along the path earlier, waiting for you," she said and cleared her throat for effect. "I saw him sitting alone on a bench reading Viktor Frankl."

"Who?"

"Morrie."

"No, I mean the Viktor guy."

"Oh. Viktor Frankl. He was an Austrian psychiatrist imprisoned in a World War II concentration camp who came out with a new philosophy of living. He wrote about it in *Man's Search for Meaning.*"

"Oh."

Guy reached over to grab an untouched slice of toast from Claire's plate, then waved to the waiter. He was starving and sorely needed his morning tea.

"Anyway, he—Morrie—was reading Frankl, of all things. We've been thinking he's a bit unhinged, and there he was reading about logotherapy."

"Logo…what?"

"Logotherapy. That's what Frankl called his theory. So, I stopped to say 'hello' and remarked on his reading, since Frankl is a favorite of mine."

"Nothing could be more natural," Guy answered sarcastically. "And?"

"He didn't say much. Just 'nice to see you'. Later, he came up to me while I was sitting here. He started by saying he doesn't meet many people familiar with Frankl."

"No kidding."

"As you were late," she paused and threw him a stern look, "I invited him to breakfast."

"Sorry. I overslept and timed things badly this morning." She didn't contradict him. "So, what did you learn?"

"I like him. He seems normal, just lonely, like Peggy told us." Her eyes drifted toward the Whispering Seabreeze home. "He's not entirely happy in the group home but at least he has a roof over his head. He lost everything in the Great Recession, and this is where he ended up. Poor guy. He used to be a math teacher someplace in Massachusetts."

"You got all this from a first conversation? Never mind," Guy answered himself. "Of course you did. Did he mention Monique's paintings?"

"No, we didn't get into that. We talked about Frankl's philosophy—about finding positive meaning in life under the worst of circumstances. Poor Morrie seems to need a new way to look at the world after it failed him." Her voice trailed off, and she gazed again toward the Whispering Seabreeze.

Guy watched her face as she struggled to make sense of her latest subject. She put so much energy into understanding strangers. She didn't just class them into neat and easy categories like he did but strove for real insights. He'd never seen someone work so hard at it. Strangers made Guy uneasy, at least, they did until Claire made things clearer. Her name, it occurred to him as he watched her ruminate over Morrie, was so fitting. Human drama followed her like gawky boys follow the class beauty and seemed to catch up with her just as clarity was needed.

After breakfast, they parted, Claire for Grace Grocery, and Guy for Creative Agenda.

Creative Agenda appeared deceptively small from its narrow Main Street façade but it stretched back a considerable length to house materials for just about every art and craft known to humankind. Guy knew he would find what he needed. On the off chance he didn't, Meilin would move mountains to get it. He had so much confidence in her that he'd stopped ordering online and transferred his full patronage to the store.

"Hey, Meilin," Guy called out, not seeing her. "Flat out of titanium white."

He approached the giant rack of oil paint tubes displayed with amazing organization. No wonder Meilin accomplished so much. Her disembodied voice rang out before her head popped from between two aisles.

"I've got plenty stocked."

She came forward, gushing with pleasure.

"I think the show's a resounding success, don't you? We're getting good press. It's putting Mayenne Bay on the map. The *Bayside Squawker* and *Central Maine Reporter* ran news releases before the reception. Community TV has been out. *Contemporary Maine* magazine is running a feature article in its digital edition. The print copy will be out next month. That magazine has reach, so this is a feather in our cap." Her face darkened. "And this after all the talk in April about pulling the plug."

"What?"

"Peggy, Roxie and I got some blowback after arguing against Leroy's executive session. Just enough well-placed people to threaten the show. Once Leroy openly backed it, the dissenters relented."

"The man whose interests you argued against saved the show?"

"Makes you wonder, doesn't it?"

"I just don't see him as a patron of the arts, no matter what he tells his groupies."

"Me, either," Meilin agreed. "Whatever the reason, he moved things in the direction we wanted."

"His support has a real up side. He'll want it to go well. I have the impression Leroy likes to be associated with success."

"That's how I see it. It's what I'm counting on."

"I've gotten much more from this show than I ever expected. Thanks for the kick in the pants to enter," Guy said earnestly.

"You're not really giving me credit for changing your mind, are you? Not when you know it was Claire." She eyed his blushing face slyly. "Gotcha."

Just as Guy set the paint tubes on the counter, the bell sounded over the shop door. Both his and Meilin's heads jerked around to see Monique burst upon them wearing her usual air of conceit as if it were a grand hat.

"Hi, Monique," Meilin greeted her.

At the sight of Guy, whatever Monique had come to buy shifted to the back burner. Meilin watched in disbelief, and Guy froze, as Monique's charm machine revved up. She slinked seductively toward him, eyes taunting, lips parted. It was the first time Guy had seen her this close up from her painted face and tight pants down to her ridiculously high-heeled shoes. He was revolted. He threw cash on the counter, thanked Meilin and made his way out the door, leaving Monique with what was very likely a new experience of being summarily ignored.

Guy fumed as he marched away and tried to shove Monique's behavior behind him. It wasn't easy. In between painting and graphic design, his heart and mind were all for his accountant-counselor. Practically everyone with eyes had seen that he and Claire were now a couple, but that hadn't deterred Monique from unabashed vamping. He growled and picked up his pace.

The night of the art show reception had ended in a long kiss and an even longer embrace just outside Claire's apartment door. Guy's steps slowed as the memory of it flooded over him, and his body responded as heatedly as it had to the real thing. He had walked her home. At the moment of parting, their eyes had locked. He flushed, remembering first the uncertainty and clumsiness of his approach and then his throbbing body as it battled with his determination not to rush things and scare off the ever-cautious Claire.

He had lowered his lips to hers—so moist and warm—gently at first and then, responding to Claire's eagerness, had fully taken her mouth to his. She pressed against him, supple, indulging, and he encircled her in his arms. Not a nerve in his body had neglected its duty that night. When they came up for air, it took all of his self-discipline not to simply scoop her up and head into her apartment. *Let her make the next move*, his prudent inner voice had urged as he had strained for control. In retrospect, it had been a good call. Claire had since become openly affectionate.

Guy extricated himself from the all-consuming memory and stopped. In his rush to escape Monique, he'd completely forgotten the varnish he needed. He swung around and made his way back to Creative Agenda, radiating indignation with each step. As he passed the alleyway between the coffee shop and art store, he caught a flash of red out of the corner of his eye. It was Monique's knitted top. She was raising her voice at someone. Guy waited until she shifted her stance to get a better look.

Morrie.

"You're trying to make a fool of me. I won't let you!" she told him fiercely.

She spun around on her very high heels, jumped at the sight of Guy, then made her escape as fast as her stilts and tight jeans would allow. Guy waited until the lipsticked bully rounded the corner, then entered the alley. Morrie had shrunk back, and his hands were trembling. Having just undergone his own encounter with the woman, Guy regarded the older man with empathy.

"You okay?"

"Yes, fine, fine," Morrie lied. "You're Claire's friend."

It was a statement, not a question. Guy nodded anyway. He guessed that being Claire's friend was an asset. Though it came secondhand, her credibility won the moment.

"I was trying to learn more about her—Monique," Morrie explained weakly, "because of her paintings."

"I see," Guy answered, though he really didn't. He was far more intrigued than he wanted to say but thought it best to leave the delving for Claire. "Well, as long as you're okay."

"Yes, thank you."

Morrie tugged at his wornout sweater, stood up a little straighter to reclaim his dignity and began making his way up Main Street.

Guy resumed his mission to fetch the overlooked varnish. At Creative Agenda, he found Meilin pouring over the Arts section of the weekend *Central Maine Reporter*, delivered minutes after he had departed the first time. The feature lauded Mayenne Bay's foray into original art. Monique's "Lupines" painting was featured prominently, as were other works, including a good-sized image of Guy's tugboat painting. A separate article was devoted entirely to Rhonda, the young, local prodigy, and her colorful cats. Photos of reception attendees were interspersed among the art. And Leroy had wrangled an interview in which he took full credit for the show.

Guy looked up from the newspaper to greet Gloria Townsend as she came through the door. It was rare to see her outside of her bed-and-breakfast on a busy weekend. She walked directly to the counter to take in the newspaper coverage. Her face glowed at the sight of the "Lupines" painting she'd acquired so advantageously featured.

"They've even named the B&B," she said excitedly. "A *Central Maine Reporter* journalist and photographer are staying at the B&B next week to cover the awards as a follow up to this feature. This show has been really good for the town."

Guy and Meilin exchanged furtive glances. They knew that Gloria's idea of what was good for the town arose from whatever benefited the B&B.

Gloria held the paper up to the light, then set it back down.

"I'm going to get a frame for this. Better let me have one copy for that, one to keep and two for the B&B lobby table," she said to Meilin and laid her credit card on the counter.

Once Gloria left, Guy reapproached the register, but his and Meilin's attention was again abruptly diverted, this time to the window. Leroy was passing by.

Meilin frowned.

"Not all ventures are beneficial to the town," she said in a scathing voice. "Leroy's project could potentially tear the fabric of what is now Mayenne Bay. He doesn't care about the fallout."

Guy's expression had turned sour. His opinion of Leroy had devolved from his earlier vague dislike to deep contempt. Leroy's rudeness and artificiality. His mistreatment of Celeste. His mockery of Guy. The list of offenses was growing. Guy was becoming wary of the condo scheme less from knowledge of the project than from the glaring fault lines in Leroy's polished persona. The developer's only redeeming act was his endorsement of the art show. Most people took this at face value. Guy didn't. What appeared to be an act of charity might have been a decoy for something else…perhaps a convenient litmus test of Leroy's influence. Guy shuddered. He feared they hadn't yet felt the full extent of the man's machinations.

Before Leroy's singular parade cleared the store window, it was disrupted by the rapid fly-by of a youth in a ski mask. On his shoulder, the bandit held a toy stuffed lobster, probably snatched from the Salty Dog Toy Store's display basket. Oversize, red claws flopped wildly as he ran. As the runner brushed by, one claw struck Leroy Hood square in the face. His self-control wavered fleetingly but just enough to give Guy his first glimpse of the man ruffled.

13

Distractions

The fourth Saturday in June marked the end of the art show and the evening of the awards presentation. To keep his nerves in check, Guy planned a tour of Mayenne Bay's garden walk with Claire that afternoon. They would lunch at her place when the glare of the summer sun bleached away the interesting shadows, then depart when the light was more suitable for painting studies. He pulled into Claire's driveway and threw the car into park. He was late. Again. Lateness was not a habit Claire prized. How many personality defects, he wondered, did it take to doom a relationship? He hoped never to know.

He opened the kitchen door with a full apology on his lips only to find Claire seated at the table with Rhonda, a convenient distraction from his tardiness. The conversation seemed to be winding down instead of up. Rhonda cast Guy a weak smile. A flush glowed on her soft, brown cheeks, and the remains of tear tracks streaked her face. She hiccoughed and drained the last bit of tea from her cup in an apparent bid to disguise her embarrassment.

The tea dregs wafted the scent of chamomile, so delightful to Guy's nostrils. Tea drinkers' noses were sensitive to the subtleties of fine herbs and flowery perfumes, which made them, in his opinion, far superior to coffee hounds. He likened the aroma of coffee to a garage band, whereas the fragrance of tea was like soft jazz. His smugness evaporated when Rhonda reached for a clean mug and filled it halfway from Claire's coffee pot. She gulped the hot stimulant quickly and rose, shoulders squared. She whispered "Thank you" to Claire and "See you tonight" to Guy, and strode from the apartment.

While they laid out lunch, Claire explained Rhonda's visit.

"We met at the bank earlier and started talking about the awards. Monique walked by—stalked is a better word for it. I wonder if that woman does anything unobtrusive. She buzzed right past Rhonda without a word."

"I didn't realize they knew each other."

"Recently acquainted through the show. Rhonda was drawn to Monique for her artistic talent and then for her...I guess I'd call it her sophistication."

Guy snorted, recalling Monique's antics at the art store last week.

"I can think of another word for it."

"Me, too, but Rhonda's just an innocent teenager from a small town. There's much that's intoxicating to her about Monique's beauty and energy and even her painting style. Apparently, Monique snubbed Rhonda several times before today. Rhonda's so well-liked generally, she's not used to such treatment. She was crushed and completely bewildered."

"That makes three people we know—Morrie, me and Rhonda—whom Monique has offended," Guy told her. He recounted his experience of last Saturday to Claire. "I'll be glad when we see the back of her."

"Don't get your hopes up," Claire warned. "She may be here to stay."

She refilled her coffee mug.

"By the way," Guy said as he set some more chamomile to brew, "couldn't you counsel without corrupting tea fans with coffee?"

"You're a snob. Both are tools of the trade. Tea calms. Coffee invigorates. You arrived at the end, after tea— late again, by the way," she observed pointedly, frowning at him. "Anyway, lots of people, like me, skip the tea step altogether." She took a huge swallow of coffee and threw him a challenging grin.

"And some never leave it. He poured the steeped beverage into his cup, dramatically inhaled the steam and took a loud slurp. "Don't expect me to convert."

They ate and chatted until the sun dropped from its pinnacle, then made their way over to the bayside end of Castle Street to begin the garden walk. The sky overhead was blue with great white, cumulous clouds that puffed in front of the blazing sun at unpredictable intervals, casting shadows that cooled the air. It was one of those fluky, sweater-on-sweater-off kind of summer days. Claire opened and closed hers in attempts to keep pace with the fickle sky.

"I wish it would make up its mind for more than two minutes," Guy complained, waving a pastel chalk over his head. "I'll never get a good color study with the light changing so fast."

Their progress up Castle Street was slow to accommodate Guy's efforts to sketch. After repeated attempts, he packed his pastels away and pulled out his camera. Through the lens, he caught sight of Peggy making her way up the street from the other end with a wagon in tow.

"What are you up to?" he asked.

"I'm getting the word out on the alternative plan to Leroy's condo project. It's an environmentally friendly housing development, tailored to the landscape, that preserves public interests and shoreline beauty. I'm asking residents to post these yard signs." She turned one over. Against a yellow background, it read in bright blue letters, "A Better Idea for Mayenne Bay".

"It's an actual plan?" Guy asked.

"Yes, and a good one, designed by Christy Chase, who is both an artist and an architect. It's drawing a lot of interest. Details are on Ken's Mainsail Wine and Cheese website."

"If nothing else, the competition is healthy," said Claire. "We know so little about Leroy's secret plan. I'll take a sign."

As Claire and Guy continued up Castle Street, it became clear from the number of lawn signs that Peggy had not overstated the popularity of the "A Better Idea for Mayenne Bay" initiative.

They were startled by a man's voice emanating from the back side of a modest bungalow.

"I'm telling you it's gone!"

A short and wizened old-timer stormed past the house toward the long flower bed that bordered the front sidewalk. The bed was full of early summer blooms and embellished with ceramic garden gnomes in varying sizes and colors. He gestured at the offending spot and waited as a very overweight woman emerged, panting and perspiring, from behind him. She heaved a breath from her huge chest and bent over her large belly to lean against a fence post. From all appearances, it was a hard job being the wife of Jay Brown. Ellie, a retired English teacher, had been at it for forty-five years and didn't appear to have mastered it yet.

The Browns' story was widely known. Jay was crusty and loud, a disposition made worse by chronic aches and pains from a life of lobstering and small farming. Several years ago, he and Ellie had sold their lobster boat to the boatyard and their farm to Thomas and Beatrice Grace, which had enabled the Browns to pay cash for their town bungalow. Though the burden of heavy labor was behind him, Jay's contrariness continued unabated. His battles with the mayor and town council, most recently against Leroy's executive session, were infamous. His tormented wife was a general object of pity.

Recently, Jay had begun trumpeting his green thumb and garden ornaments to any willing audience. He placed his hopes on his ceramic gnomes, purchased just this year, to improve his chances in the annual garden contest.

"Which one is gone?" asked Ellie.

"The female with the yellow cap."

He pointed to the corner of the flower bed nearest the driveway. A small depression in the ground amidst the irises was the only evidence that a chubby dwarf had once occupied the spot. Jay paced back and forth in front of the violated bed with the anxiety of a mother bird.

"Today of all days with the garden walk going on. They'll think I've lost my edge, those judges. I'll never win a prize ribbon now. It's that little thief. I know it."

"You don't know anything of the kind," his wife countered.

"I'm calling the police."

Jay headed for the house. Ellie lumbered and huffed after him, her tone both incredulous and sardonic.

"Sending the town into orange alert for an abducted garden gnome? Like the police have nothing else to do."

The Browns disappeared into the bungalow.

"That is one daring bandit if he's crossed Jay Brown," Guy whispered to Claire from the spot where they waited in the shadows.

"Poor Ellie," she murmured.

He gently took her arm and steered her past the fracas to another splendid bed of bearded irises one house over. Claire had done enough counseling for one day, in his estimation.

"After Peggy, then Jay, I've lost the thread of our conversation. What were we talking about?" asked Claire.

"Monique."

"Oh, yeah. Do you wonder, under all that glamour, what it is she doesn't want us to see? It's the same with Leroy, always dressed to perfection. What's beneath the mask of the paragon? Those two would make a great pair."

"I'm more intrigued by Monique's behavior to Morrie. What did the man do to earn such contempt?"

Claire crossed her arms against her chest.

"Nothing, I'm sure."

"Claire, just because he reads Frankl doesn't mean he's incapable of antagonism. He might just be an annoying fan."

"That isn't enough to generate the degree of anger Monique displayed. Morrie may be needy but he wouldn't behave offensively." She began to gather momentum. "He…"

"Okay, okay," Guy cut her off and held up his hands in surrender, hoping to dodge her awakening temper. He hadn't yet born the full brunt and would just as soon avoid it. "But you hardly know him."

"I've spoken with him enough to form an impression. Peggy thinks well of him, too. He's shown a quiet interest in Monique's paintings and in the artist herself, nothing more. Why would that offend her?"

"No idea."

Guy pulled out his sketchbook again and focused on completing his sketch before the sun made a fool of him again. Claire held back her next question until he closed the pastel box.

"Other than the argument you witnessed, have you ever seen Monique and Morrie together?"

"No. Not even in front of her paintings."

"Me, either." Claire released a sigh of disgust.

"Either way, Monique's reaction in the alley was extreme, and her behavior to you in the store was nauseating."

"Yeah, I thought so."

Over the next hour, Guy made two more disappointing sketch attempts. By this time, the sky was beginning to gray, and his mind shifted to what, if anything, the awards presentation had in store for him. Unable to keep a clear head any longer, he threw in the towel, and they headed home to dress.

***

"You look beautiful," Guy said, back again in Claire's kitchen.

Claire wore a tea-length, butter-yellow dress that accentuated the curves of her slim body. Her auburn hair was brushed back from her face, emphasizing the bright, hazel eyes that had first captivated him. Guy's eyes roved over her and lingered on her long neck and soft shoulders until she drew on her pale blue shawl. He reached out with both hands and pulled her toward him. Though his heart was pumping, he managed a gentle embrace, careful not to wrinkle Claire's clothing in the process. He'd been coached by his sisters that starting the evening by creasing a woman's attire was a serious faux pas, even if done out of passion. And Claire was the most fastidious person he'd ever met.

"I've never seen you in a dress before. It's a good look on you."

"Thanks. I had a rare inspiration tonight. Don't get used to it." Her cheeks warmed with his compliment just the same. "You look nice, too."

Guy accepted Claire's words but heard them with skepticism. His blonde hair was neatly combed, and he had exchanged his painting clothes for navy blue pants, an offwhite polo shirt and his best pair of loafers, the finest choices in his limited wardrobe. He doubted Claire was impressed but hoped his appearance was, at least, passable. He was sure it was adequate for the awards presentation. Attire would run the gamut from summer shorts and thong sandals to black dinner dresses and heels. Dress code in Maine was open to broad interpretation, and Guy, for one, loved the lack of pressure.

Under increasingly dark clouds, they slipped into his car and headed for the event that would mark the end of Mayenne Bay's first official step into the art world.

"I love to see what people wear at events like this," Claire said. "Clothes reveal a lot. Take Monique, for example. She'll wear something tight, scanty and distracting. Morrie will dress for comfort. John-Pierre will be untidy." She continued in this vein until they reached the high school.

"So, what do our clothes say about us?" Guy challenged her as they climbed from the car.

"For one thing, you don't enjoy formality. It would be hard to get you into a tux."

He nodded.

"And I'm trying to impress my date with my femininity and sophistication."

"Mission accomplished."

She tossed her shawl dramatically. Guy laughed, took her hand and led her to the door.

14

Signs of Trouble

For the awards presentation, Roxie and her team of volunteers had relocated all the art show entries to the high school cafeteria to accommodate the volume of art and the anticipated crowd at a single venue. The 3-D display sat just inside the entrance to the left. On the wall alongside it hung the abstract paintings. The large collection of representational and impressionist work was spaced tastefully along the remaining walls.

Bruce Raymond, Mayenne Bay High School's art teacher of twenty years, had been chosen to serve as judge. The cafeteria windows, papered over all afternoon to give him privacy during his deliberations, were uncovered a few minutes before five o'clock, just after Mr. Raymond affixed the last award ribbon. At the same time, Roxanne flung open the cafeteria's double-doors in invitation to the public.

Guy and Claire expected high attendance, at least by Mayenne Bay standards, and arrived early hoping to view the entire body of work before the crush. Many others had been seized by the same idea. Well before the hors d'oeuvres and drinks were laid out, the great room held enough visitors to generate a significant din. The cafeteria served amply as an exhibition hall, however lacking in esthetics, but was woefully deficient in acoustics. Even at this premature hour, the chattering echoed off the cement-block walls and was unprofitably countered by everyone further raising their voices to be heard.

Roxie and Meilin stood at the entrance to greet guests, flanked by the mayor and Leroy. Peggy posed like a sentry next to the cash box by the door to collect the donations requested for entry and sell tickets for refreshments. She wore a pale green skirt and pink blouse, but no one was fooled into complacency by these soft tones. Her commanding, every-penny-counts expression drew liberal donations for the library and lots of ticket sales. Guy conspicuously tossed some bills into the box, purchased two drink and refreshment tickets and guided Claire inside.

The pair circumnavigated the room in their habitual clockwise direction, dodging the shifting, gesticulating crowd as they roamed. At the 3D exhibit, a set of three baskets, each exquisitely laced with porcupine quills in the old Micmac fashion, had won first prize. Carved maple bowls took second, and a woven silk tablecloth took third. Honorable mention went to a handthrown set of pottery.

The abstract collection was easier to appreciate in this spacious venue than in the confines of Ken's wine shop. Guy and Claire stopped to congratulate Christy Chase, whose "Wave Meets Shore #4" took first prize. From there, they moved to the remaining art, chatting with exhibitors as they went, until they stopped in front of John-Pierre's disordered paintings. A large, green "Third Place" ribbon draped from one of them.

"Unbelievable," Guy uttered under his breath to Claire as they stared at the chaotic attempt at a seascape. "I never saw it coming. He'll be unbearable after this and want to tell you all about the hidden meaning of his winning creation."

"Pierre may have found his comfort zone in the art

world, but I can't understand the award, not when other work in this room reflects so much more technical skill."

Guy answered more for himself than Claire, training his astonishment to remain within bounds before it amplified into indignation.

"Art judging is always subjective. There's no universal set of rules to define 'best'. So, Pierre had as much a chance as anyone."

Claire craned her neck to locate the odd man.

"How ironic Pierre is nowhere to be found in his moment to shine, don't you think?"

There was a sudden commotion over by Monique's work that drew the crowd, including Claire and Guy, in her direction. She stood, sporting a tight, red mini-dress and four-inch heels, with a beaming Gloria, before the "Best in Show" ribbon dangling from the "Lupines".

Guy stepped forward and extended the expected professional courtesy.

"Congratulations, Monique. 'Best in Show' plus two sales. You must be feeling great tonight."

The crowd applauded in agreement. Gloria reached up and possessively took her purchase from the wall as Guy headed around to her side to take a closer look. Monique's eyes narrowed as she followed his progress.

"Gloria, put that back on the wall!" she ordered sharply before Guy could reach the B&B owner.

Gloria started, then quickly and clumsily did as she was bid, leaving Guy no choice but to retrace his steps back to Claire. Monique turned her back on him with a sniff of dismissal just as Leroy appeared carrying two drinks.

"Here you go, Honey," he oozed.

He extended one to the prize-winner and planted himself at her side, emptied hand at her back. Monique took the offered drink in one hand and tucked her opposite arm snugly around Leroy's. They posed together like two movie stars in front of the "Lupines" award.

Claire and Guy stared. When had this happened? The sight rankled Claire after Monique's recent flirtation with Guy, though she thought Monique and Leroy a predictable pairing. In this opinion, she was not joined by everyone. Sandra, conspicuous with her trademark French twist, stood among the spectators just behind the couple, visibly stunned, mouth open. She turned abruptly and exited the building.

"Our illustrious mayor wasn't expecting to see Leroy with Monique, it appears," whispered Meilin, who approached Guy and Claire from behind. "She just left."

They all stared at the place where Sandra had stood.

"Monique was pretty rude to you, Guy," Meilin said. "It's odd for an artist to alienate admirers of her work, and she, of all people—I'd have thought she'd want the attention."

"Monique's rebuff of Guy had nothing to do with art. Guy snubbed her in your store, so she's punishing him," Claire asserted. "Anyway, I'll wager she's not here for her art no matter how talented she is. Her paintings are props. They lend an exotic aspect to her persona. If you want an artist enthusiastic about his work, John Mills is your man."

"That doesn't make sense, Claire," Guy said. "Unlike John's, Monique's work shows real talent."

"Are you honestly saying you've never heard of an artist who behaved irrationally? Think of the personality. Monique's not used to rejection. Anyway, even if she does like art, it's probably on the back burner while she focuses on snaring Leroy, which she seems pretty close to doing."

"To Sandra's chagrin," finished Meilin.

"Chagrin or just surprise?" Guy asked.

"Both, I think," Claire answered. She was standing on tiptoes now, straining to see. "Morrie isn't anywhere near Monique's paintings tonight. Maybe she scared him off, too, after that business in the alley."

Guy regaled Meilin with the full story of Morrie and Monique in the alley as the threesome passed by Rhonda's cat paintings. Two had received awards: "Second Place" and "Honorable Mention". They stopped to congratulate the beaming young artist before they finally made their way to Guy's painting display. Since the "Tugboat on the Harbor" sale, "The Cove" had also sold. "The Point" remained unsold but bore the honor most coveted by Guy, the result of votes collected since the show opened: the People's Choice ribbon.

Guy's face lit up. Claire pecked his cheek.

"Well done, Guy," said Meilin. "I have to say I'm not surprised to see your talent acknowledged."

"Are you the artist?" came a voice from behind. It was the *Central Maine Reporter* journalist with a photographer in tow.

"Yes," Guy said.

"Really nice work," the reporter observed, echoed by the photographer, and then proceeded with the interview.

Claire and Meilin excused themselves to get drinks while Guy answered questions and posed awkwardly for a photograph. By the time the women got through the long refreshment line, the reporter had finished with Guy, photographed and interviewed Rhonda and arrived at Monique's display. Claire waved Guy forward, and they moved a bit closer to listen in. The tall beauty struck a provocative pose in front of her prize ribbon but bristled at the interview questions.

"What made you choose wildflowers for subject matter?" inquired the reporter.

"I like them," Monique snapped, startling the man.

Seeing the shock on his and others' faces, she instantly caught hold of herself and transformed from unnerved to unnervingly seductive right before their eyes. It was a performance worth recording. The reporter was no match for Monique's skills at provocation or deflection and made his escape in obvious discomfiture, photographer fast on his heels. Monique lifted her chin high, as if daring anyone to comment, and breathed audibly when Leroy stepped protectively to her side.

"She's really on edge," Claire whispered, "and so reliant on Leroy. I wonder what's happened."

Guests continued to pack the cafeteria. Meilin, Guy and Claire leisurely circled the crowded room several more times. When they again rounded to the vicinity of John-Pierre's paintings and prominent award ribbon, he was conspicuously absent.

"Now that he has a bona fide bragging right, I thought he'd be right in front of his ribbon. He should be easy to spot in his bright whites and beret." Claire lifted herself on tiptoes again. "Oh!" she exclaimed.

"What?" asked Guy and Meilin in unison.

"Look at him. Over there at Monique's little gathering. And…he's all dressed up."

Meilin, who was even shorter than Claire, also rose onto her toes.

John-Pierre had evidently taken pains over his appearance this evening and donned an ill-fitting suit and gaudy tie. His scraggly white hair was slicked back against his bared head, and his face, though heavily whiskered, was free of paint smudges.

"And mooning," Guy declared with an eye roll. "He's caught in her web, poor guy. I don't think she even sees him."

They watched as Monique fluttered her plumage, ensnaring the men—they were all men except for Gloria—in her circle of admirers, while Leroy stood steadily at her side.

"She does seem braver when Leroy's there," Claire

said. "You know, aside from Rhonda, people are acting kind of weird tonight. Sandra left abruptly. John Mills is inattentive to his prize ribbon. Monique is agitated. And Morrie is not to be seen."

As if in response, Monique's groupies shifted, revealing Morrie's small form in green hovering well outside the circle.

"There he is," Claire gestured discreetly. "He's keeping a safe distance tonight."

Due to the incoming rainstorm, the crowd dwindled early. Buyers were permitted to take their purchases home. Participating artists would have a two-hour window early next morning to pick up any unsold submissions.

The expected deluge blew through the area overnight and left its aftermath in the high school parking lot on Sunday morning. Guy pulled in at seven a.m., just as the doors opened, withdrew a single box in which to pack his unsold painting and hopped over the patchwork of puddles to the door. The entire art show committee, he could see through the window, was gathered for the artists' arrival.

"What do you mean it disappeared?"

Gloria's shrill voice rose distinctly above all the noise, and her grievous tone echoed off the bare cafeteria walls. Guy automatically veered toward her.

"I've looked all over," Peggy answered, wringing her hands and running her eyes over the room nervously. "I just can't understand it. The building was locked all last night."

"I just heard back from Monique," Meilin informed them, shoving her cell phone into her back pants pocket. "She's on her way in right now. She didn't take the painting home. Well, we knew it was a long shot."

"I checked the hallways and restrooms," announced Roxie, approaching them. "Not there."

"Is a painting missing?" Guy, approaching from

behind, asked the obvious, unwilling to believe his own ears. "This is Mayenne Bay, not some crime-saturated metropolis. There has to be a rational explanation." He searched the dismal faces around him without a clue what it could be.

"The two you sold were taken by the legitimate buyers last evening before closing," Meilin hurried to reassure Guy. "All the others, in fact, are accounted for, except the 'Lupines' painting. It's gone. Gloria is the buyer. She had to leave early to take care of her B&B guests last night and didn't take it with her."

Guy swung around and scanned the room. The cafeteria hummed with leisurely, almost sleepy, activity. He could see nothing amiss. No strange or guilty faces. No signs of haste or furtiveness. Artists were mechanically, almost hypnotically, boxing up their unsold work in the open room for all to see. Even John-Pierre, once again in his customary white painter pants, was at work in front of his own display. The whole room radiated normalcy.

"Were there signs of a break-in?" Guy asked.

"Not that we've found, but we've called the police to be sure," Meilin replied gravely.

"What a sad end to a great event. I hope it's found quickly," he said before he headed to the back of the room to collect his painting.

He took this opportunity to approach John-Pierre.

"Hey, Pi—John. I didn't get to speak to you last night. Well done on the third place ribbon," he lied in the name of artists' etiquette.

John-Pierre jumped at the sound of Guy's voice.

"Yeah, uh, thanks," he muttered carelessly, oblivious to Guy's outstretched hand.

Guy pulled his hand back, unfazed. Not once had he ever observed John-Pierre attending to social courtesies. If there was any surprise, it was that he didn't grab this chance to wax eloquent about his award-winning work.

Instead, he remained on his knees, packing his canvases amidst a confusion of boxes and paper wrappings. Not one had sold despite the award ribbon. Perhaps the old man was dejected, believing a sale to be a stronger validation of his talent than an award. Guy looked away and rolled his eyes. He was starting to sound like Claire, looking for hidden meaning in everything. John-Pierre was an eccentric, end of story.

Guy recalled John-Pierre's ardent expression when gazing at Monique and suddenly felt a rush of sympathy for the smitten artist. She hadn't paid the least attention to John-Pierre…ever, as far as Guy knew. If she had, Guy was sure it couldn't have been any prettier than the way she'd treated Morrie or himself.

He didn't disturb the man again.

He moved to his own painting, "The Point", and took it off the wall, disappointed Sandra Edgecomb hadn't purchased this canvas depicting the bay and her own waterfront home. She was known for her pride in her place. Guy had hoped for both her admiration and her patronage, especially in view of the People's Choice award. Neither had materialized. But then, she had left unexpectedly early.

He closed his box and stood up just as the furor over the missing painting was reaching full pitch over by the entranceway. Gloria was beside herself. The painting had not been cheap, and she had counted on it as an enticement to visit her bed-and-breakfast.

As he listened to her tirade, Guy caught the flash of John-Pierre's whites as the outlandish artist slipped his stack of boxes out the side door the very moment Monique entered through the front.

Well timed, Guy approved him silently.

Escorted by Leroy, nose in the air, Monique joined the committee and Gloria, exhibiting only indifference over the lost "Lupines". Guy saw no sign of the hole in the pit of her stomach that he would have felt had his own painting gone missing. He shrugged her apathy off to the self-centered person she was. Gloria appeared completely nonplussed. She could expect neither help nor sympathy from the artist.

"I'd better get paid," asserted Monique, glaring at Meilin.

"All artists will be paid by check over the next week or so, as we informed you when you applied," Meilin replied in a business-like tone. "Right now, we have to…"

"I don't care about the painting!" Monique interrupted, right fist on her hip. "That's your problem. I delivered my paintings, and they sold. I want full payment. And my prize money, too." She flashed a large diamond ring on her left hand as she waved it to emphasize her point, then scanned the cafeteria. "Where's that little worm, Morrie?" she demanded loudly with another motion of her glimmering hand. "He's been obsessed with my paintings, standing in front of them for hours."

The room fell completely silent.

"What?" asked Roxie, Peggy and Meilin almost in unison, the pitch of their voices unnaturally high.

"Morrie," repeated Monique. "He's been harassing me the whole show, hovering around my work and cornering me."

"Maybe he took the 'Lupines'," asserted Leroy, bluntly articulating Monique's intimation. He positioned himself next to her, and she took his arm.

The others looked aghast.

"Morrie would never…" began Peggy.

"No, he wouldn't," Meilin agreed.

Roxie shook her head.

"Well, I want something done!" Gloria shrieked, now in a further heat over Monique's coldness as well as her loss. "I want that painting recovered. That's two thousand dollars of my hard-earned money. Do you know how hard it is to make that kind of money from a B&B? If Morrie didn't do it, he won't mind being found and questioned."

None of the committee members could think of an argument to counter Gloria's demand. Fortunately, Officer Ben Tripp arrived in time to save them from a reply. Guy used this convenient distraction to make a quiet exit as John-Pierre had so wisely done.

15

Above and Beyond

In his haste to escape the cafeteria fiasco, Guy, for the first time ever, arrived at Claire's place far sooner than planned. She answered the door barefoot, hair askew, wearing a bathrobe hastily tied around her waist. He melted at the sight.

"You're early," she said groggily and self-consciously ran a hand through her hair. "You're never early. What's happened?"

"Everything's fine," he answered quickly to quell her alarm.

Relieved, she turned and headed for the hall.

"I'll be out in a minute."

The front doorbell rang before Claire was halfway to her bedroom.

"What time is it again?" she asked, yawning widely.

"Way too early for company," Guy responded.

"Except yours, you mean." She threw him a smirk.

The bell was followed by knocking and a male voice calling Claire's name. Guy yanked the front door open. Nothing could have prepared him to find a soaking-wet teenager swaying and shivering on the doorstep. It took a few seconds for Claire's brain to catch up with the sight.

"Grayson!" she exclaimed belatedly and motioned for him to enter. "Grayson, this is Guy. Guy, Grayson." The men nodded. "Grayson lives up near Machias. Our mothers have been friends for years."

Neither Claire nor Guy had seen or heard a car pull up to the house. And, this…this boy…could not be more than fifteen years old, far too young to drive. How on earth had he gotten here? Before closing the door, Guy poked his head outside for some means of transportation and glimpsed a muddy, red racing bike leaning against the tree.

"What the … did you ride all the way here on your bike…in that rainstorm?" Guy asked.

"Yeah."

Grayson breathed an exhausted sigh.

"Through the night?"

"Yeah."

Guy's mouth dropped open, then closed again.

"Grayson, what's going on?" Claire asked urgently.

"Can I move in with you, Claire?"

Her eyebrows arched, but she said nothing in reply. Instead, with the sangfroid of an emergency room nurse, she walked to the hall closet and returned with a towel and a small blanket. She waited until Grayson dried himself. Then, she tossed the towel on the floor, drew the blanket over his shaking shoulders and moved him to the kitchen where she pressed him down into a chair. Spent from the night's ride, he sank easily.

Claire delivered him a glass of water, put the tea kettle on to boil and began to pull ingredients from the pantry. When, in the few troubled moments that had preceded, she had found mind space to think of breakfast, Guy couldn't tell, but he was grateful for her clarity. What could possibly induce a young man to leave his home and ride his bike all night in foul weather to see her? This mystery would have to be solved, but there would be no chance while hunger had a hold on Grayson. By the time Guy had this figured out, the dry ingredients were already measured.

Claire's presence alone seemed enough to trigger a full download. While she mixed and greased, the young man babbled like an over-wound toy. Guy knew Claire was sifting for more than lumps of flour; she was listening for clues—"morsels of honesty", she called them—the kind people reveal when their inhibitions are overcome by distress.

Despite her unkempt appearance, there was nothing disordered about Claire's mind. Her mask of nonchalance alone was worthy of a consummate thespian. Grayson played his role as if reading from a script. He gradually transitioned from run-on sentences to punctuated thinking. It was like a synchronized dance between the two; the closer Claire came to pulling muffins out of the oven, the more subdued Grayson became, his venting as cathartic as it was revealing. Guy listened but didn't move a muscle for fear of disrupting the flow.

Finally, Claire set a basket of steaming corn muffins, a butter dish and homemade jam on the table, then poured two cups of coffee and a cup of tea for Guy. She dropped into a chair and sipped coffee while the teen filled his empty belly. Guy could vouch for the very ordinary ingredients in those corn muffins, yet their effect was nothing short of miraculous. After eating a half dozen, Grayson pushed back from the table, warm and satiated, and said no more. His entire body relaxed against the chair, signaling his readiness to shift from monologue to dialog.

All this occurred before Claire had uttered a single syllable.

"You've said a lot of harsh things," she began, leaning in and settling a hand on Grayson's. "Is it really so bad or is that just fatigue talking?"

"The bastard corners her until she cries," Grayson said of the man living with his mother, his voice trembling with emotion. He squeezed his fists tight, and tears filled his eyes. "Jim pinned her to the bed last night. They were arguing about me. He hates having me around because I defend her." Claire's eyes widened. Guy squirmed. "That was the final straw. I just couldn't stand to watch anymore. I stepped in and pulled him off her, the effing bully. Then they both started ragging on me for interfering. That's when I took off." His voice cracked when he uttered these last words.

"Has Jim ever hurt you, Grayson?"

He shook his head to answer "no".

Claire breathed out her relief, incomplete though it was.

"He's too afraid to try my strength, especially when I'm mad. He's a coward except with Mom. That's why he wants me out or at least pushed aside, so he can control her." He released a sob and yelled, "She's wasting her life with him!"

"But she stands by Jim—not you—and is determined he should stay," Claire summed up the sad reality.

"Seems like it."

It didn't take a master chef to see that the combination of Grayson, his mother, and her boyfriend was not a recipe for a happy household. Grayson had argued with Jim and, unsupported by his mother, sought asylum with Claire. He'd entered her place fiercely condemning Jim, but this last evidence was even more damning of his mother. There was no doubt she had poorly chosen her present companion, but the man was obviously there with her permission. As a teen, Grayson was mature enough to understand and to broil with indignation, but powerless to shield his mother from herself.

Guy, at a loss over what to do or say, rose and rounded up dishes while Claire spoke with Grayson.

"You'll have to resign yourself to your mother's choices, however ill-advised, whether or not you remain in her home." She drew a deep breath. "And you have to go back…today."

Guy saw a flash of that cobalt-blue punch Claire held in her repertoire and dropped the sponge.

"But, can't I…"

"Grayson, you're only fifteen, an unemancipated minor. You have to go home, at least for now, until we see what we can work out." He opened his mouth to protest again, but Claire held up her hand to cut him off. "We'll be right by your side."

She stole a glance at Guy in a silent appeal to join her. He nodded his agreement then turned his head away, lips tightly pressed together. His hopes for time alone with the adorably disheveled Claire had been overset by the arrival of this impulsive and angry boy. By the time they returned, his plan for an intimate Sunday would be hijacked altogether. He was aware his feelings were selfish, but that didn't make acquiescence any easier.

"Now, call your mother," he heard Claire instruct Grayson, "while I shower."

By late afternoon, Guy and Claire were on their way back home from Machias. Not a word passed between them during the first hour of the ride. It had been a long and trying day and the most intense of Claire's encounters Guy had witnessed so far. The tenuous truce she'd negotiated was better than outright warfare but it left Grayson in a home where he could never thrive.

Guy looked over at her weary face and felt something like resentment over the extreme toll the day's exertions had taken on her. He broke their long silence and reached for her hand.

"This has worn you out. It isn't good for you."

"Maybe not," she conceded, eyes filled with tears. "But what could I do? This is family or, at least, close to it. Grayson is a boy. And I've been in his shoes. His mother isn't the only parent making bad choices. The only difference is I no longer have to live with mine."

"But, Claire…"

"Grayson has no safe harbor and turned to a family friend. That's far better than other choices a teen could make." She turned to face him. "Are you saying I should have turned him away?"

"Of course not," Guy answered. Truthfully, he wasn't sure what he was saying, but he realized this wasn't the moment to tax her further. "It's just that…," he fumbled for words, "…you take on too much."

Claire fell silent and stared hard out the window.

Guy recalled the luncheon in Oyster Bay and Claire's worries afterward about backfire from her coworker. That had been concerning, but today's ordeal had been far worse. For the first time, he fully understood how significant a personal price she could pay for her bleeding heart. By association, he was paying a price as well.

"Grayson's such a good kid," Claire resumed softly. "We couldn't just leave him without trying to improve his circumstances. Now, the adults know I…well, we…are watching. And Grayson knows I'd take him in if it comes to that." She squeezed Guy's hand and then released it slowly. "I'll be fine. I always am, after a while."

She dropped her head onto his shoulder and closed her eyes. They drove the rest of the way home without speaking, but Guy's discomfort persisted. He wasn't so callous as to blame the beleaguered Grayson for reaching out, and his heart ached for Claire, but the last eight hours—time he and Claire had meant to spend together— were lost. The evening, too, if he judged correctly from her present condition. He hadn't signed up for this kind of thing, this counseling run amok. He abruptly checked his indignation. He was exhausted—not an ideal state from which to judge clearly.

At Claire's place, Guy made dinner while she relaxed at the table with a glass of wine. She perked up a bit at the smell of the garlic, onions and herbs permeating the kitchen, then drew herself up straight while Guy regaled her with the story of the missing "Lupines" painting. By the time he placed two steaming vegetable and Jarlsberg omelets on the table and sat down, Claire had heard the full tale as he knew it. Her fork hung suspended in the air for a moment, dripping cheese.

"You mean Monique and Leroy accused Morrie outright—just like that? That's really low."

She sounded like herself for the first time since Guy had interrupted her sleep early that morning, though her eyes hadn't yet regained their usual sparkle.

"I thought so, too. Selfishness, I expect from Monique. Meanness, too. But, this…as if they'd planned it…Leroy jumped right in and added fuel to the fire. Neither appeared bothered about the missing painting or Gloria and certainly not about the impact their careless remarks might have on Morrie. Monique was too busy flashing her new rock. That woman leaves a bloody trail."

"Leroy, too," added Claire. "Celeste, you, Sandra, Morrie and who knows who else?"

Guy immediately regretted these last comments. He wanted to steer Claire away from other people's problems for the time being, for both of their sakes. Fortunately, she showed no interest in pursuing them further. He washed the dishes and left her to another glass of wine and a hot soak in the tub in solitude. "Getting back in my shell", Claire called it. This was a part of Claire Guy understood completely.

16

Speculation

Claire and Guy had arranged to be off work on the Monday after the awards presentation, a decision both prescient and welcome, especially following the Grayson episode. They met for breakfast at the Fish House but didn't linger, anxious as Guy was to get to the water's edge to catch the morning light. The bay was a stunning, sapphire blue. He went straight to work on his canvas. After making two rounds of the park, Claire sat next to him in her folding chair and cracked open a brand-new book on art therapy.

"Good morning. You're Claire Munro, correct?" came a voice from behind them.

Claire marked her page and twisted around to meet the gaze of a young policeman. Twenty-one or two, she guessed from his boyish face. He held his hat under his arm, leaving his thick, brown hair at the mercy of the sea breeze.

"Yes. How did you know?"

"Meilin Li gave me your name. She said you spend time down here." His eyes flicked over to Guy as if to indicate the reason. "I'm Officer Tripp. Please call me Ben."

"Hi, Ben." Recognition lit her face. "You're the new recruit…Bobby Tripp's son, right?"

"Yes."

His aura of authority deflated a bit when reduced to the offspring of the town attorney. He circled around the bench to face her.

"So nice to meet you in person, Ben. Are you investigating an abducted garden gnome?"

"What? Ah, no. We found the first gnome in the seat of a police cruiser, unharmed. We also found the one with the yellow hat hidden in some bushes at the park. Both have been returned to Mr. Brown."

A corner of Ben's mouth twitched. "Unharmed", he had said in a business-like tone, as if the ceramic figures were human, but his eyes sparkled with amusement. He resumed his questioning.

"I understand you're acquainted with Morris Appleton."

"Yes. I've spoken to him a few times. I was hoping he'd show up this morning." Claire peered around Ben. "He usually comes to the park to read."

"I've heard as much. He won't be here today. He was hospitalized last night. Collapsed."

Claire jumped up, inadvertently dumping her new book from her lap to the ground. With a rueful frown, she bent over, picked it up and dusted it off.

"Is he alright?"

"Yes. Just needs rest."

"Thank goodness," Claire breathed, sitting down again, spine erect with attention.

The young policeman repositioned his notepad and pencil.

"I wanted to ask you some questions about him."

She looked at him expectantly.

"What is your relationship with Mr. Appleton?"

"We're recent acquaintances. I met him a few days after the art show opened. We had breakfast once at the Wharf Café. We talked about books, mostly, but also his living circumstances."

"Anything strike you as remarkable?"

"He lost everything in the Great Recession and hasn't recovered from the experience. That's pretty striking, don't you think?" She turned reflectively toward the rippling water and, in a softer voice, continued, "Sorry, Ben. It's just that I can't help feeling for him. He's been alone and living in diminished circumstances for some time. He's a bit of an outlier here as a consequence, which has led people to prejudgment. I know he's an avid reader, was once a math teacher, likes art and has an interest in psychology." She paused. "Why are you interested in Morrie?"

"Mr. Appleton is a person of interest in relation to a missing painting."

"You must be kidding." She stood up again and tossed her book aside for emphasis. "I heard his name was raised in connection with the painting but I give it no credence. You have to consider the source of that insinuation." She looked hard at Ben, recalling the last time she'd seen Morrie. "Morrie arrived late to the awards presentation. He stood back from the crowd looking calm and certainly more composed than on other nights."

"What do you mean by 'more composed'?"

Claire cringed, regretting her hasty words. Much as she hated the idea, she perceived her trust in Morrie would be discounted unless she revealed more.

"When he stood in front of Monique's paintings at the opening reception, there was an intensity about him, or maybe you'd call it a fixation." She slowly recounted her observations of Morrie from that night through the present day, concluding with, "Ben, I really don't think he's morally capable of stealing a painting. Nor would he have the energy. And he's really smart. He wouldn't be so stupid as to stand in front of a painting making a spectacle of himself— in a very identifiable sweater, mind you—and then steal it.

Something about that painting definitely captured him, though—well, both of Monique's paintings and maybe even Monique herself. His interest in the show definitely centered on her work."

"I witnessed all the same things as Claire," volunteered Guy, who had put down his brush to join the conversation. "I also saw Morrie with Monique the afternoon of the awards presentation. They were arguing. Well, she was, anyway. She said she wouldn't let him make a fool of her and stormed off. He was pretty shaken afterward. Monique is not above revenge in my estimation, but Morrie doesn't have it in him…nor theft, for that matter. I arrived at the cafeteria just as the theft was discovered. Monique and Leroy blamed Morrie baldly and without any apparent basis."

"You're one of the artists from the show, right?" Ben asked Guy.

"Right, sorry. Guy Gardiner." He extended his palm, and Ben accepted it.

"Monique told me she never met the man before awards night," Ben said, scribbling rapidly.

"Untrue, as I've said. They definitely spoke that afternoon before the awards," Guy insisted, "though it may have no bearing on the missing painting. And Morrie was in front of her paintings almost every night. She never acknowledged him as far as we could see but she couldn't miss him. On Sunday morning, she referred to him as 'obsessed' with her work. She claimed he'd 'harassed' her and 'cornered' her. Those were her own words exactly. Hard for me to forget, they were so outrageously false. Morrie hung in front of her display and approached her at least the one time, but I never detected anything untoward."

Ben continued writing. Claire chimed in.

"Morrie is odd but decent. His interest in Monique's work has been singular, on the level of a quiet enthusiast.

The painting was on the wall the night of the awards presentation. He was in plain sight in front of it. From his personality, small stature and weak health, I just don't see him breaking into a building during the night to steal a painting."

"There was no sign of a break in," Ben reported.

"How could he have taken it, then?" Claire asked.

"No idea yet." Ben flipped through the pages of his notebook, then looked up. "Well, my thanks to you both. Will you be remaining in the area for the foreseeable future in case I have any other questions?"

"We live here," they replied in unison and gave Ben their phone numbers.

Ben thanked them and turned to make his way up Main Street, leaving Guy and Claire to stare after him, mystified. Once Ben was out of earshot, Guy spoke first.

"I know he's obligated to pursue all possible leads but he's wasting his time on Morrie. What would possibly have been Morrie's motive? Fascination with a painting doesn't inevitably lead to theft. Where would he hang it in a group home? He's poor, but if he stole the piece for money, he'd have to fence it. He may be sophisticated in math and psychology, but I just don't see the art underworld in his repertoire. And the painting of an unknown artist wouldn't get him much no matter how good it was. Two thousand dollars is a great sale price for Mayenne Bay but nothing like a high-end art market."

"If the painting wasn't valuable, the thief wasn't interested in money," Claire reasoned. "And it's not like Monique is famous or anything so that the painting would be a prize to possess for its origin alone."

"Someone might just want the art to look at. That's what art is for, ultimately."

"Yes," Claire agreed, "but we're talking about Morrie. He'd have to hide the thing. Seems plain stupid to take a painting to look at when you can never actually see it. The thief must have had some other motive. What about bringing disrepute to the show? The committee has enemies."

"Possible, but unlikely," Guy replied. "It's been good for the town. Everyone sees it now."

They both stood without speaking for a minute.

"How about revenge?" Guy asked. "Morrie's not the only one Monique hurt."

"True. There's also Rhonda, Pierre, the mayor and you. Rhonda is too sweet. Pierre is too disordered in his brain. And I doubt Sandra would risk her reputation. You don't have it, do you?" she teased.

"Technically, the painting belonged to Gloria at the time it disappeared. Maybe the crime targeted her."

"Does she have any enemies you know of?"

"None that I knew of before the theft, though she may have gained some after her lousy behavior yesterday morning in the cafeteria."

"Wait! Maybe it was the notorious masked bandit."

Guy gave this serious consideration.

"The painting is medium-sized—a bit clumsy for a kid that small."

"Would a theft increase the value of an artist's paintings from the notoriety?" Claire wondered.

"Could be, but what kind of increase can you expect from a two-thousand-dollar painting?"

"We've come full circle, then."

"Yup, and remember we're talking about a modestly-priced canvas by an unknown painter in an obscure art show."

"Better hang onto our day jobs."

They both laughed heartily. Guy returned to his easel. Claire stood up.

"Do you mind taking a break to go see Morrie? I'd

like to make sure he's all right."

"I really can't, Claire. I've got to finish this before the light changes."

Less than an hour after her interview with Ben, Claire rapped her knuckles on the doorframe of Morrie's hospital room. He lay there alone staring out the window, looking shrunken and depleted.

"Morrie?" Claire began gently. "May I come in?"

His head turned slowly.

"Claire, how nice to see you," he answered weakly. "Yes, please come in."

"I couldn't think what you might want," she said as she approached the bed. "I took a chance on this." She pulled a book from her mini-backpack: Viktor Frankl's *The Unheard Cry for Meaning*. "It's a loan from my personal collection."

"Thank you, Claire." His voice choked with emotion. "I'll take extra good care of it."

"I also brought you this," she whispered conspiratorially and handed him a bag holding a coffee and a warmed lobster roll. "Hospital food will kill you." They both laughed at this. "How are you, Morrie? You've given us quite a scare."

"I'll be all right. After all my losses these past years, I tend to tire easily and don't have much reserve. And lately, I've wasted too much of it on Monique LaBelle."

"Yes, you've seemed really taken by her paintings. What's going on?"

She held her breath. If Morrie exhibited admiration of Monique's talent, he could destroy her certainty about his innocence.

"They're good. Very good. I couldn't take my eyes off them."

Her heart sank.

Morrie pointed toward a pile of books under his

green cardigan on the window sill.

"Can you grab those?"

Peggy had visited before Claire in her recognition that, more than anything, Morrie would like books for his convalescence. Claire retrieved them and set them on the bed next to the wan man. Morrie selected a book on American impressionist painters in Maine and opened it to a spread of color plates.

"See these?"

While he nibbled at his lobster roll, Claire carefully sifted through the images.

"Very striking. What in particular do you want me to see?"

"I was close to my grandfather as a boy and visited often," Morrie began. "He had American impressionist paintings all over his house. Some of my most cherished childhood hours were spent wandering from painting to painting. I played on the living room carpet in front of a large painting of wild blueberries in bloom. When I think of that painting, he comes back to me."

"Is that why you were so interested in Monique's work? Because her paintings recalled your grandfather?"

Morrie bobbed his head, then his face darkened.

"I liked the paintings, but they also upset me. I grew up in a turbulent family. At my grandfather's house, I escaped all that. He taught me so much about art." He choked and said heavily, "I'd only just begun high school when he passed away suddenly. His place—my home away from home—was unceremoniously dismantled and sold at an estate sale along with all the artwork. It broke my heart. Monique's paintings…the wild flowers…they're like my grandfather's pieces. It's been so long since I've felt a sense of home anywhere. I could stand in front of them for hours. Well, I guess I did."

A tear glistened in his eye.

"Oh, Morrie, I'm sorry and so glad you told me so I understand."

Claire sat with him for some time in vicarious grief and also in rising anxiety. If she understood him correctly, he had just revealed a possible motive to possess the "Lupines" painting. After a time, she judged it safe to probe further.

"Morrie, you were mumbling to yourself the very first night of the art show."

"I've gotten so used to being alone, I talk to myself a lot. It was an emotional experience to look at those paintings. All the losses I've endured one after the other— my childhood, my grandfather, my parents' divorce, the art. Then, in the recession, my job, my life savings, my home of fifteen years. I had my own art collection, too, all lost in bankruptcy. The memories overpowered me at the sight of Monique's work." He looked contritely into Claire's eyes. "I apologize if I was discourteous. I was insensible to everything but the feelings those paintings evoked. They transported me back to the last time I really felt good about life."

He closed his eyes and dropped back onto the pillow, a signal to Claire that she should tax Morrie no further today. She stood up.

"Did you tell the policeman, Ben, all this?"

"Yes, of course, and I'm sure he thinks I'm raving. Everyone already thought I was a bit unbalanced before this."

Claire started to contradict him, but he held up his hand to stop her.

"It's true. You know it is."

"It's worse than that, Morrie. The 'Lupines' painting has been stolen, and you're actually a person of interest in the theft. Monique and Leroy both suggested you took it. Did Ben tell you that?"

"Yes, and the way my life's gone, it's not surprising."

"Morrie, you need sleep. I promise to visit again when you're more rested. And I assure you that neither I nor Guy thinks you are crazy or a thief."

"Thank you."

"Don't thank me until you hear the other half of the deal." Claire spoke now in a business-like voice as she returned the stack of books to the windowsill. "If you promise to concentrate on getting better, I'll keep you informed of what's going on." She grabbed his green cardigan. "And I'm taking this home to mend it. Deal?"

"Deal," he answered as his eyelids closed.

17

Bon Appetit

"Well? How is he?" Guy asked Claire without turning from his easel.

Claire relayed her entire conversation with Morrie. She worried that Morrie had incriminated himself by admitting his admiration of Monique's work. It would take time to ferret out the actual details that would either indict or exonerate him. The warm spot she had for him made her stubbornly hold out in favor of his innocence. She knew it made her own judgment suspect, but Morrie was alone, poor and suffering. She determined to do what she could to help him, all the while knowing it could end in disappointment.

"I told him I'd visit again. I'm hoping to help him get cleared. Hanging in limbo in his present state of health can't be good."

"It's not enough to be a counselor. Now you're turning sleuth?"

There was an unusual edge in Guy's voice. Claire had sensed something had been chafing him all morning. She doubted it was Ben, Morrie or the painting. Perhaps it was residue from the trying day with Grayson. She had felt drained herself, but wine, a hot bath—the fragrance of eucalyptus oil rising from the steamy water—and a deep sleep had rejuvenated her. Guy might not bounce back as quickly. Not everyone had her resilience.

She didn't reply. Instead, she cast worried glances at him and watched as he worked tension from his jaw. She was tempted to confront him but feared the attempt might backfire if he hadn't yet formulated his own thoughts.

Only as they were packing up did conversation resume, though not about Morrie.

"I've been asked to host the next art club meeting," Guy announced. "Could we do it at your place?"

Claire looked up from packing her bag.

"Why my place?"

"The group won't fit in my loft. It'll be just snacks and drinks after suppertime for about two hours."

"Okay, then. When?"

"Friday night."

"That's only four days away. I'll have a lot of work at the office this week after taking today off. I won't have time."

"I only just found out myself. Meilin called while you were at the hospital to say she landed a special guest artist she's been trying to get for months: Geoffrey Bristolwaite. Don't worry about food. I'll take care of all that. And if you need help cleaning or anything…"

Guy knew he was safe making this offer. He'd never seen a hair out of place at Claire's apartment.

"If that's the case," Claire relented.

"Anyway, the meeting will be just the right place for a counselor. Everyone's upset about the missing 'Lupines' painting. Gloria's downright livid. It'll be an opportunity for grievances to be aired."

Guy's tone, uncharacteristically sardonic, put Claire on the defensive.

"Yesterday, you told me I take on too much. Just

now, you complained about sleuthing. Now you're setting me up?"

She folded her arms and looked at him icily. It was more like boring a hole through him, really. He cringed, took two steps back and held up his hands.

"Sorry, that was out of line."

Claire breathed out tension while she waited, sensing another shoe yet to fall.

"There's one more thing."

"Just the one?"

She still held her arms against her chest.

"Geoffrey mentors aspiring artists but is very selective. I'm hoping to convince him to mentor me. His work is exceptional. Dinner out would be nice, but it would be so much more conducive to eat in."

"And you want to have dinner at my place before the club meeting," Claire finished his speech.

He said no more, aware he was in the dog house for his earlier cheekiness.

Try as she might to harden her resentment, Claire found it crumbling. The prospect of planning and preparing a formal dinner was just too appealing. She had just entered a French cooking phase, and her mind already whirled at the possibilities. Her pursed lips dissolved into a half smile which erupted into bubbling enthusiasm.

"If I work extra late all week, I should be able to take Friday afternoon off," she offered.

Guy reached over and grabbed her in a hug that lifted her feet from the ground.

"This'll be fun," she giggled as he set her back down.

***

Not until late evening on Wednesday were Claire

and Guy able to meet at her apartment to review a menu of multiple courses ending with dark chocolate mousse for dessert. They drew up a long list of ingredients for Guy to purchase and agreed to start cooking at noon on Friday.

"The French really have it down. Courses pace the meal," Claire assured Guy. "Plenty of time for conversation about art."

At this proof of her understanding, Guy took both of her hands and kissed them.

By Friday, the mysterious tension Guy had radiated all week had faded behind boyish excitement. All afternoon, he overflowed with giddy anticipation and rehearsed the questions he wanted to ask Geoffrey, signaling to Claire just how much he staked upon the evening's success. She threw herself into making a meal to match his high hopes.

About an hour before the Bristolwaites were due to arrive, Claire slid four picturesque sundae dishes of dark chocolate mousse topped with fresh peppermint leaves and raspberries into the refrigerator, drew two beautifully browned French baguettes from the oven and slid the duck in to roast. While the oven worked its magic, she laid a tablecloth of the red, yellow and cobalt blue colors of her kitchen, stood back and smiled. Even the meal itself would be a work of art.

Meanwhile, Guy set out flatware and plates, made the salad, then turned on the hot water for the first wave of dirty dishes, leaving Claire to the assortment of French cheeses, a task he happily ceded to her. She sampled each one as she fussed with their arrangement on the cheese board, then dotted it with fresh sprigs of parsley and basil leaves.

"It's beautiful, isn't it?" she asked.

Guy's response was lukewarm.

"I know cheese is essential to a French meal and all that, and as co-host, I should have sophistication consistent with the cuisine."

"But?"

He sniffed the board and turned his head away as the combined odors assaulted his nostrils.

"But, Claire, the bleu cheese alone smells like a locker room. I don't understand it. With over four hundred types of French cheese, why do people focus on the most pungent?"

In response, Claire popped a piece of bleu cheese into her mouth and closed her eyes in ecstasy.

"Who was it that described cheese as 'the corpse of milk'?" Guy asked.

"I think it was James Joyce."

"He had it right. I'll fall back on the Laughing Cow."

The front doorbell rang. Guy dried his hands and moved swiftly to welcome Geoffrey and Caroline Bristolwaite. Geoffrey was taller than Guy and muscular, in his early forties, with a bit of gray at his temples. Caroline was short and skinny with wavy hair, dyed reddish brown, hanging loose at her shoulders. Each was comfortably dressed as though primed for an evening of relaxation and enjoyment.

"Wine, Geoffrey? Caroline?" Guy asked in a pitch higher than usual.

While Guy poured, they exclaimed over the colorful table and the delightful smells emanating from the vicinity of the stove—fresh bread and herbs, roasted duck and lots of garlic, not to mention that plate of smelly cheese. Claire gave them a rundown of the evening's menu, then insisted on handling the finishing touches herself. She encouraged—almost shooed—the other three into the living room to view the paintings Guy had brought for Geoffrey's critique.

When Claire turned from the counter back to the table, she was surprised to see that Caroline hadn't followed the men. Instead, she'd seated herself at the table wearing an expression like she had just sucked a lemon. Claire placed a basket of warm bread, a dish of sweet butter and a bowl of salade Niçoise on the table and attempted to make conversation with the sour woman, to no avail.

When the men returned, clearly in harmony with one another, Guy visibly started. Claire's broad smile never wavered, but she used the eloquence of her eyes to convey to him that something wasn't right. She watched in dismay as Guy tore his gaze from hers in a clear refusal to read it, determined to dwell only on pleasant prospects tonight.

Within minutes, Caroline's moody spell dissipated as though it had been an illusion, and their mouths were easily alternating between conversation, wine, bread and salad. Claire decided Caroline's low mood had been nothing but a momentary aberration. Even a practiced people-reader was bound to err from time to time. Happy, for Guy's sake, that this evening was one of those occasions, her spine relaxed.

The lively talk about the current state of the art market slackened, and the discussion shifted to more personal topics, a natural progression among complete strangers who want to get better acquainted. Caroline's shoulders began to stiffen, and she withdrew in almost imperceptible degrees from the conversation. Her lips pursed. Seeing this, Claire attempted to signal Guy, but he remained focused on Geoffrey, not the man's temperamental wife. Just as Guy filled his mouth with a final forkful of salad, Caroline broke her silence loudly and shrilly.

"I've had my fill of art. I'm leaving Maine and Geoffrey," she announced stiffly, "to move to Florida."

Geoffrey froze.

Guy choked. *What the hell?*

Caroline's words stung like a jarringly dissonant chord. She shifted one of her shoulders at her husband in defiance reminiscent of Monique LaBelle. Neither Guy nor

Claire missed Geoffrey's expression. This was more a pie-in-the-face than a morsel of honesty. A chill settled over the table.

Claire stood up and moved to busy herself at the stove. Unobserved by the Bristolwaites, she rounded and looked meaningfully at Guy for some initiative. These were his guests. It was up to him to reverse the gloom. Guy caught her meaning but, if he felt any compunction to rescue the situation, he either wouldn't or couldn't. If something wasn't done, his anticipated evening with the renowned artist would soon fall to pieces. Claire managed to eke out words enough to break the paralysis that had seized the room.

"The second course isn't ready yet," she lied in a falsely pleasant tone with her back to them all. "Why don't you resume your art review in the living room for a bit?"

Guy winced. Claire was a terrible bluff, the worst imaginable poker partner. Admittedly, though, she did what no one else seemed able to do: She changed the dynamic of the room. Guy and Geoffrey obediently rose from the table and exited. Caroline remained frozen, looking straight ahead.

When the men left, Claire dropped down next to her and looked into the woman's face.

"Caroline."

No eye contact. No answer.

"Caroline," she repeated.

Caroline didn't budge.

From the disjointed exchange she overheard in the living room, Claire surmised that the overcome Geoffrey was unable to string together two words of sense. He returned to the kitchen, eyes cast down. Guy followed, dejected. He scowled at the insensible Caroline, then threw a searing look of disapproval at Claire's hand on Caroline's arm. The men reseated themselves without a word.

In that short interval, the electric charge among the party escalated from uncomfortable to excruciating. Claire rose again and returned with a platter of steaming roast duckling topped with wild blueberry sauce and encircled with braised endive, which she passed to Caroline. It was the only thing she could think of to move the evening along. Aside from one "please pass the salt" and the painful clinking of flatware on dishes, the main course was consumed without a sound.

Guy and Clare sat at the little table trapped in a dissonance not their own, Claire in bodily agitation, Guy shut down. Claire struggled to contain the ever-accumulating emotional energy. She swallowed too hastily to enjoy the excellence of her own cooking, then took refuge again in activity—pouring wine, setting the kettle to boil and making room on the small table for the plate of French cheeses.

With two courses behind them and the cheese now in circulation, the wine had flowed. Guy didn't indulge in alcohol, so he was always in an advantageously sober position to observe its effect on others. Claire still held the remains of her first glass, a sign that all was not right with the world. Geoffrey and Caroline had been less fastidious, as evidenced by the second cork on the table. Geoffrey sported a bit of pink in the nose and cheeks, and Caroline had eyes like glass—like tiny glass beads, actually, a bit scary.

Cheese knife in one hand, bread waving in the other, the woman suddenly and obscenely launched into a full elaboration of her scheme which, it was painfully obvious, failed to include her husband. In vino veritas. Geoffrey's reaction could have melted the cheese board.

Claire neglected the Brie and Camembert and nimbly shifted from hostess to referee hoping to moderate the couple's sharp exchanges across the table and rescue the evening. She cautiously injected mediative words into the cross-fire, poised to pounce on the slightest hint of conciliatory spirit. Sadly, there would be no progress toward peace between Geoffrey and Caroline this evening.

Claire served the to-die-for dark chocolate mousse, with espresso coffee and, of course, tea. By this time, a constrictive quiet engulfed the table as Geoffrey and Caroline, emerging from their angry clouds, became conscious of how much they had exposed themselves to complete strangers. They dipped into the dreamy dessert, heads down, probably tasting nothing. Guy remained glued to the spot in sullen silence.

Not until the dessert course did Claire fully surrender her naïve hope for a recovery. She watched in misery, wordlessly invoking the chocolate to live up to its reputation for mood alteration, but even chocolate failed to deliver the Bristolwaites' salvation this night. Their taut expressions revealed an inner struggle for composure and, finally, an urge for a face-saving departure. There was pathetic irony in the fact that their conspiracy to exit was the one thing they managed to do in sympathy with one another since they first sat down to salade Niçoise.

18

Impasse

The onslaught of art club members began just as Geoffrey and Caroline made their well-timed escape from Claire's kitchen. Guy plodded mechanically to the sink to address the disordered aftermath of a marital conflict over a four-course meal. Perceiving his low mood, Claire flipped on her social switch to compensate, spread drinks and snacks on the coffee table and took the lead with the club.

"We're so sorry," she extemporized as she greeted them. "The wife of the scheduled speaker was unwell, and the couple had to leave."

The claim was true enough that Claire could say it with a straight face. No one raised an eyebrow. With Geoffrey a no-show, Meilin abandoned the agenda, setting the group free to speculate on the preoccupation du jour, Gloria and her missing "Lupines" painting. Fortunately, Gloria didn't show, leaving the other members free to speculate, nosh and drink without impediment. Not a single soul cornered Claire to unload problems. It was just as well. She didn't have the energy tonight.

"Guy," she began when they were again alone.

He shook his head and pressed his lips together. She placed her hand on his arm. He withdrew it. His movements

157

tightened, and the corners of his mouth turned down with exaggerated effect like the face of a sad clown. It was so dramatic, it was almost comical, but he was far from laughing. They performed the final clean-up without speaking.

Claire waited expectantly for him to breathe a deep sigh and join her on the couch to talk the evening through. He didn't. Instead, he became more and more morose, a side of him Claire had never before seen. Uncertain of her ground, she suppressed her own discomfort and made no attempt to cheer him. *Let him find his own way*, she told herself, hoping it was the wiser course.

Guy boxed up his paintings and made the necessary trips to and from the car in a dampening silence, eyes pointed to the floor. Claire moved to the window as he pulled from the driveway in what she judged to be all-consuming self-pity. Tears of hurt pricked her eyes. He hadn't complimented her cooking. He hadn't commended her hospitality to his friends, her efforts to salvage the dinner or her management of the art club meeting. He hadn't thanked her for, well, anything. In fact, he hadn't even said good-bye. All she could do was hope for a better tomorrow.

There was no word from Guy the next morning, nor all day. No visit, no call, no text. Claire shuddered but reaffirmed her pledge of non-interference, convinced that approaching him before he was ready would not be fruitful. Again, she took refuge in action. She tended her herbs and did laundry. She brought leftover roasted duck, cheeses and French bread to Morrie, now returned to his room at Whispering Seabreeze, and lingered long afterward over a game of Scrabble. It was almost ten o'clock by the time she checked her depressingly dormant phone one last time, slipped between the sheets and drifted off to a fitful sleep.

She awoke to a Sunday as overcast as her spirits. There was nothing she could do about Guy at the moment, so she decided to concentrate on Morrie. He hadn't improved to the degree Claire hoped after a week's convalescence. She was convinced Monique's unfounded finger-pointing was at the root of his slow progress. Something had to be done. First, she needed more information. Meilin, she determined, was a logical place to start. As it was Sunday, there would be lighter customer traffic at Creative Agenda, and Meilin just might have a few minutes to spare.

Claire arrived just as the store opened and greeted Meilin. To her dismay, Guy came through the door directly after her. One look told Claire he hadn't recovered from the dinner party. Though his demeanor could no longer be described as morose, his manner was subdued, and his body language constricted. He reddened at the sight of her. Seeing this, Claire ignored him.

"Anything new from Ben on the 'Lupines' painting?" she asked Meilin.

"They searched Morrie's room and found nothing. No surprise there. Gloria's still in a stew. It's a shame to have such a shadow cast over the show. Ironically, business all over town is even better since the news of the theft. Rubberneckers."

Guy rolled his eyes, and Claire shook her head in disbelief.

"Meilin," Claire changed the subject carefully, "do you have the images of the paintings Monique initially submitted with her application?"

"Yes, of course. We kept all images for a historical record and to use for publicity. You know that from handling registration."

"May I see them again?"

Meilin frowned but acquiesced.

"Sure, but you're going to tell me why, right?"

She reached for her tablet, searched for Monique's paintings, then turned the screen to face Guy and Claire.

"Here's the "Lupines" painting. The next tab is the "Beach Roses".

"Thanks. I needed to confirm my memory that Monique exhibited the very same paintings she submitted as samples," Claire explained and closed the tablet.

"Yes. There was no rule against that. At least half the artists did the same."

"Have you ever seen any other work by her?" Claire asked. "Her bio was cryptic. Does she have a website or studio or gallery representation that you know of?"

"Not that I know of. Of all the artists, only Guy, Christy and Rhonda have an internet presence, and none of them has a public exhibit to my knowledge. The show didn't require this." Meilin stared hard at Claire. "What's this all about? We really don't need any more bad press."

Claire hesitated. She was fishing, she knew.

"I'm worried about Morrie. He's back home but not much better. Monique's accusation is wearing on him. She has certainly been there for all to see—more exhibition than we'd like sometimes—so it's hard to argue she's hiding anything. I just thought there might be something about her or her work that would give us a clue to the painting's disappearance. Morrie tried to learn more about her, if you remember, and she blew him off. The reporter couldn't get anything out of her either. I guess this line of thinking is going nowhere, but I wanted to start at the beginning."

It was a feeble explanation. Claire felt she was barely wiggling out of the situation, but Meilin looked satisfied. Guy practically sneered and he spoke with painfully strained levity.

"Watch out for her, Meilin. She can't leave things

alone."

Claire's insides jolted at these words but she said nothing in reply. She stepped out onto the sidewalk, headed for the nearest bench and sank down, seething at Guy's rudeness. At least now, she had an inkling of what had him twisted in a knot: He saw her as interfering.

A gray-haired man with a large coffee and a Mayenne Bay historical town map in his hand dropped heavily onto the bench next to her, making it creak. Claire looked up and smiled, their proximity making anything less a discourtesy.

"Good morning," the stranger said with a slight drawl as he pulled the lid off his coffee cup. "Y'all don't happen to live here, do you?"

"Yes, I do."

"What a beautiful place." He took a deep breath of sea air as if to give evidence to the fact. "It's my first visit to Maine. Always wanted to see it. I'm originally from West Virginia. I'd heard the two states were alike, except for all the water, of course." He chuckled and looked around him. "It's true as you head west."

"Really?" was all Claire said. She was struggling to prevent her anger at Guy from tainting her tone with this perfectly nice stranger. "Mayenne Bay is a sweet town. You see some of the best of Maine in a place like this. Where do you live now?"

"Virginia. Moved there when I got out of the service. Finally got the chance to come north."

Their chat lasted for about twenty minutes during which the Army veteran, who did most of the talking, shifted from simple chat to real disclosure in Claire's company. His appreciation of being stateside again, amidst such natural beauty, sharply contrasted with his vivid memories of the battlefield. Claire let him run on for his own sake but kept one eye trained on the Creative Agenda storefront for Guy's exit.

When Guy finally emerged, purchases in hand, he took one look at Claire sitting on the bench with a stranger, dramatically rolled his eyes and headed for his car in the parking space across the street. The Virginian had already wound up his story, so Claire politely took leave of him and followed Guy.

He heard her footsteps behind him.

"Done snooping?" he snorted, dropped his bags into the car and slid into the driver's seat.

Her gait faltered.

"What?"

Guy had yet to be acquainted with Claire's inner pit bull—the brute force of her temper. It now threatened to foam at the mouth. Uninvited, she hopped into the passenger side of his car and turned on him.

"What is wrong with you? You walked out without a word Friday night. Not even a 'thank you' after all my work. And I haven't heard from you since. Now, your words drip with sarcasm."

Guy was angry enough to overcome his surprise at her sudden attack and find the needed words.

"Yours would, too! Look, Claire, you're the best thing that's ever happened to me but you're not allowing this relationship to grow."

"What?"

"You don't have to entertain the problems of every stranger in town."

"What?" she repeated. "If you're referring to the man on the bench just now…" Her voice lowered almost to a whisper but threatened to quickly gather steam. "That man is a veteran with years of experience, including war time. He was a surgeon in the Army, like in a MASH unit. I was riveted. You would have been, too, if you'd given him the time of day. What he's seen. And he hasn't fully recovered after all these years. Are you telling me a twenty-minute conversation letting a man like that unload is too much of an intrusion into your precious life?"

Guy flinched and had the decency to look sheepish for a moment before he regained his train of thought.

"This isn't a relationship; it's a therapy session every other day. Renée. Rhonda. Morrie. A whole day with Grayson. All I wanted was a chance with Geoffrey. You had to meddle with Caroline, and then…"

"Meddle with Caroline? What are you talking about?"

"You were sitting right next to her with your hand on her arm when Geoffrey and I returned to the kitchen. You couldn't leave things alone. You had to pry. And then the whole thing fell apart."

"I didn't pry. I touched her arm to soothe her. She was way out of line but clearly struggling. Anyway, they were on the rocks well before they came in the door."

"You kept trying to referee their argument."

"I was trying to salvage the dinner that was supposedly so important to you."

"You're getting off the point!"

"What, exactly, IS the point?" Her voice was louder now, and he shrank back a bit but didn't lose momentum.

"You have to get involved in everybody's business, be the great rescuer, like you just did with that vet."

"You know that's an exaggeration. He didn't need to be rescued. He just wanted to talk. And he spoke to me first."

Tears of anger were now forming in the corners of Claire's eyes.

"Right."

Her face contorted.

"What are you saying?"

"I'm saying I'm tired. Tired of your sticking your

nose in, tired of letting everybody else pull us away from what we're doing, tired of the interruptions, the lost opportunities, the drain on our lives."

"Drain on your life? You're being melodramatic. Besides, some of the people I helped are your friends." She stopped, then added almost inaudibly, "I thought you understood."

"What I understand is that your interference Friday night turned a difficult situation into a nightmare."

"So, we're back to the infernal dinner again. You blame their marital problems and Caroline's effrontery on me? You hold my efforts to save the evening in contempt?" She choked on her tears. "And this after your plan to set me up to counsel the art club that evening? You're a hypocrite!"

Guy flinched a second time at this sally, and his face glowed red, but he didn't allow her arguments to change his mind.

"Maybe you should become a licensed counselor and get this savior complex out of your system."

Claire sat as stunned as if he'd slapped her face.

"I didn't realize how much this bothered you," she said in an eerie voice. "I thought you loved this about me, that people were drawn to me, and that I help them. You called it a gift when we first met."

"Not anymore."

Her face twisted.

"So now what? You want me to give up helping when someone needs it?"

Guy said nothing but stared straight ahead.

"Sitting there like a block of wood, seems to me you have a lot in common with Caroline. Maybe you should join her in Florida." Then she filled her lungs and yelled, "IF IT'S PEACE AND QUIET YOU WANT, I'LL LEAVE YOU TO IT!", with a temper so explosive Guy was surprised the airbags didn't go off.

ARTIFICE

She got out of the car and slammed the door.

19

Sandra's Lament

On Monday, the first of July, Sandra walked intently toward her office, resolved to shake off once and for all the sick feeling that hung in her belly like a bad meal. The high humidity of the morning foreshadowed an oppressively hot day, and her clothes were already damp with perspiration. She arrived early, more than an hour before the office opened. The place was mercifully empty, as she had hoped, having a great deal on her mind to sort out before she could comfortably greet her staff. She set a travel mug, filled to the brim at the Main Street Coffee Bar, on her desk and moved to the window, her customary spot for contemplation.

A full week had passed since she had slipped away from the art show awards. She had spent that week on vacation in Kennebunk. The time and distance from Mayenne Bay, the beautiful resort, the sack full of beach-reads—none of these had managed to dispel her discomposure. It had simply festered in the hot sun then hitched a ride with her back home.

Motionless, except for her convulsing jaw, she gazed out. The early heat penetrating the old panes was nothing compared to the heat of mortification that burned her insides. It had ignited on awards night when Leroy and

Monique had first appeared together as a couple. The sight had been jaw-dropping for the crowd but completely overpowering for Sandra. She'd been at pains to maintain her self-possession until she escaped the building. Even today, the memory turned her face scarlet.

She inhaled deeply, released a long, controlled breath, and rubbed her temples. Leroy had always made her feel welcome, respected and admired. He'd sought her out, chatted and flirted. In return, she had seen no reason to hide her attraction. Why should she? She was unattached, and the man was gorgeous. His intelligence and self-assurance were strengths that had always appealed to her. She had wanted him, plain and simple, and hadn't shied from letting him know. Leroy hadn't made a move, but neither had there been the slightest hint of an interest elsewhere.

Then, Monique appeared on the scene. No one in town seemed to have known her prior to her diva-like entrance at the art show reception, and not much had been learned since except that Monique and Leroy were now an item, and Monique wore his diamond ring on her finger. How had that happened? When? Had Leroy fallen head over heels, smitten like so many others in the seductive artist's orbit? Sandra doubted it. Leroy didn't seem the type to fall; he was far too deliberate. More likely, he'd known Monique beforehand, even as he'd been publicly escorting the mayor around town, smiling, pressing close and taking her hand on his arm.

She laughed bitterly.

During her solitary hours on the beach, she had replayed her encounters with Leroy over and over in excruciating detail. Their shared excitement for his project had been real, but the rest of the energy between them had been borne of Leroy's power to please and the intoxicating rush of Sandra's own libido. A wave of nausea rose up in her throat, and her chest burned, but Sandra didn't shy from these sensations. She allowed them full sway over her being to bring her foolishness home. She had received Leroy's attentions, even reveled in them, like a hormone-befuddled teenager.

In the throes of this delirium, she had accepted his assertions at face value and openly supported his intentions for Mayenne Bay with only perfunctory due diligence. She had defended his callousness as the detachment and calculating acuity necessary for success. She had kept the public at bay with a confidential executive session and ignored the potentially disastrous conflict of interest between herself and an aspiring developer. She had even chastised Jack Wayne for his unannounced meeting with Leroy on the wharf when she, herself, was guilty of blurring the lines between municipal and private interests. All these things Sandra had done when others, like Meilin, Peggy, Roxie and Jay, had argued for transparency and further investigation. She closed her eyes to avoid looking at her own reflection in the window, repulsed by her offenses.

Leroy had tested her loyalty, first with his entreaty for closed-door deliberations, and later with his hint of a second town in contention for the condo project. In both instances, she had responded like a faithful puppy and bolstered support among the council. Later, he had advocated against the naysayers vying to shut down the art show, a cunning test of his direct influence on town officials. Only in hindsight was she able to see his maneuvers for the masterful manipulations they had been. The mayor of Mayenne Bay had been off balance at critical moments when discernment was needed and had taken the bait, hook, line and sinker.

"Sandra," she said aloud, with grimaced face and tight fists, "you allowed yourself to be handily played."

She moved to her desk and sank down in the chair under the weight of her transgressions until something—

perhaps being back in the mayor's chair—gripped her and straightened her spine. She, Mayor Sandra Edgecomb, summa cum laude graduate, successful businesswoman and elected politician, was no limp fish. Above all else, she had always held herself accountable. Though it would be far easier to blame Leroy, the pressure of campaign promises or even hormones, she would not now permit herself the luxury of playing the victim. She had allowed blind attraction to supplant reasoned judgment and had actively participated in her own deception. With the harsh truth out on the table, the cool voice of the confident leader resurged.

You were elected to lead this town, not to hide or collapse when you have egg on your face, it chided. And it was right.

Sandra stood up tall and found her resolve. She walked over to the mirror behind the office door, finally able to look herself in the eye. Her understated appearance and somewhat androgynous figure recalled to mind the colorful and voluptuous Monique LaBelle. The perfect ornament. Despite the diamond ring, Sandra doubted Leroy, who calculated every move, had lost his heart. Monique was either made of similar stuff or tragically clueless.

"Really, Sandra," she told her reflection, "you should be celebrating your escape. Let the rumor mill work overtime speculating on the mayor's unrequited love. They'll soon learn, though your feet are made of clay, you're not the type to crumble."

Her newfound clarity might not win her re-election but it restored a modicum of her dignity.

Another stark realization followed—she seemed to be on a roll now—as the unfiltered truth unfolded, layer by layer. Having helped Leroy clear the town council and launch his project, she had outlived her usefulness. For months, he had cultivated key connections all over Mayenne Bay, imperceptibly extracting the reins from the mayor's hands while publicly bowing to her authority. By the time awards night rolled around, he must have felt himself in control and secure enough to drop all pretense. Sandra deduced that things must be going very well. Leroy wouldn't have cut her off otherwise.

She moved back to her desk and drew his presentation handout from under a stack of papers. The cold comfort of his business plan was all she had left of the man now, but the promise of his scheme still warmed her imagination. Economic development was an imperative, not a choice, in Mayenne Bay, even if its originator was repugnant. Sandra cautioned herself not to toss out the baby with the bath water. The town council, chamber and others had examined Leroy's proposal and given it their stamp of approval. Investors had lined up to get a piece of the action. There had been inspections and permits. The project itself may have true merit. But Sandra would not entertain any more wishful thinking, nor would she rely any more on the opinions of others. She sat down, took several sips of steaming coffee and opened to the first page. She would go through the entire thing again, this time with a clear head.

Outside her office, she could hear the usual Monday morning stirrings indicating Sally had arrived. The aroma of hazelnut coffee—Sandra's favorite—permeated the air, her assistant's subtle signal of solidarity. Sally was wise to everything that had happened to her boss. Though they hadn't spoken of it directly, Sandra suspected this included her delusions about Leroy. Of all the people in the office, Sally would be the first to perceive the changes in Sandra this morning.

Aside from wordlessly sliding a fresh mug of the coffee onto Sandra's desk, Sally tactfully spent the first few hours of the morning performing tasks at her workstation to give the mayor time to herself. Only as the clock struck ten did Sally venture to reappear in the office doorway with the week's agenda, the backlog of mail and several phone messages.

"This last one is from Chief Manning," she said and pulled the message slip out from among the others to emphasize it. "He's hoping you can come over to the station."

"Now?"

"Yes, if possible."

Sandra hesitated.

"I presume he didn't say why."

Sally shook her head.

"Would you please call back and let him know I'm on my way?"

Sandra was unable to account for the chief's summons but grateful for the chance to break away. Grasping the message, she reached for her bag and coffee mug, then made for the door. She managed to slip out into the muggy air just in time to avoid Jay, whose agitated voice emanated from the lobby. The last thing she needed right now was to endure more complaints about the disappearance of his damned garden gnomes. As she walked to the station, Sandra reflected that Chief Manning would only request an immediate visit in an extremity and wondered what else could have happened to overturn her peace. He wasn't one to make waves lightly.

When she entered the office, the chief, a tall, balding man of commanding presence whose years behind the desk had padded his middle, stood up to acknowledge her. He immediately drew her attention to the man and woman occupying two guest chairs. The pair were of medium stature with dark eyes, jet-black hair and brown complexions. The man wore khaki shorts, a pale-yellow polo shirt and soft leather loafers. The woman had her long hair pulled back in a ponytail and wore black capris, a loose pink blouse, and sandals. They radiated comfort and confidence and smiled warmly at the mayor in greeting.

"Mayor Edgecomb, good morning," said the chief as he gestured to the remaining empty seat. "I'd like to introduce Mr. Juan and Mrs. Maria Rodriguez from Austin, Texas."

Sandra turned to the couple, shook hands with each, then looked questioningly at the chief.

"Mayor," he said, "I think you need to hear their story."

20

Confessions

The demands at the office were light this first week of July but they provided enough distraction to keep Claire's mind from her personal troubles—enough that she planned to work straight through the July 4th holiday on Thursday. She didn't miss the irony of taking refuge from life at work, when it was supposed to be the other way around.

After hours on Monday, she didn't go home, nor did she head for the Wharf Café or the Fish House or any other place where there was a likelihood of meeting Guy. Instead, she made her way to the Main Street Coffee Bar to grab a salad at a safe distance from their regular haunts. The place was entirely empty in the lull before the evening crowd, except for Claire and the waitstaff. Perfect. She was free to mull in peace or to fall back on the book in her bag if her brain stalled. She planted herself on a bar stool and gave her order to the young barista: goat cheese, walnuts and roasted beets on fresh spinach and a huge black coffee.

After yesterday's confrontation with Guy, Claire had stormed home, anger spewing from her insides like her body was expelling venom. In a sense, it was. She met no one along the way, which was just as well. That kind of venting was better done alone. She felt a guilty twinge for her lack of self-control but pushed this scruple aside. What was the alternative? Should she turn her fury inward and become dark and nonsensical like Guy? No. She would clear her emotions like a good rain cleaned the air. It had taken the better part of Sunday afternoon for her to work off the worst of it. Just past five, she had stood in her polished, dust-free living room, knuckles on her hips, and surveyed the super-clean with approval, gratified at least that her surfeit of energy had been profitably spent.

After a hot shower, she had poured some wine and sat down on the couch. For what had to be the hundredth time, she ran through the events of the dinner and her argument with Guy. He had been selfish and unreasonable. He had twisted things. She thought so now no less than before, but with each replay of the argument, she regained calm and, though apprehending the stakes, had made a plan to avoid Guy.

The barista delivered the steaming brew with her gaze on something behind Claire. Claire glanced into the mirror over the bar and spied John-Pierre staring intently at her back. He'd come into the place noiselessly and now stood as still as a statue in the middle of the dining room floor as if uncertain how to proceed. Claire twisted around to greet him, then turned her back again. She wasn't looking for company this evening. This was the downside of her magnetism for troubled people: It didn't have a pause button for times when she needed to recharge and it followed her everywhere. She cringed as she heard the hesitant shuffling of John-Pierre's shoes grow ever closer.

He arrived at her stool and hovered at her side, clearly struggling for speech. It occurred to her that this was the type of interruption Guy had complained about. She dismissed his disapprobation. *You chose a public place to eat—a popular coffee bar in a small town,* she reasoned in her head. *How can anyone have an expectation of solitude here? Anyway, Guy's not here.* A wave of sadness threatened to follow this defiance, but she repulsed it.

"What is it, Pi—John?"

"I…I…"

He glanced at the blatantly curious barista.

"Want to join me at a booth?" Claire guessed.

"Yes…yes."

He brushed back greasy, overgrown strips of white hair. Claire grabbed her coffee and bag, nodded to the barista and slipped down from her stool.

The last time she'd caught a glimpse of John-Pierre, on awards night, he'd been all dressed up and was—what had Guy called it?—"mooning" over Monique. The man walking beside her now was back in casual clothes, though not his usual, white painter attire, and agitated beyond what Claire had ever seen. Aside from the usual degree of dishevelment and the fact that he'd just made his hair stick straight up into the air by the stroke of his hand, his appearance wasn't remarkable. His body language, however, screamed distress.

They slid onto benches across from one another. John-Pierre held up his hands to decline Claire's invitation to join her for either food or drink. At this, she leaned back, sipped her coffee and waited expectantly for a story that, she guessed, would heavily feature the antics of the infamous and alluring Monique LaBelle.

"I was walking by and saw you at the bar. I hope you don't mind."

He stopped speaking to wait for her reply.

"Of course not," she fibbed.

Claire examined him carefully. She had suspected for some time that this eccentric man was extremely lonely. She was aware, too, that no matter how ludicrous his behavior, she had treated him with a respect few others had displayed. This alone may have drawn him to her. She leaned forward to convey her interest in whatever he had to say then held up her hand to stop him as the nosy barista approached on tiptoe with both ears wide open.

"Thank you," Claire said and reached assertively for the salad plate, leaving the young woman no choice but to return to the bar, well out of earshot. "Sorry, John. Go ahead. But do you mind if I eat while we talk? I'm starved."

He waved his permission, so she speared a seasoned beet and popped it into her mouth.

"I need to be sure what I say doesn't get spread about. People say you can be trusted."

He studied her.

She swallowed and locked eyes with him.

"I can't promise you absolutely because I don't know what you're about to say, but I'm not one who generally blabs."

John-Pierre considered her for another moment, head cocked to one side, the loose strip of white hair flopping comically. Claire stuffed another beet in her mouth to control the corner threatening a grin. She was spared further effort by John-Pierre who, without further hesitation, launched into his story.

"You know that old man, Morrie, I think. He seemed…so taken with Monique's paintings…and even Monique…" he faltered and gripped the table, flushing furiously, "…you know, like…the rest of us." Claire nodded. "And now they're after him for theft. I've tried to tell him, you know, that boy-cop, Ben, that Gloria's purchase of the 'Lupines' was a relief to Morrie. Morrie told me. He had no money to buy it but was excited he'd be able to visit the painting at her B&B."

He stopped to draw breath.

Claire could see why Ben might have reservations about testimony from this quirky painter.

"That's very good to know. I'll see what I can do to

help get the message across. Is that all you need?"

John-Pierre squirmed.

Claire sat back.

"Monique," he resumed speech, "well, you've seen her."

"Indeed," came Claire's benign reply before taking a forkful of salad. She wasn't sure what direction his exposé would take from this meagre beginning and didn't want to influence him.

With his disorganized mind, disjointed speech and heightened emotional state, it took the better part of an hour for him to relate his full story in a way Claire could understand it and then another hour to unravel his problem and plan a course of action. It was seven-thirty by the time she left him and raced to squeeze in a visit with Morrie. Of one thing, Claire felt sure: Guy would certainly have wanted to be a fly on the wall during John-Pierre's recitation no matter what he said about involvement in other people's problems.

She made her way to Morrie's apartment where she found Meilin before her sitting in an easy chair eating wood-fired pizza and sipping red wine. Morrie grinned with pleasure at the sight of Claire's face peering from behind the partially open door and waved her in. Meilin slid over to make room.

"Meilin has something particular on her mind tonight," observed the astute man.

"I do," Meilin agreed, taken aback. "How did you know?"

Morrie cast a mysterious smile. All three laughed, then Meilin began to explain.

"Claire's timing is uncanny because she's the reason for my coming. She came into my store yesterday asking questions about Monique's work." She turned to Claire, whose eyebrows were raised. "I hope you don't mind, but you really piqued my curiosity."

"Not at all."

"Claire wanted to find out more about Monique, like where she paints and what else she's painted. I think you're interested in her work, too, Morrie."

Morrie swallowed and gave an abridged account of his grandfather's paintings for Meilin's benefit.

"Though all I had to go on was my memory, I was so excited! I looked up Monique online right away but could find no information about her. I asked around, went to the library. Even Peggy found nothing. So, I approached Monique and was instantly— and rather rudely, I might add—rebuffed."

"So that's what happened in the alley," said Claire. "Morrie, she's been rude to everyone except Leroy. You can't take it personally."

"But her reaction to me was so out of proportion. And the next morning, she insinuated I was a thief. I admit to being engrossed with her paintings and curious about her, but theft? That was a low blow."

"It was," agreed Meilin. "I haven't heard a single person aside from Leroy and Monique suggest you'd steal, Morrie."

"I'm glad. Ben had no trouble suspecting me, though." He made a face. "They make these kids cops before they have real sense."

Both women stifled giggles at this.

"Actually, Morrie," Claire corrected him, "Ben seems smart and pretty reasonable. And you're only a person of interest at this point."

"Don't be too hard on him for inexperience or for doing his job," Meilin added.

"As if I would steal the painting for money," Morrie continued, ignoring their defense of Officer Tripp, "or even just to own it. The idea is ridiculous. Where would I put a stolen painting in a shared home? I'd be found out immediately. I was so glad when Gloria bought the 'Lupines'. At least I'd be able to visit the B&B. And now, they're gone, and the 'Beach Roses', too."

"Morrie, you have to move on," Meilin urged, "or you'll never heal. This whole thing is eating you alive."

"How can I move on when I'm still a suspect in the community?"

Neither woman had an answer.

Meilin caught sight of the clock over the sink and jumped.

"We have a special committee meeting tonight at Creative Agenda to collect thoughts about the art show, a sort of post mortem. Art club members are invited. Too bad the theft is overshadowing our success right now because, overall, everything went really well."

"Let's hope it gets solved quickly so it doesn't blight the show's sequel next year," Morrie said.

Claire took her leave at the same time. She rolled past the coffee bar and peered in the window looking for Ben. He was seated at the far end of the bar in his conspicuous khaki uniform. She parked at home and rushed over, hoping to relay to Ben John-Pierre's vindication of Morrie. To the right of the bar's entrance, she caught sight of John-Pierre's fidgety silhouette lurking in the alleyway shadows. After Gloria, Rhonda and several other art club members passed by heading for Creative Agenda, he hurried up Main Street in the opposite direction.

Claire swung open the door of the Coffee Bar. The place was packed, so the din was appreciable. Only half the chatter was in English. The Coffee Bar had secured the regular patronage of the Mayenne Bay French Club by hosting its meetings and catering to its preferences. Table centerpieces featured a quartet of American, Acadian, Quebecois, and French flags and a small vase of fresh flowers. Next to these sat a basket of French bread, a dish of sweet butter and plates of French cheeses and crudités. Each place setting included a traditional demi-tasse cup for French espresso.

The club members spoke openly as people often do when they feel certain they can't be understood. Around the tables, to peals of laughter, Celeste strutted before her compatriots in comical mimicry of a pompous monarch, calling herself "le roi le-ROY". Having some knowledge of French from her college years, Claire listened. Words like "fou", "cretin" and "idiot" flew across the room in a variety of French accents, and there was a tongue-in-cheek debate about how to honor "son Altesse Royale". Claire doubted Leroy had a clue of his infamy.

With a lingering smile on her lips, she moved to the young policeman, full of purpose. When she arrived at his side, Ben was trading light banter with the flirtatious barista and sipping a cappuccino. It was easy to understand the barista's attraction. Ben was bright, friendly and quite good-looking. His body was lean and muscular. And then, there was the inevitable draw of a man in uniform. A badge-bunny barista. If Claire judged correctly, however, the attraction was not reciprocated by Ben.

"Hi, Ben," Claire greeted him. "Mind if I take a few minutes of your time?"

She regarded the barista expectantly. The teen made a face and disappeared to the other side of the bar. Ben motioned to Claire to take the stool next to him.

"So, you see," she wound up her report a few minutes later, "Morrie is not your man. Both Pi—John and Meilin can corroborate this as well as I."

Satisfied, Claire dropped nimbly from the bar stool, intending to go home. It had been a long day. The weekend's emotional strain coupled with the efforts of her new Guy-avoidance campaign had worn her out.

Ben stalled her, clearly not picking up on either her intention or fatigue.

"Um, are you in a hurry?"

In answer, Claire climbed back onto the stool and wondered what could possibly come next. The little barista? Difficulties on the new job? Trouble in the town? Another gnome? She never could predict the topic of conversation. It was what made people so fascinating and kept her open to their approach.

"I think you know Rhonda…you know, the cat artist?"

Ah, Claire apprehended quickly, *so, that's why it's uphill work for the barista.*

"Yes, I do."

"I met her through my investigation of the art theft," he explained shyly. "Met her again, I should say. I graduated with her brother, Leon, and knew her distantly from school."

"And now Rhonda's a rather beautiful woman," Claire finished for him.

His face colored. Even the uniform couldn't disguise his boyishness in this moment. In a confusing jumble of sentences, the smitten cop unloaded his heart and ended by asking for Claire's advice. For the second time that evening, she turned her attention to a near stranger. She was glad Guy wasn't around to witness the double-duty she was pulling.

After taking leave of Ben, Claire trudged home. When she reached the door to her apartment, for the first time ever, her solitude overtook her. She had lived alone since well before her move to Mayenne Bay, but never before had singlehood felt like this.

In this very dooryard, she and Guy had kissed—her first kiss in years. It had evoked a memory of her last kiss along with the unsavory man who had given it, an imprudent ardor gone wrong. Guy's breath against her face, his lips on hers had effaced that old shadow and supplanted sour with sweet. The afterglow of that single embrace had warmed Claire for hours. How could the passionate man on her doorstep and the reproachful man in the car be one and the same person?

She forced her feet to step forward into the gloom and stood stock still in thought in the dark kitchen. In the hours since she and Guy had separated, so much had happened. How she would have welcomed his humor and understanding. She shook her head to stop this train of thought.

"The last time you were with him," she reminded herself aloud, "he was very short on both."

She went to her bedroom, removed her clothes and dressed for bed in listless, mechanical motions, then slid her heavy body between the cold sheets.

It was time to call old faithful, her cousin, Daniel.

21

Lifeline

On Tuesday, the last week in July, just over three weeks after she'd slammed Guy's car door with gorilla force, Claire was stunned to receive a text from him as she pulled into work. Her heart leapt, hoping for a kind word. Just as quickly, it sank.

"'Lupines' painting found B&B lobby," was all it said.

Claire swelled with pleasure knowing how this report would lift Morrie's spirits, then stared down at her phone. Guy's clipped message, an off-putting mixture of thoughtfulness and brevity, reawakened her pique. She would not, after their serious dispute, resume dialog by text. Nor would she beg for details. An acknowledgment, at least, was in order out of common courtesy. No more than that.

"OK," she thumbed back to Guy, then immediately dialed Morrie.

"Have you heard, Morrie?" she asked him as she headed for the office door.

"Yes, Ben called. It's really good news!"

Claire marveled at the newfound energy already evident in his voice.

"Morrie, I'm just about to start work. How about I

bring you some lunch today? We can talk about it then. I'll be there just past noon, if that works. Keep an eye out for my car."

"Great!"

Claire smiled to herself. Morrie had improved with bed rest, but this catapult into good humor was no mere coincidence. Here was proof of how much the accusations against him had suppressed his spirits.

"I'm so glad you're finally out of the woods," Claire told him later as he opened the car door in front of the Whispering Seabreeze. "Get in."

Morrie obliged and buckled up. She handed him a bagged lunch from the Coffee Bar.

"Where are we going?" he asked.

She smiled mischievously, the headed up Park Street, turned left onto Castle, right onto Crest and right again onto Bay Street, which led to the driveway of the Town's End Bed and Breakfast.

"I thought you'd like to see the painting again with your own eyes."

Morrie shot her a grateful look and scrambled out of the car with unprecedented alacrity. Claire was not above wanting to see it herself and followed right on his heels. Gloria, having heard the tires on the gravel driveway, waved them over excitedly from the front porch.

"The 'Lupines' painting. It's been found!"

Gloria Townsend was Gloria Esposito by birth. She'd come to Maine from New Jersey seventeen years ago for a college education and never left. Her dark, curly hair and Mediterranean complexion contributed to her overall good looks, which had drawn Steven Townsend to her side shortly before her graduation. They married and settled into the bed-and-breakfast business together, giving it their shared surname.

The B&B was a remodeled, six-bedroom Victorian

house which the Townsends had bought at a bargain price. It sat on the water's edge at the end of Bay Street, for the hardy, within walking distance of Mayenne Bay's town center. Built in 1819 by a prominent sea captain, it had served his descendants for a time as a vacation home and was eventually abandoned, until it was snapped up and revitalized by the Townsends.

The couple had taken side jobs and invested all their earnings to make the B&B work. They added a large deck off the back and installed a dock to provide water access for the inn's kayaks and paddle boat and moorings for visiting boaters. They painted the clapboard siding an uplifting, buttery yellow with white gingerbread trim, which made it easily identifiable from land and bay alike. Inside, Gloria decorated in pastels to maximize the reflective light that flooded in from the large windows. The furnishings and décor were sparing, which generated an airy ambiance that soothed and unwound their guests. The B&B's comfort, shoreline location and striking views now drew tourists from all over.

Just as they had begun to see a return on their labors, in the year Gloria had turned thirty, she discovered Steven cheating with one of their out-of-town guests. The B&B was the one thing Gloria sought in the messy divorce that ensued. She retained her married surname solely because it tied her undisputedly to the business, which remained her only financial means and her only passion. She'd been running it herself for five years now, and she protected and promoted it like her life depended on it, body and soul, which it did.

Gloria viewed her purchase of original artwork as a crowning achievement of her business success. She proudly led Morrie and Claire to the former parlor where the painting already hung in a place of honor on the wall over the antique check-in desk. It was highlighted by a picture-light that made the colors pop. Gloria stood beside the canvas flushed with self-importance as Claire and Morrie approached.

"I found it tucked behind that bookcase when I moved it to vacuum," Gloria told them, pointing to the spot. "I couldn't believe my eyes. I shift the heavier furniture to clean only once a month or so. There's no telling how long the painting was sitting there or even how it got there. The police are clueless."

"What a mystery," declared Morrie. "And no damage done as far as I can see."

"None at all. Someone's idea of a prank, I suspect."

"I'm so relieved the whole thing ended as it should," Morrie said, "and the painting is in its proper home." His eyes shone with a light Claire had not detected in all the time she'd known him. "One day, when I'm back on my feet, I'm going to collect art like this again."

"It's too bad Monique is so off-putting, with everyone so prepared to admire her work and even acquire more," Claire mused. "Of course, this assumes that whatever lurks behind the diva mask is worth knowing."

"When a person makes herself a mystery, people fill in the blanks," Morrie observed. "I found out first hand that being too private and leaving everything to appearance can fan speculation."

"Yes. People make all kinds of assumptions."

She looked to Gloria for consensus, but the woman's arms were crossed over her chest, and her face was taut with disapproval. Having heard about Gloria's dark side, Claire decided she and Morrie had stayed long enough. They thanked her and headed for the car.

"Did you notice Gloria's reaction to our discussion of Monique's mystique?" Claire asked Morrie.

"No, I was looking at the painting."

"She was unnerved. I think Monique's bad behavior

and the theft have got under Gloria's skin."

Morrie heaved a huge sigh.

"I hadn't thought about the effect of all this on Gloria. I should have been more sensitive."

His breathing signaled to Claire that Morrie, whose mended green sweater hung very loosely on his thin frame, needed rest. She drove him back to the Whispering Seabreeze. Morrie waved and plodded heavily toward the door, lunch bag in hand.

After work, Claire sat alone in her kitchen picking at apples and cheese with Guy's text of the morning open in front of her. Curt. Impersonal. No response needed. A hit-and-run. What made him send it at all?

During these weeks apart, she had wracked her brain for a single thing she should have done differently at the disastrous dinner with the Bristolwaites, to no avail. Nor could she bring herself to regret the time she spent helping others. She just couldn't. It was too integral to her being, much as art was for Guy.

Daniel had understood this when he'd visited her the weekend before last. And with the conversation centered on Claire and Guy rather than Daniel's personal finances, Daniel's usual sagacity and clearheadedness were back in control. He even suggested that Claire walk away from Guy.

"Jesus," Claire had said, dropping her head into her hands. "I said the same thing to my mother."

Daniel's voice became stern.

"Let's get something clear. You are not and never will be your mother. You need to see this, Claire."

She looked up, slightly heartened.

"Guy was out of line, and, if the man hasn't called you in weeks…"

It seemed an age to Claire and yet she wavered about what to do.

"But in the short time I've known him…"

"Listen to yourself!" Daniel interrupted her. "How many jerks do you have to date before you get it? Mick the Prick almost broke you."

He popped one of Claire's homemade chocolate-chip cookies into his mouth and got up to refill his coffee mug.

Harsh as Daniel's counsel could be, Claire clung to the lifeline of their friendship when her own self-ministering failed her. He'd been her steady confidante and safety net for years. She couldn't resent his impatience. Her relationship with Guy wasn't the first messy entanglement he'd coached her through.

"Guy acted like a jerk once," Claire argued, almost pleaded. "Just once. That's not a pattern. It doesn't make him a prick."

Daniel eyed her skeptically.

"Except when he is. Are you actually about to repeat all the good stuff about him and talk yourself right back into his life after he twisted you up?"

Claire couldn't respond to this—not articulately, anyway. She had come to Maine with plans for a single life. Then came Guy, unexpected, funny, kind. He had introduced her to the world of art, cooked for her, treated her with respect. He had understood her like no other man but Daniel, until the day he didn't. Confusion clouded her face.

"Aside from this one…absurdity, Guy doesn't resemble the other men I've known at all. There's so much more to him. He's given me so much. I haven't been the same since I met him."

"That's an understatement," Daniel returned. "Claire, giving men can be jerks and not worth pursuing. They can hand you flowers with one hand and slap you with the other. God, have your mother's choices taught you nothing?"

"You're right, it's just that it's not so black and white to me. Guy didn't mistreat me every day, like the schmucks Mom dates or the other men I've known. He's fallible but he's not mean. Am I so different? I can swing from anger to comforting a stranger and back again in the same minute."

"Okay, so he's human—a low bar, by the way—but a human who hasn't contacted you and who's made no apologies," Daniel reminded her.

"I know. It's just…I really like him. I wasn't even looking for someone. You know that. Guy came out of nowhere. Before the dinner fiasco, I thought he and I might be headed someplace good."

"This vacillation is so out of character for you. You'd be better off plucking daisy petals and reciting 'He loves me, he loves me not'. I'm not really sure what you want from me at this point. Look, Claire, I love that you look for the best in people, but Mr. Wonderful obviously has a dark side."

"It seems that way, but I could say the same thing about myself. I was enraged afterward."

"In response to a betrayal by a man you trusted. You're not volatile all the time."

"That's exactly my point. Was Guy's behavior, like mine, just a moment of weakness after a deep disappointment or was it an indication of a hidden beast inside?" Tears filled her eyes. "I'm so tired, Daniel. The uncertainty alone is a drain. The game of avoidance is exhausting. It even feels childish to me now."

"It's no wonder you're worn out." He squeezed her hand. "All this conflicting emotion plus a serious curtailment of your life. You're a naturally open person, Claire. You face things and resolve them. You're not one who hides out. This isn't like you. You have to draw a line in the sand, set the boundary for what you will tolerate going forward, with or without Guy."

Claire conceded this point. What had begun as a necessary period of separation to think things over had turned into a month of heart-rending. She'd survived but, in her right mind, couldn't call this living. Being constantly on the lookout for Guy made her edgy. How much more time could she allow this uncomfortable existence to persist?

"I'll give him just another week or two, before I totally give up."

"If that's how you want to handle it, fine. Just know I'll be clocking you," Daniel said, rising. "Listen, I've got to hit the road. Will you be okay?"

Claire nodded.

He bear-hugged her and, armed with a large travel mug of coffee and a handful of cookies, threw her a sympathetic parting glance and headed out.

The scene with Daniel dissolved, returning Claire to her phone screen and the morning's text from Guy. She rose and began to reorganize her pantry. An hour later, she remained firm in her view that Guy had wronged her, with both his scathing rebuke of her helping hand and his lack of contact since. Today's text counted for nothing. Did he feel justified? Remorseful? Had he given up? She had no way to interpret his silence. Impatient as she was for closure, Claire reaffirmed that she would not break the impasse between them. She may have slammed the door, but that was only after Guy had broken with her. It was up to him to come forward. And he had better do it soon.

22

Guy's Mess

The same weeks that Claire had endured in turmoil had not gone well for Guy. He couldn't settle down to work, a movie, gardening—anything. He struggled with his graphic designs and reworked his latest canvas until the paint was so thick, he had to scrape it all off and start all over again. His loft had fallen into complete disarray. Dirty dishes were stacked precariously high by the sink, and a mound of soiled laundry was bunched against the wall. His desk was barely visible under all the project clutter, and a heap of unfinished paintings sat on the floor collecting dust. Even his appetite was off—a clear sign, if ever there was one, that all was not right in his world.

He knew full well the root of all his malaise and derangement lay in Claire's absence from his life. He relived his last moments with her over and over again. He had winced when the car door had slammed but, afterward, had continued to buzz with righteous indignation. He had pushed Claire hard, but maybe, just maybe, he had thought, she would wake up. Everything they did together shouldn't end in a counseling session. Some things were better left alone. For a few minutes after she stormed away, Guy had sat completely still, savoring the power he felt, for once, of having said exactly what he'd been thinking when he'd been thinking it. But when he reached for the ignition, his hand had fallen short, and he'd leaned back against the seat in intense disquiet, a disquiet he felt even now.

He wasn't the type to sort his feelings out by sweating at the gym or puffing through a marathon. Nor did he go on a cleaning frenzy, like Claire, as was obvious from the state of things in their respective homes. In desperate times like these, Guy was an Oreos-and-milk man, which explained the half-devoured package in front of him and the trail of crumbs on the floor.

"Damn!" he said aloud, staring into his glass.

He slid two fingers into the milk to retrieve the offending cookie and popped it into his mouth. Milk trickled down his chin, and he drew his sleeve carelessly across it. His problem wasn't lack of focus; it was unremittent focus…on Claire. He reached for another Oreo and dunked it, but instead of eating it, waved it in the air, throwing specks of milk as he paced the floor and talked to himself.

"Against all odds, she was attracted to you. Why? You have no idea. You just ran with it. And then, in your stupid self-absorption, you broke it." A rush of heat covered his neck and face. "Like a little kid!" he yelled and stamped his foot like the angry boy he'd been. "And, what, if you're honest with yourself, is your real complaint? Not that you lost an art mentor. No, Geoffrey Bristolwaite is out there somewhere painting and approachable." He shoved Geoffrey's image aside and looked hard at his own in the window glass. "What then?"

For at least the hundredth time, he relived his words to Claire in the car. "I'm tired of you sticking your nose in…of the interruptions and the drain on our lives," he had said. Could he have been more selfish? Of all the hours they'd spent together, how many had actually been interrupted? Darned few. And Claire had done much good in those hours. She'd helped people—or tried to—including his friends. What had she said before slamming the door? Guy repeated her words in an agonized whisper, "I thought you loved this about me". The pain he had heard in her voice at the time made him cringe even now.

"You do love her for it," he told the man in the window and brushed this argument aside.

He was getting to the final layer of the onion now. He could feel it in his gut, squeezing and churning the sickening overdose of milk and cookies. He leaned his forehead against the wall as he wrapped his mind around his emerging confession.

"Oh, God," he moaned and swallowed hard. "Geoffrey was your ticket to amount to something, something worthy…for Claire."

Cold gripped his chest. His throat constricted. From the very first day he had met Claire—articulate, well-read, educated and professional—this gremlin, born of his own sense of inferiority, had gnawed his insides. Only after dinner with the Bristolwaites was it revealed for the monster it was.

"Say it," Guy told his image in the window. "Say it!" he repeated in a raised voice. "You demanded more from Claire…because you, yourself, don't measure up." His entire being deflated. "And now she's gone…because of you." He pounded his fist against the wall and shouted to himself. "Idiot!"

The force of the punch crushed the uneaten cookie in his hand, spilled Oreo-polluted milk onto the floor and scattered the birds from the bush beneath the windowsill. He looked down and stared at the crumb-and-milk puddle, stunned at his own ferocity.

Not naturally blessed with self-awareness, Guy had always tended to leave his feelings to the indefinite workings of time. Occasionally, they leaked out in inappropriate ways, as Claire and the birds down below learned to their detriment. But getting to the third row of Oreos in a single sitting—this was a bad sign. The difference today was, whereas normally he couldn't manage much more than a stutter, he was sorting his emotions like a pro. With words. Out loud.

"You owe this to Claire." He slapped the wall with each word: "She…showed…you…how!"

The very act of peeling away emotional layers on his own was a gift from the woman he had so unceremoniously dismissed from his life. For what? To teach her a lesson about relationships. He fell back onto the couch and dropped his head in his hands.

Panic suddenly seized him. He reached for his phone and pulled up his calendar. He had broken with Claire in late June, and July was almost over. He had to do something to fix this before it was too late, if he could. He jumped up and began pacing again. He hadn't run into Claire over these weeks and guessed she'd been avoiding him. There would be no leaving things to chance this time, hanging around, hoping they'd meet someplace. No, this was going to take something intentional. Not a text. Claire would be angered by a mere text. He'd understood her clipped "OK" in reply to his news about the "Lupines" painting for what it was. Not a call, either. He was awkward on the phone, and it just wouldn't be enough. Something personal.

It took only a few seconds more to decide.

Guy grabbed a dirty shirt from the laundry pile, threw it over the spilled milk, then moved directly to his easel, where he unwrapped a small canvas and fastened it in place. A rose, he thought, a red rose, and he began pulling out paint tubes and setting up his palette. He sifted through his reference material from the garden walk, found nothing suitable and ran a hand through his hair. Desperate times, he told himself. He checked the window for any sign of Annabelle. Her car was gone. He dashed outside to her prize rose bush, cut the stem of a perfect bloom with his pocketknife and ran back upstairs. *Just one*, he reasoned. *She won't miss one.* He stuck the bloom in a vase of water, grabbed his brush and began blocking out the painting.

As he dashed stroke after stroke onto the little canvas, Guy brainstormed the best time and place to deliver it to Claire. Not a public place. Not her apartment, either, or she might feel hemmed in. He finally determined that the best spot would be the office parking lot when she finished work. It would be fairly empty and, allowing for the painful possibility she might not want to see him at all, leave room for escape.

He threw a glance at the clock. It was already twenty past eleven. Even at this early hour, at his slow painting speed, it would be close. He plunged ahead and only just put the finishing touches on the painting at four-thirty. He was out of time. He wasn't entirely satisfied but he signed the canvas anyway. He threw his brushes in the can of oil to soak, peeled off his sticky gloves and looked down at himself. He would have to go as he was, in his paint-milk-and-Oreo-splattered clothes. So much for good impressions.

Just before five, Claire's usual quitting time, Guy pulled into the parking lot of her office and breathed relief at the sight of her car. He stationed his vehicle directly behind hers, got out and leaned himself against her driver-side door, staring unblinkingly at the building exit like…a stalker. What woman wanted to venture into a parking lot while a man lurked at her car, especially a man who had been hurtful?

He backed away to his own car and watched as a number of Claire's colleagues exited. When she finally appeared on the stoop and spied Guy, she stood stiff as a statue. He celebrated for a split second—she hadn't anticipated him—then chastened himself and waited anxiously for her second reaction, the one that mattered. Wearing the most contrite face he could muster, he looked, he was sure, as pleading as a puppy. Whatever. As long as it worked. Would she backtrack into the building? He held his breath.

With her first step forward, Claire looked down, Guy was sure, to hide her emotions and gather her strength. He couldn't blame her. After all, she had no idea what he had in store for her. Cautious as she was, she was probably on her guard for another rebuke or an irreversible break-up. When she spotted the canvas he was balancing in the palm of one hand, a look of unfeigned curiosity overspread her face. Guy's fair face was a brilliant shade of red, probably embellished by a few paint smudges of the same color, but he didn't turn away.

"I wanted to…I was…just going to… bring you this."

The words he had rehearsed in the car evaporated from his brain. He could only hope she would understand his meaning despite the awkward delivery. He wiped his spare hand on his pants and extended the hand holding the painting.

"It's wet," he cautioned, then abandoned any further attempt at speech.

Without a word, Claire reached for the little canvas board and took it gingerly by its edges. It was a fresh painting of a single red rose with petals opened wide to the sun. Now, she, too, seemed lost for words. Her fingers detected the slip of paper Guy had taped to the back, insurance in case his slug-tongue made a reappearance. "I'm sorry" was all it said. Tears filled her eyes.

Guy stole a glance at Claire then looked down and said all at once, "Claire, I was an idiot. I'm so sorry."

He stopped talking and waited.

In answer, she slid the painting carefully onto the roof of her car, then stepped forward, leaned into him and laid her head on his shoulder.

"Will you let me take you to dinner tonight?" he whispered in her ear, careful to stroke her hair with his clean hand. She nodded her head "yes", and Guy thought his shirt felt damp. The pit bull was nowhere to be seen. He hadn't expected it to be so easy.

23

La Ferme

Several hours after their reunion in the office parking lot, Guy sat opposite Claire before a crisp, linen tablecloth at La Ferme Restaurant, just a few miles north of Mayenne Bay on Route 1. Owned and operated by the Grace family, La Ferme featured organic, farm-to-table cuisine. Its menu and prices were more upscale than the downtown eateries, but Guy meant this evening to make a statement. Reconnection with Claire deserved no less in his mind—in fact, it demanded more—and he wanted her to see this from the get-go.

Celeste arrived to take their drink order.

"Celeste! I had no idea you worked here, too," said Claire.

"A woman has to make a living," Celeste joked. "Besides, I get a free meal. Wait until you taste the food."

She headed for the bar to get their drinks.

Guy had never before eaten at La Ferme but knew it by reputation and history. About five years ago, with their grocery thriving, Thomas and Beatrice Grace had sought to branch out into food production. They'd been obstructed on their first two attempts to purchase farms by sellers who refused to deal with persons of color. The Graces had persisted and found a third property through a willing seller, Jay Brown. This land, they reworked into a sustainable, organic farm that now supplied both Grace Grocery and La Ferme with quality, local foods. If the grocery was any indication, Guy was sure he and Claire could expect an exceptional meal.

Celeste delivered wine for Claire and a frosty tea for Guy, then laid the menus before them. After she left, Guy slid a small white box with a red ribbon across the table to Claire. It bore a label from the Seafoam Candy Shop.

"What's this?"

"Dark chocolate. A mood enhancer and a bald-faced bribe. Completely shameless, but I'm not taking any chances tonight. I've missed you. And it's all been my fault."

"You did behave stupidly."

"Yes."

"And really hurt my feelings." She looked hard into his eyes. "You accused me of goading Caroline, as if I wanted to sabotage your chances with Geoffrey."

"Yes," he cringed and shook his head. "I acted like a frustrated juvenile. I didn't understand myself until this very morning. All I saw was lost opportunity and…well, I was embarrassed. I wanted so badly to impress you with my prospects. I was such a jerk."

Claire's eyebrows arched in surprise.

"And I never thanked you for all you did that night."

"No."

"I'm so grateful for all of it. And I'm really, really sorry, Claire."

"Apology accepted," she answered and straightened her shoulders. "Now, it's my turn."

Guy braced himself.

"First, I like you for yourself, not your prospects. Second, just so you know, I have a juvenile side myself. I spent almost an hour choosing something to wear tonight so I could show you I was worth your pains."

"You are," he assured her and took her hand.

"Third," Claire resumed, "I have to admit that, though your delivery left much to be desired, your message wasn't altogether without basis."

"What?"

"Guy, I'll never stop my interest in people. It's in my very being, like art is in yours. And I will help, if they ask, and I'm able. Sometimes, it won't be convenient. You need to accept that, or we can't be together." There was no mistaking her meaning. Guy had been ready for it and made no objection. "That said, I don't mind if you watch out for me, let me know if I'm getting in over my head. I aim for good Samaritan, not messiah." He looked surprised. "And we can agree that certain hours will be sacred and uninterruptible. Like tonight."

She smiled at him. Guy's heart leapt, and he reached for her other hand.

"Really?"

"Yes, really. It's only right."

"So, you forgive me?"

"Yes, I forgive you, though you can't always rely on chocolate to soften me," she said archly. "It didn't work for Geoffrey and Caroline, remember."

"No, that bit didn't work at all," he admitted.

"There's one more thing."

Guy's eyes opened wide, and one knee started bouncing nervously under the table.

"I hate losing my temper. I'm sure it wasn't much fun on the receiving end. We're going to disagree. It's inevitable. But we have to talk things out like adults and not just wait until you implode and I explode."

"That's easy for you to say," he answered and pulled back into his seat more comfortably now that he knew what he was dealing with. "You have no trouble finding words for what you want to say. When I get upset, I clam up, sink into a funk and eat junk food. I can't paint. I can't work. I can't speak. Everything gets jumbled in my head. That time in the car was a rare exception."

"Which is why you need to make sense of it by talking. Remember Grayson? It might begin as gibberish but it will end in clarity. Will you promise me you'll work on your shutdown response? In turn, I'll work on my anger." She looked at him with eyes full of tears. "I really didn't like being apart."

He reached over again and squeezed her hands.

"Me, either," he agreed. "And I promise."

She pulled her hands away and drew the white box toward her.

"I'm not sharing the chocolate, though."

They both laughed. The ease in their conversation was back, and they began to catch each other up on what had happened during their time apart. After Guy finished his list of work, art and apartment woes, Claire told him about things at the office and Morrie's recovery.

"He's getting stronger now and toying with the idea of a job."

"The return of the 'Lupines' painting had to be a boost," Guy said. "As usual, the rumors are flying. I'll be glad when they find the culprit, though I wonder, can we call it a theft if it's been returned?"

Claire dropped to a whisper and leaned forward conspiratorially.

"Actually, I know how the painting got back to the B&B."

"What? Ben said he hasn't caught the thief."

"I hope he never does," she said slyly then took a long, slow sip of wine to keep him in suspense.

"Of course, we want the thief caught!"

Claire shook her head.

"After you and I argued that day in the car, I decided to take some space."

Guy grimaced.

"I ate at the coffee bar where I thought I'd be unlikely to run into you. No sooner had I sat down when Pierre came in. After hemming and hawing, he decided to confide in me. I thought it would be just the venting of a broken heart, after the way he'd mooned at Monique. Then, right in the middle of his story, he told me he knew who had taken the 'Lupines' painting!"

"Who was it?"

"Pierre himself."

"What?"

"You heard me right. Pierre took the painting."

"Did he tell you why?"

"Not in so many words. His mind was so confused, I was lucky to get the facts straight. He was attracted to Monique and ignored by her. So, take your pick: heated passion or cold revenge or mere impulse. The only thing I can say for sure is that it was not premeditated."

"But it's back. He found a way to return it."

"Yes. He said he was sorry the moment he took it, then realized how hard it was going to be to right the wrong without getting caught. Our friend Pierre isn't what you'd call a clear thinker," she concluded wryly.

Guy looked dubious.

"Come on, Claire. We're supposed to believe he meant to return it? You're buying into his tale."

"I think he was telling the truth. Why else would he have confessed unprompted? First, he acted rashly. That's not hard to imagine of Pierre, is it? Then, he discovered his conundrum holding the goods, further complicated by Gloria's distress and Monique's baseless accusations against Morrie. Even if he didn't regret the theft, give him credit for regretting that Morrie took the heat. Pierre was genuinely pained about that. He may be befuddled but, underneath, Pierre, well, John Mills, is a pretty good guy."

"If you say so," Guy conceded. "But that doesn't tell me how he found enough clarity to return it."

"I helped him hatch a scheme."

"You did what?"

"I helped him figure a way out," she repeated. "He confessed to me the evening of the post-mortem art show committee meeting. He hung out in the alleyway until Gloria showed up for the meeting, then slipped away to put the painting in her B&B reception area. The main door is usually open. He hid it behind furniture so she wouldn't find it right away." She smiled triumphantly. "That last part was my idea."

"Nice little reverse-caper, Claire. And you didn't tell Ben?"

"No. Pierre's not a hardened criminal. He's more pitiful than anything. I told him I'd report him if he didn't return it promptly. He did, so that's that. So far, you're the only other person who knows the truth."

Guy let out a low whistle. Just when he thought he really knew her, Claire surprised him again.

"You really took a chance on him."

"I know, but he was so pathetic."

"How did he steal it? Nobody's been able to figure that out."

"At the end of the awards presentation, he heard Meilin and Peggy talking about Gloria not picking up the painting until the morning. So, he hid at the school until everyone left, took it down from the wall and slipped out the side door."

"Pretty slick, if I can be allowed to admire a theft. No break-in required. I'd never have guessed he had it in him. No wonder he was so quiet the next morning during pickup hours. You realize you're denying Ben the Rookie a chance to shine by solving his first case, right?"

"He'll survive. Now he can focus on the masked bandit and gnome kleptomaniac." She stood up. "As you've plied me with wine, I need the restroom."

Guy watched her slender figure walk away from the table, marveling at her audacity and elated they had come together again. Now at his ease, he took in the tasteful restaurant décor and well-dressed waitstaff and wondered how there could be enough regular clientele to support La Ferme's pricey menu year-round. At least now, in season, on a Friday night, the place was full.

A familiar voice sounded from behind an overgrown dieffenbachia. Leroy Hood. Guy caught sight of his well-combed, dark hair and the shoulders of a navy-blue dinner jacket between the leaves. That probably meant Monique was somewhere in the vicinity.

He looked around expectantly but saw only Claire returning from the restroom.

"Monique is in there crying," Claire reported as she slid back into her seat.

"So, that's why Leroy is sitting by himself. What happened?"

"I'm not sure. When I stepped out of the stall, there she was. Not the diva we're used to. She's wearing a simple blouse over black knit pants—nothing sexy. Her hair is flat, and her mascara streaked. She says she's fine. I don't buy it but I couldn't press her in a public bathroom. Besides, I just promised you this was sacred time for us. So, I soaked a paper towel with cold water to cool her face and left her with an offer to help if she wanted it."

"Good," he said, entwining his fingers with hers. "Um, about the helping thing." His face was sheepish, and he cleared his throat. "I have a confession to make. I had a little counseling session of my own…this morning…out loud…with my reflection in the window glass."

A corner of Claire's mouth threatened a half-grin, but she repressed it and said nothing.

"I realized, after I'd eaten an entire package of Oreos and worked through— I think for the first time in my life—my feelings out loud, that you're the one who taught me how. It was like I could hear your voice in my head walking me through the onion layers. What a hypocrite I was to demand you stop helping others while I was benefiting from your guidance myself."

He hung his head.

"Hearing voices is not a good sign in anyone, Guy, any more than cookie binging," she said in mock seriousness as her thumb came loose from their clasp to rub the back of his hand.

His head shot up to catch the amusement on her face.

"I'd better stick close so I can keep an eye on you."

"Yeah, you'd better," he grinned.

24

Sandra's Secret

While Guy and Claire celebrated their reunion at La Ferme well into the evening, their mayor remained tied to her desk, hard at work.

That morning, Sally had delivered the morning mail to her boss with an expression of disquiet.

"Sandra, it happened again," she said.

Sandra had sighed and placed a reassuring hand on Sally's shoulder.

The citizenry had got wind of the closed-door council meeting called for August 1st next week—the second executive session this summer. Speculation was blowing through Mayenne Bay like a Nor'easter. Residents cornered Sally and Sandra from every direction, demanding information. For cover, the mayor had told the council the topic was a sensitive legal matter. The true details remained confined to Sandra, Chief Manning, legal counsel Bobby Tripp and Sally, who remained tight-lipped against persistent efforts to pry those lips open. Leroy's project, his slight of the mayor, the "Lupines" painting—these were old news. Sally's discomfort aside, Sandra wasn't sorry for the fickleness of the rumor mill; it took the focus off her love life.

"People seem more agitated over this session than the last one," Sally said.

"They're bound to be, Sally. They had an idea of the topic last time. Now, they're completely in the dark. I'm really sorry. It'll be over soon. I could never manage without you, you know."

Sally's pursed lips stretched to a weak smile at the compliment, signaling her continued compliance. Sandra rose and moved to the office window to consider their dilemma.

Since May 2, all council meetings had been open to the public as usual and had centered on Leroy's waterfront building project. In June, he had provided a cursory status report, and the council had reviewed a survey of the canning factory grounds. In July, the Environmental Protection Agency spoke about the presence and safe handling of hazardous materials that would be exposed during demolition.

It was at the July meeting that Louis Rainwater had made his appeal. He stepped to the microphone with an entourage: his son, Robert, several tribal members, Peggy representing the Mayenne Bay Historical Society and an agent from the Maine Historical Preservation Commission. In the five minutes allotted for his address, he succinctly reminded the council of the genocide and forced diaspora that had been perpetrated upon his Wabanaki ancestors. He cited sources indicating the Wabanaki had regularly frequented Mayenne Bay's shores and even camped there. He ended with a formal request for an archeological exploratory before commencing with the factory's demolition.

"I don't propose that development be stopped," Louis concluded, "because I understand its importance to the town. I ask only that the site be properly inspected and cleared of artifacts prior to commencement of work. No such examination was performed, as it should have been, before the factory was originally built."

During Louis' address, Sandra had cast surreptitious glances at Leroy knowing the study would mean a project delay. On one hand, her most pressing priority, the well-being of Mayenne Bay's present-day constituents, outweighed the importance of relics of any kind from a bygone era. Yet, she knew this for the over-simplification it was. An archeological find would further validate the Wabanaki presence in this community and beyond. Should the council fail to accede to Louis' reasonable request, the alternative would likely be a litigious contest over tribal rights. Sandra, like the council, supported Louis' petition.

Sandra knew the upcoming meeting, by contrast, would do more than merely chafe or delay; it would take the council into uncharted waters. She broke from these reflections to close her office door, then slid into the chair behind her desk and extracted two large, brown envelopes from her locked desk drawer, one from Chief Manning, the other from Attorney Tripp, and broke their seals. She had until next Thursday evening to absorb the full import of their contents and estimated it would take all day plus a good part of the evening and weekend. After one last swig of hazelnut coffee, she set to work.

***

On Saturday evening, the art club convened at Gloria's B&B in celebration of the returned "Lupines" painting. The place was packed. Invitations had been extended to supportive non-artist guests including Sandra, Claire, Roxie, Morrie, Ken and Ben. Between public interest over the painting and requests for tours of the B&B, Gloria was, for a change, upbeat.

Monique was conspicuously absent.

"I had my fingers crossed she'd resurface tonight," Claire whispered to Guy, "though which persona, the Narcissistic or the Tragic, was anybody's guess."

"I'm not sorry for a Monique-free evening," he said.

He handed Claire a glass of wine, then grabbed a flute of champagne in one hand and sparkling grape juice in the other and made his way over to John Mills, the club's newest member. Claire watched approvingly as Guy offered John-Pierre the champagne, then tapped it with his own glass.

"Cheers, John. This is a night to celebrate, isn't it?" she heard him say. "The painting's been returned, and no harm done. Look at Gloria's smile. And Morrie's. Looks like everyone has moved on."

John-Pierre offered no reply to this neat little speech, but his shoulders relaxed perceptibly as he drew a sip of bubbly.

From the reception counter, just below the painting, Meilin called the room to order. With Peggy, Roxie and Sandra at her side, she lifted her champagne flute high for a toast.

"With the 'Lupines' painting hanging in its rightful spot in the beautiful Town's End B&B," she said to calls of "hear, hear" and a smattering of applause, "we can finally fully celebrate the success of Mayenne Bay's first art show. To the artists!"

"To the artists!" the crowd repeated, and they all drank.

"To the buyers!" Peggy added, lifting her drink.

The crowd echoed and drank again.

"With the proceeds, we'll expand the art section in your honor and digitize the old card system. Thank you for contributing your work to benefit the library."

A wave of excited murmurs crossed the room.

"Let's do it again next year," called Roxie over the

hum.

The company applauded her suggestion before it dispersed for more drinks and chatter.

Sandra took this opportunity to slip out before she could be cornered about the executive session.

Claire approached Meilin.

"Monique's not here tonight, though her work is the centerpiece."

"I haven't seen her at all lately," Meilin said.

"Are you talking about Monique?" squeaked Rhonda, who happened to be within earshot.

Her art success and recent hook-up with Ben had made her a bit giddy—that plus the two glasses of champagne she'd already drained. Ben stood with her, steady hand at her back, clearly enjoying the uninhibited Rhonda but also bearing a gently protective demeanor.

"Did you know Leroy calls her Nicky? A nickname…or a love name. I heard him say it," she giggled.

Meilin smirked, unable to disguise her cynicism, but Claire answered, "That's the sweetest thing I've ever heard about Leroy and Monique."

Rhonda giggled again, and Ben steered her away.

"Rhonda's not used to drinking, I see," Meilin chuckled. "Good thing Ben's a decent guy, or we'd have to worry about that young woman tonight." Her eyes followed the couple to the sofa where Ben seated Rhonda with tender care.

"Anything new on Leroy's project?" Claire asked.

"It's on track as far as I know, except for the delay for the archeological study," said Meilin, her face rueful. "Rumor has it, Leroy also has a private marina scheme that's picking up steam. The man is as ambitious as he is unscrupulous."

Claire ruminated for a moment.

"Meilin, do you know for a fact he's unscrupulous? I

don't like him much either, but arrogance and love of money don't necessarily go hand in hand with bad dealing."

"I don't have any hard proof, if that's what you mean," Meilin said stiffly. "Just my gut and things I pick up from people."

"But the rumor mill is the worst place to get information."

"We can't trust what's being circulated officially. Sandra called another executive session for Thursday night. No hint on the topic or attendees. No one is talking. Another blow for government transparency."

"But it could be about anything. My guess is it's the tribal artifacts. Very touchy politically."

Guy joined them. Claire slid her arm through his in welcome.

"On one hand, I don't miss Monique. On the other, it's too bad she's missing so much appreciation of her work," he said.

"I'm relieved she's not here," said Meilin. "She dominates the room and usually offends somebody."

Guy shot an "I told you so" look at Claire, but Claire had softened toward Monique since their meeting in the La Ferme restroom.

"I've recently had a chance to see Monique with her guard down and saw a very different person."

"Did you?" Meilin sniffed her disbelief.

"Yes. I think the sophistication she presents to the world may be a pretense. What if, under that movie star persona, there's a person—well, not as sweet as Rhonda, but far closer to normal on the spectrum?"

"Nobody normal is going to attach herself to a man like Leroy," declared Meilin.

"Oh, I don't know, Meilin. Leroy is good-looking, charismatic, intelligent and self-assured. Even our mayor has been captivated by him. His appearance of wealth alone could be enough for some women."

"Appearance?" Guy looked his surprise at Claire.

"Well, we don't actually know his net worth, do we? He has to exude financial soundness or he won't make headway with the affluent in this town. Only the council is in possession of the facts."

"I wouldn't nominate him for a congeniality award, but he'd be unlikely to win backing from town officials if he was all form and no substance," Guy said.

"Maybe it was the other way around, and Leroy was first drawn to Monique," Claire suggested. "She's beautiful and has attracted a number of admirers."

Meilin rolled her eyes.

"I can understand admirers of her talent more than her looks," Guy said.

"Funny," Claire countered, "but her talent is the one thing I can't make sense of. To hang on the arm of a man like Leroy takes a certain personality. Monique has fit that bill to the Nth degree. Her art, for Leroy's purposes and seemingly for her own, is superfluous. So, why paint?"

She looked expectantly at Guy and Meilin for an answer.

"Income," Meilin began.

"A living wage from art can be hard to achieve. Other than Mayenne Bay's show, how is Monique earning money?"

"Maybe Leroy is supporting her, so earnings aren't important," Meilin suggested.

"That could be. What really nags me is that her work is so good and, at least here, she has exhibited little interest in it or even in being an artist. She doesn't talk art. She doesn't support the art club. We haven't seen her in the act of painting anywhere."

"She could have painted the 'Lupines' and 'Beach Roses' in the studio, Claire, from photos or studies, as I've often done," Guy reminded her.

"True, but where's the studio?"

"Not everyone has a separate studio. I live in mine," he reminded her.

Claire nodded and bit her lip but persisted, "I don't feel like we have all the pieces of the puzzle. Is her innate talent so prodigious that she could just whip out two fabulous paintings at will or did she have to practice hard to get this good? If the former, what made her do it if she has so little heart in it? If the latter, where's her other work?"

"Just because we don't understand from the face of things doesn't mean there's underhandedness about her," Meilin answered.

Claire thought this argument could apply to Leroy, too, but held her tongue.

"We have no idea what's going on in Monique's life, other than Leroy," Meilin continued. "If the committee had concerns about an artist, we'd have investigated. We've already endured a theft. I don't want the show tainted further, Claire, or future shows jeopardized, just because one of the artists is enigmatic or unsociable or…"

"…dating a slimeball," Guy finished for her.

They all laughed, glad for the comic relief. Only now did Claire awaken to the reason for Meilin's defensiveness.

"Sorry, Meilin. You're right to be protective of a good thing. I have nothing against Monique per se, just a curiosity about the gaps in her story."

Meilin appeared mollified, but Claire thought her essential point was well taken. They should be careful about voicing reservations aloud. Unbridled curiosity and injudicious remarks lead to unintended consequences. Morrie's experience was proof of that.

25

Joint and Several

During the drive home from the B&B, Claire continued ruminating on the glamorous artist and the controversial real estate developer who, jointly and severally, were so baffling.

"I've glimpsed the human side of Monique but haven't detected a hint of humanity in Leroy," she said.

"Leroy is here to build a condo, not to make nice with the natives," Guy said as he swung the car onto Harborview Street. "He wears his ego like a badge, displays his girlfriend like a prize and swaggers around Mayenne Bay like he owns it, which he seems intent to do. Looking for compassion in him may be a lost cause."

Claire digested Guy's words as they rolled into her driveway.

"Want to come in for tea?" she offered.

Guy shut off the ignition.

Inside, they settled onto the couch, drank tea and wine and chatted until well past midnight when idle talk dissolved into delightfully passionate words for each other. Guy did not return to his loft that night.

The next morning, he lay stretched across the couch tenderly stroking Claire's hair as she lounged against his bare

217

shoulder inside a cocoon of summer blankets.

"I wonder if the 'A Better Idea' campaign will gather enough steam to disrupt Leroy's project," Claire mulled aloud.

Already, at this early hour, her inquisitive mind was threatening to kick into gear. She made a motion to rise up, but Guy pulled her back to him, unwilling to let her disrupt their euphoric mood so soon. He'd exercised a great deal of patience and forbearance waiting for such a night and clung tenaciously to its remains. Just as Claire opened her mouth to speak again, he pulled her to him, said softly, "We'll talk later," then planted a deep kiss on it. They spent another amorous hour on the couch until Claire gently, but firmly, disengaged herself from Guy's arms.

"I'm going to shower. Want to start breakfast?"

"No. Let's go to the Fish House. I'm feeling lazy."

He pulled her back to him for one more full body embrace before releasing her.

"The Fish House it is," she called over her shoulder as she practically skipped her way down the hall.

He watched her from the couch, hands behind his head in happy indolence, savoring the newfound depth between them. If there was a word for how he felt just now, Guy would never find it. Following Claire's lead, he got up and made his way down the hall to find his clothes. He, too, would have to shower. It occurred to him just then, as he heard the bathroom door click behind Claire, that there was a way they could save time.

They were soon freshly dressed and settled at their favorite booth at the Fish House over steaming breakfast plates delivered by Celeste. Claire returned to the subject of Monique.

"Why do you keep pressing on about her?" Guy asked.

"She's a mystery. And I can't get her distress out of

my mind. It unsettles me when things are unresolved."

"You must be unsettled a lot, then," he teased. "You need to work on this."

She ignored him.

"We're missing something," Claire resumed, brow furrowed. "I keep coming back to the idea that the artist can't be disentangled from her art or vice versa. Yet, Monique is weirdly detached from her artwork and has only two paintings to her name."

"Claire, I have lots of work—you saw the piles at the loft—that I've never shown anyone. Monique may have the same. When you're self-taught, confidence can be a big issue."

She pondered his point silently as she munched on toast and sipped coffee. Happy for the break in conversation, Guy dove into his eggs, hash browns and English muffin, then greedily pulled the side of bacon toward him. His appetite this morning was bigger than usual. While he ate, he stole glances at Claire, who stared pensively out the window off and on, and, for the thousandth time, he drowned in the light of her hazel eyes.

"I'm going to paint a storefront today," Guy announced once he and Claire stepped off the wharf onto the Main Street sidewalk. "I'll be on the corner in front of Grace Grocery, just across from the Salty Dog."

"I'll join you after my haircut. Shouldn't take more than half an hour."

"You've got to have the only hairdresser who keeps Sunday hours."

"And for that, she snares a lot of clients."

She pecked Guy's cheek and turned into the little building near the wharf that constituted Mayenne Bay's premier hair salon. It was a free-standing, former shed, not more than twelve by sixteen feet, run by Amy Davis, a tiny woman, barely five-foot tall with waist-long, light brown hair. Amy had attended stylist school right after high school and rented the little shop immediately upon passing her license exam. She retained its original name, Free Choice Hair Salon, as well as its respect for clients' preferences, which had drawn Claire to the place. At Free Choice, she was safe from pressure to adopt the latest fad.

Claire pulled open the door, stepped inside and greeted Amy, whose hair hung in corkscrew curls held back from her face by a simple barrette. Amy was seated facing the door from behind a small table arrayed with nail polish in every possible color. She looked up to welcome Claire, then leaned in again to work. Claire sat down and watched with interest as Amy delicately pressed decorative decals onto long red nails extended from a pale hand bearing a familiar diamond ring.

"Monique? Is that you?" blurted Claire.

Monique jumped in her seat but, with her hand in Amy's grasp, didn't turn, so that Claire's question landed at her back. The artist was draped in a worn, over-sized sweatshirt over yoga pants. Her red hair hung in limp strings, making it clear that Amy had not had a hand in its care this morning. For the second time, Claire felt she was getting a glimpse of the woman beneath the façade.

"Hi," was all Monique said.

It was more than Claire had expected.

"These last few are a bit tacky," Amy told Monique. "I'll have to dry them before I apply the decals."

Just as she reached for the hair dryer, the phone rang. She excused herself to take the call and stepped over to her desk to access the appointment schedule on her tablet.

"We missed you at the art club celebration last night," Claire told Monique. "Your beautiful 'Lupines' painting was the talk of the evening. Have you gone over to the B&B to see it hung?"

Monique was not destined to answer. Just as Amy returned to dry her nails and apply the final decals, Leroy burst into the shop.

"Nicky, aren't you done yet? I have things to do," he barked loudly, ignoring the salon's other occupants.

Monique sprang to her feet, knocking her chair backward to the floor. She jammed a hand into her jeans pocket, ruining the damp nails, and threw cash onto the table. In her haste to leave, the toe of her shoe caught on the fallen chair leg. She stumbled to her knees with a grunt.

"Oh!" cried Claire and Amy together and started toward her.

Leroy was quicker. Without a word, he strode over, grabbed Monique by the wrists and pulled her to her feet. She let out a cry. Disregarding the shocked faces of the two onlookers, he pushed the red-faced woman straight out the door, one hand grabbing the back of her neck and the other her shoulder. Amy and Claire stood for a few moments staring at the door.

"That seemed pretty rough to me," said Amy, all concern.

"Indeed," was all Claire said, using her word of choice when she needed to temporize.

Leroy had behaved like a brute. His use of Monique's nickname, "Nicky", however it may have begun, hadn't resonated from his lips with affection. Claire moved dazedly into the salon chair and caught Amy's face in the mirror. They each wore the same worried expression.

Thirty minutes later, Claire made her way up Main Street toward Guy's easel, the sea breeze gently lifting her freshly cut hair. Even from this distance, she could see his brush moving across the canvas with vigor. She smiled, understanding the source of his energy this morning. They had turned a corner last night through their intimacy. Her whole body thrilled at the memory. Every step she took radiated an exhilaration that even her worries over Monique couldn't dampen. Later, when she and Guy were alone, they would revisit their first night of lovemaking. Claire would watch his blue eyes, knowing everything he felt would be right there when words failed him.

When she reached him, Claire positioned herself as close as possible to his side to relay all she had just seen and heard at the hair salon.

"Leroy was rough on Monique. And she's fraying at the edges."

"Meilin has always maintained Leroy is a bad character," Guy said.

"Right, but without any proof. Until now, he seemed possessive, but Monique looked comfortable enough. In the salon, he was a full-blown bully, and she was clearly overpowered. I'm surprised he'd allow his image to be tarnished by such a public display. Maybe he's fraying at the edges, too."

They were approached by Morrie, whose face bore a childlike excitement, making him look younger than Claire had ever seen him.

"I have really good news! I've been accepted as a substitute math teacher at the middle and high schools. It's on-call work for what's left of summer school with the promise of more in the fall, a first step, after a long hiatus, toward something like normal. Believe it or not, those Frankl books helped," he said and gave a slight bow of acknowledgment in Claire's direction, "not to mention all the kindness I received."

"You realize you're about to pay it forward, taking on adolescent math students," Claire warned.

"Don't I know it. I'm ready. It'll feel good to contribute to a community again."

"Why don't you join us for dinner tonight and tell us all about it. We're planning homemade pizza. We can toast to your new job."

"I'd like that. I finally have something to talk about besides Monique's work and Viktor Frankl."

"Amen to that," quipped Guy. "I want to be able to stay awake during dinner."

Claire rolled her eyes.

"Swing by my place at five o'clock. It's just around the block there on Harborview. On the left, Number 23, bottom floor. I'll have popped a bottle of red by then, and we'll be eating around six."

Guy's eyes glowed as he turned back to his painting. Claire had held to her promise and set the hour of Morrie's arrival late enough to reserve several hours of downtime for just the two of them.

26

Coming to Grips

On her way to open Creative Agenda, Meilin stopped to view Guy's painting and caught the tail end of Morrie's other news.

"Gloria lets me visit the 'Lupines' at the B&B whenever I want," he announced happily. "I'd visit the 'Beach Roses', too, if Leroy and Monique hadn't taken an aversion to me."

"What do they have to do with the 'Beach Roses'?" Meilin inquired.

"Leroy bought it."

"Leroy didn't purchase any paintings at the show," Meilin said flatly.

Claire looked up in unfeigned surprise.

"Really?"

"Yes. The 'Beach Roses' was purchased by someone else—someone anonymous."

"Anonymous?" chorused Guy, Claire and Morrie.

"Now I am intrigued," added Guy without skipping a paint stroke.

"That's curious…and too bad," Morrie said. "I held out a small hope I'd reconcile with Monique and see that painting hanging in her house someday."

"Peggy took the check but kept the name to herself. A lot of people mistook Leroy for the buyer. He didn't bother disabusing people of the notion, though, did he?" Meilin's tone was disapproving.

"I wonder how we could find out the buyer's name," said Claire.

"People buy anonymously for a reason, Claire," Meilin reminded her. "Anyway, why do you care?"

"This is an unknown admirer of her work, another piece of the Monique puzzle."

"I wonder if little Nicky herself knows who it was," Guy mused.

"Who?" asked Morrie.

"Nicky," Claire repeated. "That's the nickname Leroy uses for Monique."

"Rhonda was a bit tipsy last night so she may not have got it quite right when she told us that," Guy said.

"She got it right," Claire said. "Leroy called Monique 'Nicky' this morning when he picked her up from the hair salon, though there wasn't an ounce of tenderness in his voice when he said it."

"Seems too ordinary a name for such a flamboyant person and artist," Morrie said.

"The last two times I saw her, there was nothing flashy about her," Claire told them. "You might wish for Monique the Ice Queen to return once you see the state Nicky the Frazzled is in."

"Oh," Meilin exclaimed suddenly. "I'm supposed to be opening."

She rushed down the sidewalk toward Creative Agenda where several customers were already at the door.

The next moment, Guy's easel was almost toppled by a four-foot tall, masked demon who pelted past, clutching a pair of hot-pink sandals, with Ben in pursuit. At the sight of the group at the easel, the policeman paused, panting and laughing and leaving the culprit to sprint unimpeded across the intersection. Claire yelped when the runner tripped and stumbled onto one knee, thinking the delay would give Ben an advantage, but Ben had already given up the chase. She watched the youngster recover, having barely lost his rhythm, and, with a quick glance behind him, disappear between the bank and toy store.

"If a young and fit cop can't keep up with him, Ben, no one will. I don't think any of the older cops have it in them," Guy laughed.

The others, including Ben, joined him. It was a testament to the general harmlessness of the bandit that they all took his home run with good humor.

"Sandals right off the summer-sale shelf in Peabody Shoes," Ben explained. "I was inside looking for work boots, saw the kid and startled him. He took off like a shot out the back door. I think, by now, he's hit every store in town. God knows where the sandals will end up, but I'm sure we'll retrieve them intact."

"Jay thinks this boy's also the culprit behind his missing gnomes," Claire said.

"That was true for the first one, I think," Ben agreed, "but not the others. The second and third gnomes were damaged, and our wing-footed bandit is not about vandalizing. He's not even a true thief—at least, not that I've seen so far. He's just pulling pranks." He looked at each of their faces in turn. "Did you happen to mark any identifiable features, like hair color? Sophie, the florist, said she saw red when he grabbed a potted plant."

"I'll bet she did," joked Guy.

"I haven't been able to make out a single thing," Claire answered, "except for the obvious stature and speed. He's looked exactly the same each time right down to the black gloves and shoes."

Guy and Morrie said the same.

Ben straightened his shirt and said, "I'll have to save it for another day. Gotta go. Rhonda's expecting me." He headed into the grocery.

"I'd better go, too," said Morrie. "I want to tell Peggy my news. See you at five," he called appreciatively over his shoulder.

Guy and Claire watched the green cardigan, fitting better now with Morrie's increasing girth, disappear up the sidewalk at a markedly energized gait.

"I don't know how old Morrie actually is," Claire said, "but he seems to have dropped years."

"It's more like Morrie was dead and has come alive," Guy corrected her. "He's that changed."

Claire left Guy at his easel in her usual upbeat mood when heading for her kitchen. It was her favorite place, where her creative juices flowed. She was one of those cooks who could imagine a successful combination of flavors in her mind and determine, just by smell, what was missing from the ingredients. Pulling an original recipe together, like her homemade pizza, was as inspirational to her as paint on canvas to Guy.

"For you," Guy said as he stepped through the door a few hours later. He swung forward the arm he held behind his back to reveal a pot of mixed summer herbs—basil, parsley, tarragon and rosemary—tied with a huge ribbon. "One of Sophie's creations. I thought you'd prefer live plants over cut flowers. Did I get that right?"

"You did," answered a spattered and untidy Claire.

Her apron was dusted with flour, and her left cheek dotted with tomato sauce. Claire landed high on the messy-cook meter, so at odds with her habitual cleanliness, but she more than compensated with flavor and efficiency. Already, the sourdough ball that was soon to transform into personal-sized pizza crusts was proofing on the counter, a crockpot of homemade sauce sat cooling and fresh mozzarella lay in a row of neat slices. Even with all this, lunch was spread on the table in anticipation of Guy's arrival.

Claire took the pot of herbs into her flour-caked hands and set it on the table, shedding crumbs across the floor as she moved, then turned and threw her arms around Guy's neck. He brushed flour from his shirt while Claire positioned the new plant among the others in the window.

They ate a light lunch of chicken salad on a plate of greens knowing tonight's dinner would be substantial, then stretched out on the couch and sank into the quiet like a soft pillow, talking over their first night together. Before they knew it, there was a knock at the front door.

Guy was first to rise and shake off his dreamy stupor. Claire stood up next, shook back her hair, smoothed her clothes and released a dramatic "ahem" to Guy to do the same. He stopped mid-stride to tuck in his shirt and plaster his blonde hair back into place with the palms of his hands before he proceeded to the door. Claire quickly straightened the cushions.

"Morrie," Guy greeted the man. "Come in."

Guy opened the door wide and waved him toward the kitchen. Morrie entered wearing a brown cardigan and holding a wine bottle he immediately handed to Guy.

"Welcome, Morrie," Claire said. "Nice cardie."

"Thank God for thrift shops with present funds so tight. I thought I'd better get a few more things to wear. Adolescents aren't very forgiving as it is. Imagine what they'd do to a teacher who wore the same, patched sweater every day." He shuddered, then added quietly, "I'm nervous enough, after all this time."

"You're going to get right back into the saddle, I have no doubt," Claire assured him. "Let's toast to your new job."

Guy delivered drinks all around, and they all called

"Cheers!"

Claire slipped the pizza stone into the bottom of the oven and flipped the temperature control to four hundred-fifty degrees. She threw a generous amount of flour onto the counter, grabbed the swollen dough ball and sliced it into eight equal portions. Finally, she began to flatten each portion into a personal-sized pizza with her fingers.

Morrie was rapt with attention and stood right next to her at the counter to watch. Guy moved over to the cutting board to chop toppings and watched for the inevitable confluence of Claire's helpful nature and Morrie's anxiety.

"What makes you so nervous about teaching after all your years of experience?" Claire asked.

"I'm so out of practice."

"Do you mean in math itself?"

"No, no. Math is like my native language, and I've already gone through all the textbooks. I'm just out of practice with people, especially young people. I withdrew after the bankruptcy to insulate myself from any more of life's blows. After living like a recluse these past years, I'll suddenly be standing in front of a new generation of kids."

Claire dusted her hands with more flour.

"How did you manage before?"

"I had so much enthusiasm about math that I barely noticed."

"You'll reclaim it all after a few months on the job. Your vitality has returned. You've come to grips to a large degree with your past. And you're going to resume the work that added a great deal of meaning to your life." She said in a conspicuously loud whisper, one hand cupped at the corner of her mouth, "I had to throw Frankl's meaning-in-life theme in there. Guy is so fascinated."

Guy gave the expected eye roll as he chopped the

last of the mushrooms, then dried his hands, found soft mandolin music on his phone and tapped into Claire's Bluetooth speakers.

Morrie shifted his attention to the meal and rubbed his hands together.

"This is looking and smelling mouth-watering. What can I do to help?"

Claire pointed him to the cupboard.

"Plates and napkins are in there. Flatware in the drawer below. Water glasses above. And I could use a refill of that delicious wine you brought, too, if you don't mind."

Guy smiled to himself. Claire measured the amount of wine she drank by the degree of comfort she felt with her company. With Geoffrey and Caroline Bristolwaite, she had barely consumed a half glass the whole night. With Morrie, she was already on her second.

Morrie refilled everyone's glasses, then busied himself setting the table. Suddenly, he touched the heal of his hand to his forehead and swung around to Guy and Claire.

"I completely forgot. I saw Monique at Grace Grocery when I picked up the wine."

They gave him their full attention.

"She looked totally worn out. Nothing like the queen who's been strutting around town. The sight of her reminded me of your story from the hair salon, Claire. I wasn't sure what to do, considering our history. Up until today, she preferred I simply not exist. I decided to approach her anyway, she looked so sad. She teared up, burned red in the face and stared down at her shoes. I had no idea what to do or say after that."

Claire's hands, which had been nimbly working the third dough ball into a pizza crust, froze in place.

"Then what?" she pressed Morrie.

"I stood there, not wanting to leave her. Her hands

were trembling, and she had bruises on her wrists."

"From Leroy's grip this morning, I'm sure," Claire growled.

"I held my ground even when Leroy came and towered over us. I never realized how tall he was 'til that moment. They left together. I'm not sure if I should have done more. Her relationship with Leroy is a private thing on one hand, but when he's hurt her like that, seems to me the boundaries of privacy aren't the same."

"Abuse is not subject to the usual rules of privacy," Claire declared, a martial glint in her eyes. "Morrie, do you have any idea how to find her?"

"No, I don't."

"I think we should try." Claire looked from one man to the other. "It would be terrible if she was open to help and no one even tried, don't you think?"

"I wonder if Meilin has an idea where she might be," suggested Guy.

At this, Claire moved immediately for her phone, leaving another trail of flour as she went. Guy stepped in front of the stove to toss the pizza toppings—mushrooms, onions, peppers and black olives—into the frying pan to pre-cook.

"Not mushy, just softened," she coached in a low voice before the call went through.

27

Intervention

"Hi, Meilin? It's Claire. Am I interrupting?"

"No, I just closed up shop and I'm heading home."

"Good timing, then. Do you have plans right now? We—Guy, Morrie and I— need to talk to you. It's important. We're having homemade pizza at my place. Can you join us? There's plenty."

"Sounds intriguing and delicious. I'm on my way."

Claire disconnected and shoved her phone back in her bag.

"Better set another place, Morrie," she instructed.

Guy moved to the sink to rinse the fresh basil. Claire worked the remaining dough balls into crusts which, one by one, were prebaked and restored to the queue on the counter. She and Morrie worked in assembly-line fashion to spread sauce and arrange slices of fresh mozzarella on the crusts. Guy put the toppings in one bowl and the herbs in another to be sprinkled on the final product. Claire turned the oven up to five hundred degrees.

"Good thing we made extra."

Guy turned to her, incredulous.

"Claire, how many times have you been in exactly the right place or prepared just the right thing as though some sixth sense guided you? How can you be so aware about so much but at the same time so clueless?"

She regarded him, nonplussed, until Morrie struck his forehead a second time.

"The 'Beach Roses'!" he said.

They turned and stared at him.

"I've been so distracted by Monique and cooking, I forgot. Earlier, I found Peggy at the library."

"Of course, you did," joked Guy.

"You know the name of the buyer," anticipated Claire.

Morrie grinned.

"Well?" Claire and Guy asked in unison.

"It was a Mrs. Littlefield. Someone from up north. She only wanted anonymity until the show was over."

"Littlefield," Claire and Guy both repeated.

Claire popped the first dressed pizza into the blazing oven and set the timer.

"That's a pretty common name, but as it's an outsider, I'm sure I don't know her," Guy said.

"Me, either," said Claire.

Meilin rapped at the kitchen door and let herself in.

"Perfect timing," Claire told her. "I'm about to pull the first pie from the oven, and it has your name on it."

"A mystery plus homemade pizza," Meilin said. "How could I have gone home to leftovers? Oh, it smells so good in here." She got right to the point. "Now, what's going on?"

"Wine first, Meilin," Morrie offered as he uncorked a second bottle.

"Thank you. That would be lovely. It's been a rough day." The other three listened patiently as she unloaded. "Sundays are usually quiet. Not today. The store was bedlam. When I opened the delivery boxes that arrived yesterday, half the stock was wrong. It took me hours to sort it out. People came in expecting to pick up their special orders. I had to disappoint them and hand out discounts like candy, just to smooth them over. Thank God Rhonda was available to help. She's so adorable. Nobody will rag on her no matter what the problem."

"Good strategy," Claire said. "You always seem so composed. It's easy to forget you live the unpredictable life of a retailer."

She motioned to Meilin to sit down and set the first pizza in front of her.

"I love the business, generally," sighed Meilin. "I try to please my customers. Some days, that simple goal is hard to achieve. Thanks for letting me vent. I don't usually have that luxury."

She dove into her pizza.

Claire relayed the details of her two encounters with Monique, at La Ferme and Free Choice, then turned to Morrie.

"Want to share your story from today at Grace Grocery?"

Morrie related the tale as he had done before. "…so that's when she left with Leroy," he finished and looked earnestly at Meilin. "We were hoping you'd be able to help us locate her."

"For some kind of intervention on her behalf," Claire completed the thought. "We may not be able to change anything, but it's important to try."

Meilin swallowed.

"I've made no secret of the fact that I don't like Leroy but, no matter how ill I've thought of him, I've never suspected him of abuse. I have no idea where Monique is but I'll check around." She gulped more wine. "Who'd have thought we'd spend a Sunday evening feeling sorry for her?"

"Not me," Guy answered.

"I'll contact Ben Tripp after we eat," Claire said.

The mood in the room turned solemn after this, so Guy powered off the music. Claire served Morrie, then Guy, then herself, flipped off the oven and sat down. The pizza was superb, but their minds were at work on how to reach Monique, if she could be found.

While Guy served tea and coffee, Claire made a quick call to Ben, then set out a plate of dark chocolate squares.

"I know we're not in a celebratory mood but I've got to have dark chocolate after Italian food."

"Why not just say you've got to have dark chocolate and leave it at that?" Guy teased.

She made a face.

"There are no moments unsuited to dark chocolate," agreed Meilin. Turning first to Claire, then to Guy, she added, "This was a wonderful meal. Delicious. Thank you. And Morrie, congratulations again on your new job."

"I hope you'll come again when we can be more relaxed, Meilin. It would be nice to talk without Monique and Leroy dominating the conversation," said Claire. "Oh! And before we forget—the 'Beach Roses' painting was bought by a Mrs. Littlefield from up in the County. Peggy told Morrie."

"You are full of surprises today. Mrs. Littlefield. Hmm. Not someone I know."

"Us, either," Guy told her.

"Well," said Meilin, rising, "if you won't be offended, I'll get moving. I could use a hot bath and an early bedtime. I'm beat."

She popped another piece of chocolate into her mouth, threw them a grin and left.

"I'd better go, too," said Morrie. "I have to be careful not to overextend. Besides, tomorrow is Monday and just might be a workday for me."

He thanked his hosts and followed Meilin out the door.

The next morning, when Claire returned to the office, it felt like stepping off a rollercoaster. Her first overnight with Guy. Her anger at Leroy. Her fears for Monique. In just two days, she had tumbled from the height of joy to deep anxiety and was reeling from it. The tranquilizing effect of passionless number-crunching was just what she needed for her disordered emotions.

Over the lunch hour, Guy phoned to relay an unexpected request from Gloria.

"Hello?" he had answered tentatively, not recognizing the B&B number.

"Guy, is that you? It's Gloria."

"Hi."

He stared in mingled surprise and misgiving at his phone.

"I'd like your opinion on a new frame for the 'Lupines' painting."

More surprise.

"Um, okay. It'll have to be late evening, the way my schedule looks. How's Wednesday?"

They made arrangements to meet at eight o'clock, generally a quiet time for the B&B and late enough to allow Guy time to meet his deadlines. Guy asked Claire to join him.

"Gloria unnerves me. I'd appreciate your steadiness on hand. I'll bring dinner to your place beforehand."

On Wednesday evening, Guy entered Claire's kitchen with two steaming boxes and found her already in comfortable jeans, wine in hand. He emptied the food onto the plates she had laid out, and the enticing fragrance of Thai spices filled the room. Claire sat down and dug in. Guy picked up his fork, rolled it with pad Thai noodles and hesitated mid-air. Thai food was never a certainty for him.

Every restaurant had its own spice range—zero, mild, medium and just plain hot. Claire's taste landed in the warm to hot zone. Guy was in the zero category, but zero, he found, didn't really exist in Thai food. "No spice," he requested every time, but heat seemed to be inherent in the cuisine. While Claire chatted easily between mouthfuls of spicy mixed vegetables with shrimp, Guy alternated his forkfuls of "zero-spice" pad Thai with sips of milk to counter the burn.

Just before eight, they headed for the B&B. They found the parlor completely empty and, as the sun had just set, dark, except for a small lamp on the checkout counter and a torchiere floor lamp on either side of the sofa. For closer viewing, Gloria had taken the "Lupines" painting down from the wall and laid it on a blanket spread across the coffee table.

"I've got some tea made, Guy," Gloria said. "I'll bring the pot out. Wine, Claire?"

"Thanks, but just a half. I've already had some tonight," Claire said as she lowered herself onto her knees next to Guy in front of the painting.

"Don't say anything 'til I get back," commanded Gloria. "I don't want to miss a word."

Guy rose and pulled the floor lamps forward to shed more light onto the celebrated canvas. They threw a diffuse glow not ideal for viewing artwork but infinitely superior to the dark shadows elsewhere in the room. There had been so much hoopla around this painting, Guy felt like he already knew it well. The truth, he realized now, was that he had never truly examined it up close. There had always been a crowd or other distraction to prevent him.

Gloria returned almost immediately with their drinks, and they all settled around the table. As Guy had come expressly to look at the frame, he started there.

"It's antique, if I had to bet on it. Wood," he

observed, "The front is aged and dirty but underneath the crud is either gold paint or gold leaf." Gloria looked her surprise, leaned forward and squinted. "Did you ever ask Monique where she got the frame?"

"No, we never discussed it."

"It might be a good idea to ask her. Older frames can themselves be valuable, if their age or craftsmanship can be authenticated. You can buy solid wood frames now, even hand-carved and gilded, but they're costly. She may have found this one at an old shop or flea market. It could have been more of a find than she realized."

"It's all beat up," said Gloria with a grimace.

"Yes, but that's part of the charm. Haven't you ever watched the *Antiques Roadshow?*" They all laughed, then Guy resumed a serious tone. "The fact that it hasn't been refinished may actually increase its value, if it's authentic. It's counter-intuitive, I know. Let's flip it over and see if there's a maker's mark." Guy and Claire leaned back to allow Gloria room to turn over the painting, then bent forward again. "Mudded on the back like American impressionists used to do," resumed Guy. "Current frame makers still do the same to emulate them. And look at this. Hand-carved initials 'E-L-C'. Interesting."

He sat back on his heels and looked from one woman to the other.

"Do you know that mark?" Gloria inquired.

"Nope," answered Guy. "I don't recognize it, but you could Google..."

"This is just unsightly," Gloria interrupted with a dismissive wave of her hand and rose to her feet. "*Antiques Roadshow* be damned. I don't care who made it or how much it might be worth. I don't want it on my wall. I think the painting would look better in a clean frame with sleeker lines. It would fit better with my décor."

"Framing is a matter of personal taste no different

than the artwork itself," Guy answered calmly, disregarding her churlishness. "Roxie does great framing work. I've used her myself. All I would caution is, don't toss the old frame until you ascertain its origin and value unique from the painting itself. Roxie may be able to help you with that, if Monique won't."

"Right, well, thanks for your advice," clipped Gloria.

She put an abrupt end to the meeting by lifting the painting from the table and hanging it back on the wall. Guy and Claire wordlessly rose to their feet and set their half-finished drinks on the coffee table. They bade Gloria good-bye and headed into town for a waterside walk under the stars.

"She didn't care what I had to say," growled Guy, "so why call me? That woman is so frustrating. That was the first time I got close enough to that painting to examine it, and she cut me short. Even in the poor light, I'd have relished the chance for more time."

"If we had stayed, you would have been hampered by Gloria breathing down your neck," Claire said.

Hand in hand, they made their way along the park path in a contemplative silence. Claire said nothing. Guy was grateful for her forbearance. Words had not yet caught up with his churning mind. All he could have shared with Claire at that moment was his vague suspicion that something about the "Lupines" painting wasn't quite right.

28

Morrie's Tale

The town council's second executive session—the August 1st, closed-door event that had raised so much fuss—came and went without fanfare. Even the coffee room at work, typically gossip central, had been mum on Friday morning.

"Anti-climactic," Claire said aloud as she got out of her car that evening.

"Claire, you're talking to yourself," said a familiar voice behind her. "It's nice to know I'm not the only one."

She spun around to discover Morrie walking toward her.

"I hope you don't mind my stopping by unannounced. I don't have a cell phone, and the public phone in the Whispering Seabreeze lobby isn't great for private talk."

"I don't mind at all," answered Claire, intrigued. "Has something happened? Is it work? Did they call you in?"

"As a matter of fact, they did." His tone was triumphant. "All week. And it went far better than I'd expected. I hadn't realized how much I missed teaching."

Claire swung the door wide, and they both stepped in. She relieved her arms of the canvas bag that served to transport necessities to and from the office, then moved to the sink to wash her hands.

"Take a seat, Morrie. Would you like a drink—water, coffee, wine?"

"Water, if you don't mind. I want a clear head."

He dropped into the nearest chair.

With heightened curiosity, Claire retrieved the water and a white Bordeaux for herself, then sat down in front of him and waited expectantly. He drank some water, inhaled deeply and began.

"When I left here last Sunday, I was sorely hoping to get some rest but found myself so unnerved by Monique's predicament that sleep was sure to elude me. I felt like I'd failed her by not being more assertive at the grocery store."

Claire opened her mouth to argue the point, but Morrie forestalled her by holding up a hand.

"I struggled to think what else I could have done. I'm certainly no match for Leroy, and Monique is a grown woman, after all. Funny though, how much closer to girlhood she seemed that day than all the other times I'd seen her. No arrogance, no rudeness, no over-played sexuality. I saw pallor, exhaustion and what was probably disillusionment on her face. From all appearances, she was completely alone, except for that bully. It made the hair on the back of my neck stand up."

He stopped to wet his throat again.

"I was absorbed in thought the whole way home. When I finally lifted my eyes from the sidewalk, I was shocked to see the Whispering Seabreeze right in front of me. I yanked open the foyer door, anxious to get inside and collapse on my bed. As usual, the place was silent as the grave at that hour. The lighting was subdued, and the lobby was entirely empty except for a single person. On the corner bench next to the bookcase sat the slumped figure of Monique LaBelle."

Claire took in a short breath.

"What?" She stood up. "Was Leroy there, too?"

"No. She was alone. She'd left him but had no place to stay, no money. So, she'd come to find me." He held his palms up to convey his disbelief. "I have no idea why she chose me out of all the people she'd met in Mayenne Bay, a man she dislikes, who has no means and who lives in a group home. All I could think of was how relieved I was that she wasn't wandering the streets or seriously battered, as far as I could tell."

"Wow." Claire said and sank back down. "This is totally unexpected, but good news, I hope. Was she alright?"

"I knew only what I could see. She looked worn out and unkempt. No make-up. Red eyes. All she had with her were a small handbag and the clothes on her back—yoga pants and an old sweatshirt, the same she had on at the grocery store earlier that day."

"And at the hair salon," Claire added and leaned in. "What did you do?"

"I didn't think either of us would have the energy to sort things out that night. I sat her down in my apartment with some water while I located the residence manager. Mary Bouchard is very caring. She agreed to allow Monique to use a recently vacated room for the night—completely against regulations, mind you—and also to let me rustle up a sandwich from the kitchen. I was thinking of Maslow's basics, you know, water, food, a hot shower and a warm bed."

"That seems exactly right to me." Claire said and exhaled the breath she'd been holding. "I can't say enough how relieved I am. Something made her trust you, Morrie, and overcome your rocky history. Thank goodness."

"I felt relieved, too. I told her to get a good night's sleep and suggested we'd figure things out in the morning after we were rested."

"I'm hoping this won't end by you telling me she disappeared during the night."

"I fully expected it, to be honest. Monday morning, there she was, waiting for me in the dining room, as planned. She looked a bit better. I'm not suggesting she was all healed up or anything, but clearly the food and rest had helped."

"Not to mention the safe room and being treated with dignity."

"Yes, I'm sure. Funny, but first thing she did was to ask me to call her 'Nicky'." Morrie seemed very moved by this. "Seemed like even she'd had enough of 'Monique'. She was embarrassed, but thankful, and apologized for her mistreatment."

"Wow," Claire said again. "This is a new Monique…I mean, Nicky. You breakfasted together at the residence on Monday?"

"Yes, and then I got called in by the school to substitute teach, as luck would have it, so I had to run. They're always last minute, you know. Monique stayed in her room 'til I got home."

He stopped short when Guy, who had graduated from knocking like a guest to letting himself in, opened the kitchen door.

"Hey, you two," he greeted them. "Done with my big project. If you don't have anything else planned, Claire, I picked up some fresh perch." Turning to Morrie, he explained, "It's Claire's favorite. You're welcome to join us, Morrie. I bought plenty."

"I'd love to. Your cooking is such a welcome change from the meals at the residence. Not that I'm complaining," he caught himself. "I'd have been out on the street if it hadn't been for that place."

"Three for supper, then. Looks like the pow-wow has already begun," Guy looked from Morrie to Claire and eyed their half-finished drinks. "Want to fill me in?"

They caught Guy up while he poured himself iced tea.

"Is Nicky still at the residence?" Claire asked, anxious to move the story along.

"Yes. Mary gave permission until we could figure out what to do. Nicky is down and broke. I thought she needed time and space to come back to herself…whatever her 'self' really is. The first thing I did after work on Monday was to walk her to the thrift shop to find a change of clothes. I thought she'd turn up her nose at the place, being so used to finery, but she was appreciative. She even picked out a pair of flat sandals."

Guy released a low whistle.

"I'm already liking Nicky far more than I did Monique."

"Me, too," agreed Morrie.

"She'll be fine financially, though, after she hocks that big rock on her hand. It'll give her a start, anyway."

"That might have been true, had it been genuine. Nicky found out it was a fake. It was one of the many things that, collectively, broke the spell Leroy held over her. She'd been trying to get away from him for days."

"That says something for her."

"Yes, it does," Morrie agreed.

"Leroy has a lot to answer for," said Claire, arms crossed in indignation.

"Though I doubt he ever will," Guy said.

"I had to leave Nicky to herself most of the time," Morrie went on. "Mary kept a discreet eye on her for me. I was assigned to a classroom for the whole week. With papers to correct, and needing rest myself, I hardly had a minute to spare. And the common dining room doesn't exactly inspire confidences. I think the solitude did her good. By yesterday afternoon, she was ready to talk."

"What else have you learned?" Claire asked.

"Our Nicky has a backstory from right here in Maine."

Claire smiled. Morrie's "our Nicky" revealed a fatherly protectiveness budding in his heart. The woman who had scorned him and almost broken his spirit with her false accusation was now, ironically, accelerating his return to a productive life.

"She's from up north," Morrie continued, "Not sure yet what brought her here, if it wasn't Leroy himself. We haven't gotten into that. I've been trying to persuade her to reconnect with family or friends—anyone who would have her interests at heart, besides us, that is. I don't know if she's acted on that suggestion or not."

"You handled everything with such a clear head, Morrie," Claire told him.

"When you've been rescued yourself, you learn how to focus on what matters."

Claire rose, pulled some sweet potatoes and salad greens from the refrigerator and flicked on the oven.

"We'd better get started," she said. "Want to handle the table setting again, Morrie? And Guy, will you do the salad? I'll prep the perch."

While the men attended to their tasks, she washed and cut the potatoes into fries, tossed them with seasoning and spread them onto a greased baking sheet. Then, she turned to the fish.

"It's so good of you to feed me again," Morrie said and wagged his finger at them. "Someday soon, when I'm back on my feet and have a place of my own, I'm going to cook dinner for the two of you."

"Deal," Claire said.

"You're on," said Guy.

Before they sat down to eat, Claire made quick calls to Ben and Meilin to inform them Monique had been found safe. Ben expressed relief. Meilin released a gush of breath that told Claire Meilin had been as worried as she. Claire felt an even greater kinship with the shop owner as she hung up to rejoin Morrie and Guy.

There was nothing Claire loved more than to witness a person changing into a better version of himself. Morrie, not long ago, had been a mere shell of his former being, a hollow, dejected man, barely participating in life. Yet, here he sat in her kitchen, full of compassion for a fellow being—one who had injured him—and imagining a future home. Monique, in her turn, was pulling out of the dark days of artifice and abuse and emerging as a more humbled Nicky. Even Claire and Guy had become improved versions of themselves since they'd reconciled. Perch and sweet potatoes were all well and good, but the soul food Claire derived from these personal transformations filled her to overflowing.

29

Overheard

Dinner at Claire's turned out to be a savory, but short, affair. Morrie was exhausted after his first week on the job and the added exertion of supporting Nicky. Having completed his mission of informing Claire and Guy about Nicky's whereabouts and eaten his fill, he headed back to the Whispering Seabreeze.

Guy and Claire speculated on Nicky's origins all through cleanup, then blocked out everything but a movie and each other for the night, aware that their respective work commitments would consume the rest of the weekend. Guy's large project this past week had put him behind on some of his smaller, bread-and-butter accounts. Claire had a series of financial reports to complete for a nine o'clock meeting on Monday with a new client. Saturday and Sunday flew by, as time always does when there are deadlines to be met.

Claire arrived at the office early on Monday for a planned interval of quiet before her client meeting. She unloaded her bag onto her desk and moved directly to the coffee room to start the first pot. Renée Pincer, whom Claire hadn't seen since their luncheon in Oyster Bay, approached timidly from behind.

"Good morning, Claire."

"Good morning."

Renée looked behind her to make certain they were alone before speaking again.

"I never thanked you for letting me interrupt your day in Oyster Bay to listen to my problems. Sorry it took me so long. I felt a little uncomfortable afterward."

"You're welcome. Honestly, I was worried you'd never want to talk to me again after that. May I ask…how are things going?"

"As you can see, I didn't take the other job. I decided time with Mom is more important."

"That says a lot about you."

Claire turned away as she suppressed a twinge of envy and a sense of despair that such an intimacy would never be possible with Hannah.

"I'd love to count you as a friend," she heard Renée say from behind.

Claire's face lit up, and she spun around.

"You would? I'd love that, too."

They were interrupted by several co-workers who noisily crammed into the little kitchen to stuff their lunches into the refrigerator and fill their mugs. The coffee hadn't finished brewing, so they hung around to wait.

"Did you hear the rumor?" one of them asked Claire and Renée.

"What rumor?" Claire and Renée asked together, then giggled.

"That guy who was tearing down the factory to build a condo—Leroy Somebody—has left town. Scarpered!"

Claire heard the news with skepticism.

"Unlikely. He's knee deep in the project, and it's about to launch."

She filled her coffee mug, cast a meaningful glance

at Renée and went to her office, unwilling to accept the office scuttlebutt at face value. Once inside, she closed her door and dialed Meilin.

"Meilin? It's Claire. Sorry to call so early."

She dove right into the rumor she'd just heard.

"Yeah, I talked to Sandra late last night," Meilin said. "Leroy's landlord is Bruce Raymond, the art teacher. Bruce stopped by yesterday to collect rent, including some payments in arrears, found Leroy gone and assumed the worst. Turns out Leroy has some unpaid accounts around town, too, which fueled everyone's panic. Sandra guessed I'd been keeping tabs on Leroy and might know something."

"Well, you were, weren't you?"

Meilin laughed.

"Yeah. Perpetual watch. Much as I'd like Leroy to be gone, Bruce is overreacting. Leroy just cleared the Preservation Commission. He can start demolition. Everything's greased and ready to go. He's probably taking a break or meeting with investors or contractors."

"That's a more credible explanation than scarpering. As for the debts, my firm supports a lot of start-ups. Not many get through without cash shortages. Bills accumulate before the money starts flowing. The fact that people jumped to the worst case scenario just tells me Leroy hasn't earned much trust."

"That's exactly what I told Sandra. People are suspicious. He's an outsider and not exactly an open book, plus he has offended many. Won't Bruce be embarrassed when Leroy shows up in his hard hat by the waterfront?"

Claire laughed and looked up at the clock.

"Look, Meilin, I have to go. I'll be in touch."

"Let me know if you bump into Leroy, will you? For all we know, he's at the Fish House right now harassing Celeste."

"Will do."

They hung up. After a quick call to Guy to give him the news, Claire closed her eyes and sipped her coffee in peace for the remaining ten minutes before her meeting. It started and ended precisely as scheduled. By eleven-thirty, she was already making her way to the Main Street Coffee Bar for an early lunch. It was her habit to take time for decompression once a stressful deadline was met. She slid onto her preferred bench by the window, where she and John-Pierre had talked, and leaned her head back to relax.

The bench backs at the coffee bar were tall and embellished at the top by potted philodendrons whose green tentacles draped lazily over both sides. This attractive divide between booths was a privacy feature of the coffee bar that Claire prized. It was substantial enough, she found, that people rarely breached its protection. One could eat unmolested. She ordered her customary spinach salad with goat cheese and roasted beets and a large black coffee, then settled herself in for an hour of quiet over some professional magazines she'd brought from the office.

"You mean it's ALL gone?" came a harsh voice from behind the barrier.

Claire jumped in her seat at the jarring tone, and her ears involuntarily tuned in.

"Yes," answered a meek voice, followed by a sniff.

A long silence ensued which meant, Claire hoped, the conversation had ended. The bench back hid her neighbors at the next booth from view but was not very soundproof with the place so empty.

"I was afraid you'd say that," answered the stern voice.

"He made me," the other whined.

"No one can make you hand over your inheritance. You gave it willingly. You never noticed, but I was here and saw with my own eyes what you were with that excuse of a man—nothing like the Nicky I know. You paraded all over town looking down on your neighbors."

"Oh, Aunt Maddy," cried Nicky. The sound of muffled sobs ensued.

Claire sat up very straight. Nicky. It was she who had given her inheritance to "him", which had to mean Leroy. That an inheritance had been squandered, Claire had never before imagined, but it certainly added to the reasons for the demise of their relationship. Perhaps Leroy was making himself scarce because he knew this Aunt Maddy was in town. That would answer.

Claire didn't want to catch wind of something else not intended for her ears. She rose, stepped directly in front of their booth and looked from one face to the other. Nicky and her aunt stared at the intruder for a few seconds. Nicky's red hair was pulled up into a simple pony tail, and her face was unobscured by makeup. She looked tired and sad, but beneath the distress, there was a loveliness Claire had never before detected. Aunt Maddy's face was scrubbed clean and glowed a natural pink. Her dark hair was streaked with gray and swept up into a knot at the back. Though her features were soft, her words to Nicky had told Claire not to be fooled by her looks.

"Hi, Monique," Claire began, not yet having been invited to call her "Nicky", then addressed both women equally. "I apologize for interrupting. I just felt it would be dishonest to let you go on with your conversation not knowing I was within earshot. I'm so sorry."

Monique opened her mouth to protest, but was forestalled by her Aunt Maddy.

"It doesn't matter now, Nicky," interrupted her relative sharply, defusing an indignant retort. "You lost your right to privacy when you strutted around like a peacock. Anyway, better to have the truth known than to leave it to the creative guesswork of the rumor mill." She stopped there and extended her hand to Claire. "I'm Maddy, Nicky's aunt."

Claire accepted it.

"I'm Claire. I know Monique from the art show where my friend, Guy, also exhibited."

Claire thought it best not to elaborate.

"Her name is 'Nicky'," the aunt replied, looking meaningfully at her niece.

Nicky squirmed.

Claire said, "Seeing you now, Nicky, I honestly think it's more suited to you. Well, I'd better…"

"Thank you for making yourself known to us," interrupted Maddy.

"You're welcome. Again, I'm sorry. I'll, um, take my salad to-go so I can leave you in peace. A word of warning. It's going to get crowded in here shortly, just in case you'd like to slip out while there are fewer prying eyes and ears." She leaned in to whisper. "And be especially guarded around that barista."

"Thank you, Claire," returned Maddy courteously. She waited expectantly, glaring at her niece.

"Thank you, Claire," Nicky echoed weakly.

Claire understood Nicky's embarrassment better, she thought, than Maddy. Not only had Nicky behaved like a spoiled prima donna and been rude to everyone, she had also openly played the minx to men other than Leroy. More to the point, she had vamped and been rebuffed by Guy. Now that the gig was up, humble pie left an acrid taste in the mouth. Nevertheless, Claire regarded Nicky's tears with pity, not disdain. Nicky wasn't the first woman bamboozled by a good-looking man—Sandra came to mind, as did Hannah and even Claire, herself.

Claire held out her hand in good-bye to Maddy, then to Nicky, who hesitated, then took it. It was a start.

Maddy announced resolutely, "We're going, too. Nicky has reparations to make around Mayenne Bay.

Where's the list, Nicky?"

A red-faced Nicky pulled a crinkled paper from her pocket and handed it to her aunt. Maddy glanced it over.

"We'll start with the art store."

Claire stepped away, collected her things and hastily exited the coffee bar with her takeout. Once outside, she stopped short on the sidewalk and looked back at the restaurant. First John-Pierre's confession, then Ben's outpouring, now Nicky's bombshell, had been unexpectedly dropped on her in there. She chuckled. Maybe she needed to find a new place to buy salad. She knew it would be fruitless to return to the office before she regained her concentration. She headed for her car, intent on the only person to whom she could confide what she'd just overheard. A quick debriefing session with Guy would do the trick.

Within minutes, she was knocking on the door of his loft.

"Hi! I…uh…wasn't expecting you," he told her awkwardly with a glance inside, as he held open the door.

She stepped in.

"Obviously," she said, lips compressed, nose wrinkled.

The place was, simply put, a mess. She looked him over. He was rumpled, unshaven and uncombed.

"So, this is the real you, is it?"

"Well, sometimes," he admitted. "Sorry." What else could he say? He'd been caught red-handed.

"I don't have much time. I'll tell you my news and go. Maybe next time I come, there'll be a place for me to sit down in here. And maybe you'll indulge me by giving yourself a shower and shave."

He nodded sheepishly.

"Then, here it is. Morrie was successful convincing Nicky to call on family. I just overheard Monique—I'm to call her 'Nicky' now—and her Aunt Maddy talking at the coffee bar. Nicky had been given an inheritance, and Leroy got his hands on it. It's all gone."

Guy released one of his characteristic whistles.

"And her aunt is taking her around town to make 'reparations'." Claire's fingers formed air quotes. "That's the term she used. I think it means she's paying all the bills Nicky racked up. Well, that's all for now. I have to get back to work. I just had to get this off my chest first." She turned toward the door, then swung around again. "Oh, and there's a rumor started by Leroy's landlord that he's left town. Meilin and I think it's ludicrous, but you know how it goes once the gossip train leaves the station."

She stepped out the door.

"Wait!" Guy stalled her. "Look, I'm sorry about this." He waved his hand toward the disorder and then looked down at himself. "I've been buried in projects. I promise to clean up my act. Can I come to your place after work if I shower and shave first?"

"Sure." Her lips were pursed.

Guy stood, miserable, at the threshold for a few minutes to watch her pull away.

Claire returned to the office but didn't stay until her normal quitting time. Having worked through the weekend, she had no qualms about cutting Monday short. She left the office mid-afternoon and stopped at Grace Grocery to grab a few items on her way home. There, she heard speculative talk in the aisles about Leroy but volunteered nothing. It was all guesswork anyway.

That evening, as if Claire's glimpse of his slovenliness wasn't enough, Guy ran late. By the time he arrived with a conciliatory offering of fruit and cheese, she was already changed into jeans and well into a glass of Douro.

"You know," she said, after kissing him and nuzzling

his clean neck and shaven face, "I really love being with you." She stopped to find the right words. "I know we each have our faults."

Guy pre-empted her.

"Like when I'm late all the time?"

"Yes, like that. Though that's not the worst."

"No, probably not. I admit my personal hygiene and the loft were out of control today. I didn't miss the tone in your reproach. When you deliver clipped answers, hands clenched, I know it means I'm on tenterhooks. If a reasonable degree of cleanliness is the only thing you really require, if you can tolerate all my other faults and eccentricities, then I'm getting off lightly."

Claire didn't contradict him.

"I'm willing to relax my ultra-clean standards," she offered in return. "They're unnatural for anyone but me. But we have to find a happy medium. Lack of personal hygiene and extreme sloppiness like that—these are things I know I can't live with. I just can't."

She looked into his eyes and perceived her answer had left him bereft of words, though the reason escaped her. He tenderly wrapped her in his arms, and she knew he was trying his best to convey that he understood. After a long, reassuring embrace, they sat down to feast on bread, fruit and cheese and all the news of the day. Guy ate as though it was his favorite meal of all time.

30

Suspicions

It didn't take long for word to circulate that Nicky had dropped her "Monique" moniker and was making the rounds with her aunt to make amends. The grapevine vacillated between harsh judgment of the arrogant, deceptive Monique and sympathy for the redeemable, victimized Nicky. At the same time, lips flapped in unreserved vilification of Leroy the Brute and Leroy the Invisible Man.

A week after the first rumor of Leroy's disappearance, there had still been no sighting of him, nor had there been any activity at the factory site. With the calendar fast approaching mid-August, Guy and Claire sat down at the Fish House to hear the latest buzz from Celeste.

"It's the same all over town. Leroy's gone. Thank God." She waved a hand of dismissal.

"How can you be sure he isn't just taking a break?" asked Guy. "He's been working that project of his night and day for months. It makes sense he'd break just before it actually gets underway."

Celeste smirked.

"You know something," Claire observed.

"Oh, yeah, I know something. I know it all," bragged the waitress.

Celeste interpreted Guy's and Claire's looks of astonishment as an invitation to share her story. She eagerly squeezed into the booth next to Claire and leaned in conspiratorially, eyes shining.

"At first sight, he was so good-looking, always dressed well, and smelled so good. Pretty quickly, he showed me what he really was, suggesting stuff and touching me. I have to deal with flirting all the time. This wasn't flirting. He thought I was just a stupid waitress, all boobs and no brains."

She waited for Guy and Claire to react to this preamble before starting again. Guy's eyes instinctively darted to Celeste's ample breasts, then over at Claire, who suppressed a giggle, but Celeste was not to be distracted from her breaking news.

"Next, it turns out he has a girlfriend. First, I thought he was after the mayor, then he latched onto Monique. All the while, he was pestering me."

"But I don't see his womanizing driving him from town," Claire said.

"Never left a tip either, le Roi du Condo, did he?" continued Celeste as though Claire hadn't spoken. "He'd sit for hours on the phone like he owned the table. It wasn't hard to overhear his conversations."

By this time, Celeste was breathless, and her listeners' eyes were wide.

"Do you mean," Claire began, "that you learned things about Leroy from his phone talk while he was here?"

"Ayup. He didn't play it low-key, did he? Always swaggering. I could tell something wasn't right. He was always trying to get money."

"But Celeste, it was his job to round up investors," said Claire, disappointed by this anti-climax. "Of course, he was asking for money."

"He wasn't so cocky on those calls, let me tell you, and he was always testy afterward. I told Patty." She tilted her head toward her boss. "She listened in. Finally, his credit card was rejected. He said he'd come back with cash. We haven't seen him since. Patty called the mayor. Then, Mr. Raymond reported Leroy was gone," Celeste finished triumphantly.

"By 'gone', you mean he hasn't been spotted for a week," Claire countered, unconvinced. "It's reasonable to expect he's taking a break or attending to details outside of town. As for the money, everybody knows he was putting deals together, and new business ventures are notoriously short of cash."

Celeste grunted.

"He had lots of unpaid bills. So does that Monique woman. She was with Leroy the whole time. Now, she's calling herself 'Nicky' and being dragged around town by her aunt."

Celeste's nose turned up in indignation.

"She's trying to start again, Celeste," explained Claire, her voice somewhat pleading. "You said yourself Leroy is attractive. Others besides Nicky have been caught up in his good looks and charm, even the mayor. Nicky is facing all the people she hurt to right her wrongs. Surely you can respect that."

"Well, when you put it that way," Celeste conceded in a much smaller voice.

She stood up and started stacking their dirty breakfast plates on her cart.

"We also suspect Leroy abused her," Claire added.

Celeste's head jerked up, and her expression changed.

"I had no idea," she said, then slowly pushed the dish cart to the next table.

"How long before that little seed you just planted sprouts and Celeste sways the whole town to forgive Nicky?" Guy asked Claire in a whisper. "I wonder if Celeste is aware she has the power to transform town opinion over bacon and eggs." He sipped some tea. "Nicky may win forgiveness, but I doubt that will extend to Leroy. His arrogance. His mistreatment of women. His squandering of Nicky's inheritance."

"But Guy, Nicky may have offered her inheritance to him freely at a high point in their relationship," argued Claire. "Start-up entrepreneurs often borrow from friends and family. And the nature of his phone calls here at the restaurant—drumming up cash— comes as no surprise. I really see nothing untoward in all this on the financial end. Something about Leroy has always seemed off, despite his impeccable appearance and aura of wealth, but, as far as the development scheme goes, nobody has uncovered anything amiss. Look how many town officials are involved in project oversight."

Guy sat mutely as he took all this in. Claire fell silent, too, as she tried to make sense of it all.

After one more refill, they left the restaurant and made their way up Main Street in the direction of Creative Agenda. It was a partly cloudy day, hinting at a summer rain. The wind was kicking up a bit, blowing in salty smells off the bay. They passed the Free Choice Hair Salon where the scent of hair products saturated the air and made them screw up their noses. Inside, Maddy and Nicky were in close conversation with Amy. This was Guy's first glimpse of the reformed Nicky. He stared at her through the window until Claire grabbed his arm and marched him up the sidewalk so he wouldn't be caught ogling.

Suddenly, Guy froze, threw a meaningful look at Claire, and broke into a jog up the sidewalk. Claire rushed alongside, uncertain what had spurred this haste. He burst into Creative Agenda, breathless, Claire on his heels. Meilin popped out from behind the shelves.

"Hey, you two," she called and started toward them.

"Hi, Meilin," they each answered in turn.

Guy's body language was conveying an uncharacteristic impatience.

"What is it?"

"Meilin, I wonder if I could get another look at the image of the 'Lupines' painting on your computer."

"Didn't you just see it first-hand at Gloria's?"

She bent under the counter for her tablet nonetheless.

"I inspected the frame but not the painting itself. Gloria whisked it away too soon. The only time I had a chance to study that painting up close was at the show, but there was always a crowd and some kind of commotion around it. The lighting, too, in the church community room, the cafeteria and at the B&B, was bad. Too much glare or too many shadows."

Meilin turned her tablet toward him.

"Here, but you're going to tell me what you're looking for, right?"

"Do you mind if I drive?"

He was already reaching for the touch screen. In answer, Meilin stepped around the counter to watch by his side. Claire also stuck close. She didn't want to miss a thing.

Guy expanded the lower right corner of the "Lupines" image.

"When we first got to Gloria's parlor, the painting was already off the wall and lying face up on her coffee table. The lighting was bad—not glaring this time, but insufficient. Claire and I pulled two lamps forward to see better."

"The lamps were torchieres," Claire interjected. "Lots of shadows."

"Yes," agreed Guy, "and Gloria's focus was on the frame, so I had to follow her lead. In the few moments before she flipped over the canvas to view it from the back, I thought I caught something." He pointed to the screen. "Look at this corner where Monique's signature is sprawled."

Both women looked more closely.

"Claire, remember I said the signature was overdone? You attributed it to Monique's 'narcissism'." He gestured air quotes. "Now we know that was an act. We just saw the unpretentious Nicky at the hair salon. It was the sight of her without artifice that flicked on the lightbulb in my head. If not to signal a huge ego, what purpose would a flashy signature possibly serve?"

"A diversion," answered Claire.

"Right. You've been saying all along that Monique's outlandish behavior has been meant to distract our attention from something. You just couldn't put your finger on what. Now we know her entire persona was an act, but what if there's something else?"

He zoomed in on Monique's signature and pointed. "This is newly painted."

"It is," confirmed Meilin. "She bought the paint here."

"It's a distraction from the paint beneath, which is what caught my eye at the B&B. This corner seemed to stand apart as if it had been done…well, if not in newer paint, then at least in brush strokes a bit inconsistent with the rest of the canvas."

"You think she touched up that area before signing?" Claire asked.

"Yes, touched up, refreshed, however you want to describe it, then added the huge neon scrawl to distract from the touch-up."

Claire was exasperated.

"Guy, touch-ups aren't uncommon. Even you make them. If Monique did this, why should she hide it?"

"Hers is different," persisted Guy.

Meilin turned to Guy, fists on her hips.

"I personally looked over every submission and found nothing amiss. I won't tolerate anything that maligns the art show."

"I'm sure you did, Meilin, but you looked at digital images and you see how hard it is to detect details even at this zoom level when we're expressly looking for them. Anyway, I doubt you bothered to enlarge sections like we're doing now."

At this, Meilin relented.

"Let me put this in context."

Claire and Meilin stepped back and prepared to hear him out.

"First, Monique hasn't given us evidence of any other work."

"Correct. I explained to you once before that this doesn't make her any different from other artists," Meilin said.

"Yes, Guy. You yourself said she may have unseen work tucked away in her studio," added Claire.

"Yes, and, by itself, that is credible for any artist, but bear with me to get the full picture," he went on. "Second, you pointed out a number of times, Claire, that Monique exhibited no interest in her submissions and has been unapproachable on the subject."

"True. She produced and exhibited two fine paintings she didn't want to discuss."

"Third, we find out Monique was an alias, and she's clearly known elsewhere in Maine by another name."

Both Claire and Meilin nodded.

"Fourth, she's been under the influence of a controlling man whose motives involving the show were…well, let's just say enigmatic, as we have no proof of anything more damning. All this adds up to an artist who isn't at all what she seems." He turned to Claire. "I don't think we can separate Monique's person or circumstances from the artwork, just as you have maintained since the reception. I'm sorry I discounted the idea back then but I think you're onto something. Monique's deception, repeated deflections and distractions add credence to what I think I'm seeing on her canvas."

"What, exactly, are you seeing?" Meilin asked, impatient, but captivated in spite of herself.

"The thing is—and add this to the points I just made—at Gloria's, the age of the materials struck me. Monique chose a timeworn, hand-fitted canvas, manually stretched over a wooden frame. The canvas itself is tacked on—canvases made today are usually stapled—and the edges are yellowed. You can only see that if you examine the back, as we did."

"What's wrong with using an old canvas?" asked Claire.

"Nothing by itself. Artists re-use canvases all the time. Maybe she found it in a flea market or estate sale, which would also explain the distressed frame."

"So, where's the problem?"

"Look here."

He used the cursor to trace a large, imaginary triangle over the lower right corner of the painting.

"My initial suspicion was that Monique overpainted an entire used canvas as any artist might do. In that case, the newer paint would cover the whole surface. Now, I'm wondering exactly how much of the original she changed. My guess—and right now that's all it is—is that she overpainted a canvas so old it couldn't possibly be her own original but only partially touched it up. She modified someone else's painting and presented it as her own. That's why she couldn't be engaged to talk about her art."

Both Claire and Meilin drew breath at the possible implications.

"This is pretty serious, if it's true," growled Meilin, "and won't look good for the show."

"I understand we want to protect the show, Meilin. Being sure of what Monique submitted, one way or another, will do that, don't you think? I admit this all sounds farfetched, and my mind may be conjuring something that isn't there."

Meilin sighed, pulled the tablet closer and took control. She tried several different magnifications of the "Lupines" image. Each yielded pixels too blurry for examination. She opened Monique's "Beach Roses" image but ran into the same difficulty.

"We'll never prove anything with this one way or the other. The resolution of these photos just isn't good enough."

"We need to see the original again," prompted Claire. "There's no other way."

"That's what I'm thinking, too," Guy concurred. "Unfortunately, the 'Beach Roses' are gone, so the only original available is under Gloria's tight-fisted control. If we could study it without her around, I don't think we'd need more than a few minutes in the right light."

"We need this resolved," declared Meilin, "but how can we work around her? She barely ever leaves the B&B and she's formidable on a good day, let alone when it comes to that painting."

"I was surprised she was willing to let go of it to have it reframed," Claire said. "Wait! Maybe it's already at the frame shop."

They all exchanged looks and dashed for the door. Claire and Guy were on the sidewalk in seconds. Meilin followed right behind, stopping only to flip her "Back in one hour" sign in the shop window and lock the door. The three jogged up Main Street, past the intersection with Crest, toward the Roxie's frame shop.

31

Exposure

Meilin's mind raced ahead. If Roxie wasn't at the shop today—usual on a Saturday—they'd have to take liberties and examine the "Lupines" painting in her absence. Roxie would hold Meilin personally accountable for this intrusion, but Meilin had to take the chance. Her position as chairperson of the art show made a prompt inspection imperative. She set her teeth and pressed on, willing to beg forgiveness since she hadn't, in her impulsive pursuit of the truth, sought permission.

A teenage clerk wearing a name tag that read "Super J" stood behind the shop counter, visibly taken aback by the sudden invasion of three panting adults. Meilin felt their good luck. Super J and she were acquainted through Roxie's participation on the art show committee. He 'd be more amenable than Roxie to display Gloria's painting in her absence. Super J retrieved the painting and laid it on the counter, puzzlement on his face.

"May we view it over by the window?" requested Meilin politely.

He walked the painting around the counter and set it on a small reception table in full daylight.

"There it is," Guy said in a hushed tone, tracing his

finger lightly across the right corner where the graduated layers of fresh paint faded into the original paint. "It wasn't just shadows."

"You're right," Meilin said and stepped around to get the light just right. "It's well done. I have to give Monique that." She colored. "After all the art work I've handled, I can't believe I missed this."

Super J stood by looking confused and increasingly anxious as he tracked the conversation.

"It looks like she may have touched up some of the flowers, too," Guy observed and ran his finger along one of the petals. "The old paint had darkened, so she brightened up the composition in key spots." He shook his head. "And I call myself an artist."

"I feel totally stupid," said Meilin.

"You're both judging with hindsight," Claire intervened. "The paintings were first judged from poor photos, then exhibited in poor light at busy venues. Look how hard it is to detect the modifications in good light even when we know what we're looking for. You had no reason to suspect trickery."

Guy and Meilin weren't appeased, and their faces reflected their self-judgment.

"Monique worked really hard," continued Claire, "and successfully, I might add, to distract everyone from her paintings. If people weren't mesmerized by her person, they were angry or, like me, found her to be an interesting case study. We were played, blinded by that oversized personality, the garish signature and the bright paint strokes. Perfect decoys. Even Bruce Raymond missed them."

"May I take it out of the frame?" Guy asked the clerk.

Super J shifted nervously from one foot to the other, then looked to Meilin, who nodded her approval. Using the tiny tool kit he carried on his key chain, Guy carefully loosened the fasteners and pried the canvas loose from the frame. He lifted it out, turned it to inspect the sides one by one, then set it down on the table.

"This painting hasn't been dislodged from the frame for some time," he noted. "See the dried material that fell on the table? And in the signature corner, the fresh paint stops at the edge. This means Monique performed the touch ups while it was in the frame."

He pulled out his phone and opened the magnifying app. Sure enough, there were tiny flecks of new paint on the frame, including the tell-tale neon orange of her signature. They took turns examining it and stepped back. With this newfound knowledge, and after close inspection in full daylight, the petal embellishments became quite conspicuous.

"Just as Monique overshadowed Nicky, these embellishments obscured the original work. The art reflects the artist," Guy said, looking at Claire.

"I'm kicking myself for missing all this," Meilin said. She pulled out her phone and snapped close-up photos of the canvas and frame, front, back and sides. "For the committee," she explained. "I'll have to call Roxie and Peggy. Both should view this first hand."

While Meilin thumbed out a text, Super J's eyes widened, and he mutely slipped back to the safety of the counter.

"We need to figure out what to do about Nicky before she and her aunt leave town," said Claire.

"We have no choice," answered Meilin. "Nicky will have to be confronted."

"First, we have to tell Gloria," Claire cautioned.

"Hold on," Guy said. "Do you think Gloria has been overly sensitive about the painting because she already discovered this?"

"She wouldn't be likely to display the piece under a

spotlight in her parlor if she had," reasoned Meilin. "No, I don't think Gloria knows."

"Knows what?"

Gloria's voice sounded from the shop entrance where she stood, framed by the doorway, hands on her hips, glaring at the sight of her beloved painting dislodged from its frame.

It took a full half hour for them to subdue Gloria's ire and walk her through their discovery. She listened with lips pressed together and arms folded across her chest and, when they concluded, flew into a passion. Super J ducked behind the counter. Claire attempted to tranquilize the overwrought B&B owner.

When Roxie and Peggy finally arrived, Guy took Claire's hand and drew her toward the door.

"We're off to find Nicky," he announced. "We'll handle things on that end."

Once they were a safe distance from the frame shop, Claire looked back over her shoulder and said, "Your art sleuthing was amazing."

"I can't take all the credit. If you hadn't kept harping that something wasn't quite right about Monique and insisting artist and art can't be separated, I don't think I'd ever have found it. I needed just the right turn of mind."

"Twisted?"

They both laughed.

"But the credit for deescalating Gloria's rage is all yours," Guy said with a shake of his head. "That woman has a short fuse."

"She does when it comes to the 'Lupines' painting. Monique's mistreatment, the theft and all the uncertainty around that painting are all bound up together. She hasn't been able to separate the artist she detests from the work she loves. And now this bombshell."

As they walked, the fury of Gloria's tempest rose up

again in their minds.

"First, I had to put up with Monique herself…her meanness," she had growled. "Then, my painting was stolen and returned by some…some phantom. Now, I'm hearing it may be a fake. Where was the committee in all this? Why is this being found out so late in the game?"

"Both good questions," Meilin had replied, wasting no time beating around the bush. "We missed it, plain and simple. I can give you all the reasons we're so late with this discovery, but they'll all sound like excuses. I'm truly sorry. Obviously, we owe you your money back."

Gloria had practically screeched in reply.

"This isn't only about money! I look like a fool. I spent weeks explaining the empty space over my check-in counter, then publicly celebrated the found painting. Now, after its story has been in all the papers, I have to tell people it's a fake? I'll be a laughing stock, and the B&B will suffer for it." As she flung these last words, her pitch was close to ear-shattering.

Gloria viewed herself first and foremost as an astute business person. The B&B was flourishing, and her purchase of the "Lupines" was meant to crown that success. The painting's disappearance had inundated her with negative attention that, in her estimation, deflated her reputation. Having narrowly survived that ordeal, she had little interest in being associated with a painting notorious for fraud.

"Gloria," Claire had intervened as the B&B owner had drawn renewed breath for a sequent diatribe. "Your emotions are understandable, but you didn't discover anything amiss until we pointed it out, though you've spent more time with that canvas than anyone."

"I'm not an art expert."

"I'm not either, but now that we're both aware of the alterations, they're easy to see even for a layperson. You would have had to be looking for them, just as we were today. Even we thought the whole thing might be a figment of our imagination."

"But…"

"Besides," Claire broke in again, "I've heard you say you love this painting. Is that not true?"

"Of course. I do love it. Otherwise, I wouldn't have bought it," Gloria had snapped.

"If you love the painting as it is, why does it matter who painted it or even when or how much paint was applied? It's striking as it is and an original piece of artwork. It just wasn't, or I should say wasn't fully, painted by Monique LaBelle. At least, that's what we're suspecting. We'll want to confirm it with her before final judgment."

Her logic had a neutralizing effect on Gloria, who sputtered something unintelligible and fell silent, though she cast Claire a black look, which had prompted Guy to step in.

"Unfortunately, I do think we're right in our assessment. We'll find Nicky nonetheless and get her to confirm or deny it."

He had thought it wiser to use "Nicky" in the moment. "Monique" would have been sure to further inflame Gloria.

"She'll just lie," Gloria had muttered.

"Not in front of her Aunt Maddy, she won't," Claire assured her.

"We promise to get back to you with what we find out," Guy said.

They left the simmering Gloria in the hands of the art show committee and set a brisk pace toward the Whispering Seabreeze. It was the most likely place, they reasoned, to find Nicky and her aunt or even Morrie, for that matter, who might know where the women had gone. They didn't have to travel quite that far. They spotted the trio already approaching from that direction.

"Guy! Claire!" Morrie called and waved. "We were just about to have lunch at the Wharf Café. Want to join us?"

"Guy, this is Nicky's aunt, Maddy," Claire said. "Maddy, this is my artist-friend, Guy." The two shook hands. "We'd be glad to join you."

Guy's acquiescence was less enthusiastic. Claire guessed he wasn't keen on being trapped at a lunch table with the former vamp. She took his arm and pressed him forward. One way or the other, discomfort would be on the menu. There was nothing they could do about that.

The party of five entered the dining room and moved to a round, six-seater in the far back corner best situated for privacy. Guy pulled Claire into the seat next to his and took her hand under the table. Once everyone was comfortably seated and had placed their orders, she squeezed his hand and pulled hers away. She was about to speak and would never get on with one hand hobbled.

"We were headed for Whispering Seabreeze in search of you."

"Was there something you needed?" asked Maddy shrewdly.

Claire met the woman's eyes but didn't flinch.

"Yes, there is," she answered. She directed her words at Nicky. "We were just at the framer's where Gloria Townsend, the buyer, left the 'Lupines' painting to be reframed. When the canvas was removed from its original frame, we had a chance to study it closely. Please forgive us if we're mistaken, Nicky, but…"

"Nicky didn't paint it," Maddy finished for her.

"What?"

Every head jerked toward Maddy.

"Nicky didn't paint the 'Lupines'," Maddy repeated, disarming them with this admission, "at least not all of it. She painted over parts."

"Right," said Guy. "So, we guessed correctly." His breathing relaxed now that the worst was out in the open.

"Nicky and I planned to visit Gloria today," said Maddy. "The buyer must be told."

"She already knows," Claire said. "She's very upset, as you can imagine. We were pretty sure but held out to confirm the truth."

"Sadly, it's true. I hope Nicky appreciates the generosity that caused you to withhold final judgment before speaking to the source."

Maddy turned to her niece.

"Nicky, you need to explain to these people what you've done."

Nicky's face burned red, and her eyes welled with tears.

"I…I…touched up two old paintings and put my name on them. I looked up how to do it on the internet. I learned a little about mixing paints in art classes."

"You learned more than 'a little' from the skill level I saw," Guy told her. "Looks like you worked the lower right quadrant and also the flowers."

"Yes. The painting had darkened with age, so I put color back."

"Nicky has been very talented at painting from a young age," Maddy explained.

"What made you do it, Nicky?" Claire asked.

"It was L…Leroy," she stammered, clearly ashamed. "He was short on money and thought he…we…could make some at the art show." She hung her head and added in a hoarse whisper, "I didn't want to do it. I'm really sorry."

"Yes, Leroy was a huge influence," Aunt Maddy agreed, "but Nicky must take responsibility for her part in this fraud, having allowed her normally good sense to be swayed." Nicky gasped at the word. "Fraud," her aunt repeated unmercifully, staring hard at her. "You must call things what they are, Nicky, or your apologies will mean nothing. Sugar-coating does not alter the essential point. Gloria is owed the absolute truth from your own mouth, a public apology and her money back, if she wishes it," Maddy finished flatly.

Nicky's posture shrank, and her head hung.

"Nicky," Claire spoke gently, "almost everyone in town is aware of Leroy's skills of persuasion, but your aunt is right, though it's unfair you have to bear the blame alone."

"We've been working all week to make amends around town," Maddy said in a strained voice, the toll taken by the week's activity evident on her face. "Carelessly racking up bills, then leaving them unpaid—with Leroy or without—is tantamount to stealing, as I have drilled into my niece." She paused to release a long breath. "This more difficult confession about the fraudulent painting I admit to saving until last after everything else was cleared up. I hoped opinions would be softened toward Nicky by her acts of restitution so that this would be disclosed in an atmosphere of…well, if not mercy, then at least not extreme bias. It was a small hope, I own. We'd planned to see Gloria Townsend directly after lunch."

Claire sat back to take stock of both the determined aunt and the sobbing niece. Harsh as her formidable management of Nicky's atonement appeared, Maddy's no-nonsense approach was dispelling any lingering confusion between right and wrong. Nicky needed no less to pull out of this quagmire.

Lunch was delivered, and everyone ate in silence until Guy broke it.

"I was wondering, Nicky, where you got the original paintings. Both the canvas and frame of the 'Lupines' look pretty old."

"The 'Beach Roses' was old, too. Aunt Therese inherited them from Great Grandma Catherine. They were in Aunt Therese's attic for years until she got sick and died. Aunt Therese willed them to Aunt Maddy, who gave them to me because I admired them." Her voice quavered as she spoke the last sentence. "I didn't really want to sell them."

"With Leroy's help," added Maddy, "Nicky gave up the heirloom paintings she adored and blew through all her inheritance from Therese."

"And hurt you, Aunt Maddy," Nicky cried.

Maddy nodded her acknowledgement of this truth. Her eyes misted, and she directed them out over the water for a few moments, revealing a small crack in her armor. Claire suspected Maddy was struggling to withhold sympathy until all the hard work was done.

"Oh, Nicky," Claire commiserated. "It's really too bad, but it could have been much, much worse. The injuries Leroy could have inflicted had you stayed with him are too terrible to imagine. We really feared for your safety."

"You see?" Maddy asked Nicky in vindication. "I'm not the only one who saw he wasn't good for you."

Morrie put a comforting hand on Nicky's. With the other, she wiped her eyes, then laid her head on his shoulder and closed them. The scene stirred the heart of every person at the table.

"Nicky's not the first young woman to lose her head to such a man," Maddy told them. "She's essentially a good person. After all is said and done to make repairs here in Mayenne Bay, she'll get back on her feet and be all the wiser. She'll have a long row to hoe, mind you, to pay back all the money her grandmother and I have laid out here, but I have confidence in her future."

Nicky sat up straight at her aunt's words of constancy, and her eyes glowed in gratitude. Her face was so girlish in that moment that Claire realized Nicky couldn't be more than twenty years old. As Monique, she had appeared at least ten years older.

"Do you know the original artist?" Claire asked.

"No," Nicky answered. "I liked the paintings for themselves, and the paint was so darkened with age, there was no legible signature."

"You might ask Gloria if she'd like to remove the fresh paint from that canvas and have it restored back to the original. That might regain her goodwill. Meilin Li at Creative Agenda will know someone who does that kind of work," suggested Guy.

"We should stop to see Peggy, too," Morrie said. "She knows how to reach the buyer of the 'Beach Roses' painting. You may want to restore that one, too."

"That won't be necessary," Maddy replied. "I bought the 'Beach Roses'."

Nicky's head jerked up. She had obviously not been in on the secret until this moment.

"What?"

"You bought back your own painting?" Guy asked incredulously.

"I did," Maddy told them. "My full name is Madeleine Littlefield."

32

Family Affair

After Madeleine paid for lunch, she, Nicky and Morrie headed for Maddy's car and the Town's End B&B to confront Gloria. Guy and Claire left to find Meilin, Peggy and Roxie. On their way, Guy pulled Claire aside against the wall of the hair salon and dialed his phone.

"Town's End B&B," Gloria answered.

"Gloria, it's Guy. We met with Nicky."

Gloria sniffed.

"Go ahead."

"Look, I know you're upset. I don't blame you. Nicky did alter the painting as we thought. She and her aunt are on their way over to see you."

"Why? Like I want to talk to them."

"You should hear them out, Gloria. They were already planning to visit you before we found them. Nicky put her signature on an old work, a family heirloom she partially overpainted. Give her a chance to explain and apologize, will you? She's trying to make things right."

Guy held his breath during the ensuing silence.

"How can that make things right? An apology doesn't fix my problem."

"If you don't want to keep the painting as it is, you

can return it for a refund or restore it to its original state. Restoration would be a way to keep the painting and have a fresh start. I'm sure Meilin knows someone who does this kind of work."

"That's going to cost me."

"It won't be cheap. But if you give them a chance, Maddy and Nicky may offer to cover the cost."

"And what if I don't like it afterward?"

"Gloria, you can work out the repair details with them," Guy answered, irritation threatening to overwhelm his composure. "I just called to ask that you hear them out. Will you?"

There was a long silence on the other end.

"Gloria?"

"What I need are repairs to my reputation! How are they going to manage that? God, this has been a nightmare."

She disconnected.

Guy and Claire, who had overheard the conversation, stared at his phone for a moment.

"I thought Gloria might be more receptive if she wasn't blind-sided," Guy said.

"It was worth a try, though I suspect Mighty Maddy will have things well in hand."

"She'll get an earful about the B&B's reputational damage regardless. Honestly, I don't know if anything will make Gloria feel whole again."

They paused outside the door of Creative Agenda.

"I have trouble understanding Gloria," Claire said. "She's got a pit bull quality, always ready to growl and bite. She's smart, successful and surrounded by friends, yet her glass is always half empty."

"Sounds like you understand her just fine."

They proceeded into the store where Meilin anxiously awaited their findings. Peggy and Roxie had returned to their jobs.

"Nicky definitely doctored both paintings," Claire announced. "She claims Leroy pressured her to modify and sell them under her name—Monique LaBelle, that is—because he needed cash."

"Nicky and her aunt are on their way to see Gloria right now," Guy added.

"Peggy was astounded and speechless," Meilin informed them. "Roxie was so engrossed in Nicky's brush strokes, she forgot to be angry with me for invading her shop. The committee is going to meet this evening after hours."

"There's more," said Claire. "Both of Monique's paintings were inherited by Nicky. Maddy is actually Madeleine Littlefield, the Littlefield who bought the 'Beach Roses' despite the alterations. Even Nicky didn't know about Maddy's purchase until just this morning."

"What a lucky catch by Maddy," said Meilin.

"Nicky's grandmother, Georgia Wilson, came up with some of the money." Claire told her. "I met Georgia a few months before the art show when she was heading north to help close her daughter's estate."

"Did they say who the original artist was?" asked Meilin.

"They don't know."

"What amazes me," Guy said, "is Nicky's artistic talent. Successfully altering a painting as she did is a formidable challenge. To have run it past so many experienced eyes without detection and under pressure…there's some real skill there. We suggested they consider painting restoration to appease Gloria. I referred them to you, Meilin, so be prepared for a phone call. I was sure you'd know someone."

Meilin nodded.

"Let's cross our fingers that Gloria's more gracious nature has surfaced by the time Nicky arrives at the B&B. It hasn't been her dominant feature lately. The soap opera won't be over until Gloria is satisfied."

"Is that possible?" Claire joked.

They all laughed.

"In the end, though, Gloria's not asking for much, is she?" Claire reflected. "She just wants the painting she purchased to be what was represented and where it belongs."

Guy and Meilin could make no argument. As there was nothing more to be said or done, Meilin returned to the demands of her store, and Guy and Claire headed home.

"Pick you up in an hour," Guy told Claire in parting and squeezed her hand.

That simple gesture fractured Claire's already fragile self-control. Today's confrontations with Gloria, Nicky and Maddy had been nothing compared to her next hurdle. This evening, Guy would take her to meet his family for the first time.

Meet-the-family neurosis manifested first in fifteen minutes of sitting on the edge of her bed and staring at the wall, then another half hour of compulsive fussing with her appearance. Claire's sense of reason told her there was nothing to justify such anxiety, but her constricted solar plexus differed. She decided to cope by simply letting the beast inside her have its head.

While she rummaged through her wardrobe, she ran through what she knew of Guy's history. He was born Down East, in Washington County, where his father was employed as an electrical designer at a mill and his mother as a bookkeeper at a nursing home. To this day, the Gardiner family lived in the same Cape Cod-style house where Guy and his two younger sisters, Joy and Anna, had been raised. According to Guy, his parents had a good marriage, and the family was close or, at the very least, not at open war with one another—a state of affairs foreign to Claire. Instead of calming her, this made her fret all the more. Claire had no experience with familial normalcy.

By the time Guy arrived at her apartment, his trim and wiry frame covered in the same jeans and shirt from the morning, at least six outfits lay discarded on Claire's bed. She appeared at the kitchen door in navy-blue slacks, a plain peach top and sandals, simplicity that belied the confusion she'd left behind in the bedroom. She was uncharacteristically tightlipped as they headed out. A normal case of nerves would have set her babbling, but this was something different, deeper, that left her mute. She was grateful for the music Guy selected to fill the void.

It was five o'clock by the time Guy cleared the final turn onto the narrow road that would take them to his parents' house. He straightened the wheel, punched off the radio and braked the car.

"Um, just so you know…you're the first woman I've ever brought home."

The fingers on his right hand tapped the steering wheel.

Claire's brow rose, and her stomach flipped several times.

"Does that matter?"

"Well, it's just that…the level of curiosity will probably be…extreme." He released an unnaturally shrill laugh. "I have two younger sisters, remember, barely out of their teens."

"Don't worry. I'm ready," she fibbed and rehearsed the names. "Joy and Anna."

"Yes. Joy is older by a year and more talkative. Anna is the determined one, though neither really comes up for air." He bit his lip. "And…um…nobody in the house is a great cook. Don't expect the gourmet food you're used to."

With that, Guy pressed the pedal and rolled the car down the road. Claire was left to marvel in silence at the uncomplicated preamble Guy thought necessary to prepare her for his family and to wonder what she would tell him were their positions reversed. How did one explain someone like Hannah or Gerald Munro?

They pulled up to the Gardiners' house. It was painted federal blue with white trim and set back off the road on a partially wooded lot, giving the place a feeling of privacy despite the proximity of its neighbors. Joy and Anna ran out to greet them even before the vehicle pulled to a full stop.

"Don't worry," Claire told Guy as they opened the car doors, "I'm ready for two Chatty Cathies over boiled beef and boxed mashed potatoes."

Claire's joke about the menu turned out to be practically clairvoyant. Dinner was a bland affair of plain, dry meatloaf heavily garnished with ketchup, mashed potatoes— though not from a box, and overcooked green beans. Mrs. Gardiner herself piled servings onto their plates directly from the pots on the range, then handed them to her daughters for delivery. Claire gave Guy a discreet, wide-eyed look when the laden plate was set before her.

"Is Guy your first boyfriend?" blurted Anna.

She and Joy leaned in to hear Claire's answer. Barely had it left her mouth when a second question, then a third, shot at her from the openly curious sisters. It took both Mr. and Mrs. Gardiner's stern looks, throat clearings and, finally, outright requests to give Claire a break, to stem the flow.

Claire gamely pressed on, forkful after forkful, as if she routinely ate enough food for a lumberjack. She chatted with Anna, Joy and Mrs. Gardiner and even teased Mr. Gardiner out of his customary silence. When the family rose to clear the dinner plates to make room on the table for dessert, Claire assisted as naturally as if she lived there.

Guy's gratitude was palpable.

The whole family were tea drinkers. Mr. Gardiner

dug through the cupboard for an old jar of generic-brand, instant coffee, mixed a mugful and heated it in the microwave. Guy winced as his father proudly delivered the beverage to Claire, who accepted the tepid, watery brew with grace.

Guy was given the honor of cutting warm, blueberry-buckle cake and placing a serving onto each dessert plate. Mrs. Gardiner added a generous scoop of vanilla ice cream on top. Dessert was the one part of the meal that Claire, had she not been overstuffed by meat and potatoes, and had her coffee tasted less like cold tin, would have most appreciated for its flavor.

When the evening was finally at an end, Mr. and Mrs. Gardiner bade Claire goodbye at the door. Joy and Anna trailed behind her to the car continuing their breathless barrage of unfiltered questions and observations about herself, her clothes, her relationship with Guy…anything they could think of. She answered what she could and evaded the rest, wanting to retain at least a modicum of privacy. Her energy was flagging, though whether due to the relentless interrogation or an oncoming food coma, she couldn't have said.

Guy pulled his sisters into hugs, giving Claire time to collapse into the car seat, then hopped in and pulled the car away. Joy and Anna remained at the end of the driveway waving furiously until the car was out of sight. Finally, Claire leaned back, released the top button of her pants and breathed out a sigh of relief.

"Does your family always eat so much?"

"Yes. It was the first thing I changed once I left home." He took her hand. "You were great, by the way. Valiant, even, in the face of my mother's huge serving spoon and Joy and Anna's jabbering. I was amazed you got a word in edgewise."

"They were dying for the scoop about me…us…so

they had to let me talk at least part of the time."

"The meal was pretty much what I had expected. Dry, bland and overcooked."

"Let's not forget the gourmet coffee."

"Thank you," Guy said, his voice earnest. "You made that so much easier than it could've been."

"You're welcome. They're your family. I was really glad to meet them. And with the ice broken now, it'll be easier next time."

Her voice dropped as she spoke, and she snuck a sideways look at Guy. He'd want to experience the ritual on her side sooner or later, and the thought of it, on top of the massive amount of food in her gut, made her almost sick. He'd have far worse than tasteless food and nosy siblings to contend with.

"Are you saying you're game enough to go back?"

"Of course. Your family is likeable, aside from their diet—blueberry-buckle excluded. Let's give ourselves time before the next visit, though. It's going to take me a month to digest that meal."

"I think they liked you."

Claire's face lit up.

"You do? I hope so. I liked them, too. Joy and Anna were a bit trying but they'll calm down now that I'm less of a mystery. Cooking and food-pushing aside, I could easily be friends with your mom."

"I think she'd like that. And you absolutely charmed my father. He would never have let us get away with teasing him like that."

"He's a character. I got the impression he likes to be wheedled out of his sullenness. I can't believe he pulled out that picture of you naked in the bathtub. How old were you?"

"Six."

"You were cuter then."

"Very funny. I swear he's been holding onto it for just this moment. I can't tell if he expected it to endear you to me or chase you off."

"I'm not going anywhere."

She laid her head on his shoulder.

They pulled onto the secondary highway to the rhythm of the windshield wipers beating against heavy rain. Guy chose this interval of ease between them for a confession.

"Claire, this morning, you likened Gloria Townsend to a pit bull."

"I did."

"I have to confess that I have thought of you that way."

She cackled.

"Really? Am I that ferocious?"

"I distinctly recall the slam of a car door that almost deflated all four tires. I have to give you credit, though. I've just likened you to a junkyard dog, and you're taking it pretty well."

33

Backstories

Guy and Claire returned from the Gardiners' house to Claire's apartment, where Guy would spend the rest of the weekend, a level of intimacy he'd kept from his family. They practically fell into bed from exhaustion. It had been a day of nerves, people and gluttony.

Morning held the promise of recovery. Claire was up with the sun. Guy awoke to the intoxicating smells of toasted rye bread and oregano. Claire was making her favorite huevos fritos a la Española—eggs fried and basted in olive oil in the Spanish style— seasoned with herbs. He rose to join her. It was fully ten o'clock before they moved from the table to put the kitchen to rights.

"How long will it take to restore Nicky's two paintings?" Claire asked. "The canvases aren't large, and only a few spots need work."

"The restorer won't stop at just removing the new paint," Guy answered. "He'll restore the whole canvas both to clear Nicky's embellishments and to remove the effects of time. Otherwise, it would end up with clean spots against aged paint. Not a good look."

"That means the paintings could look totally different after restoration."

"Definitely."

"And the work will cost more."

"Definitely."

"And it could be weeks before we have the results."

"Or months."

They passed a lazy midday at Claire's, grabbed a late afternoon bite, then headed for the park at six o'clock. The setting sun would provide a giant display of light and color over the water. Guy planned to capture the evening drama on canvas.

Meilin stopped by his easel on her walk.

"Hi, Meilin. What's the word on the restorations?" he asked.

"Looks like they're going ahead. My restorer-friend, Aaron Cline, is available, so the work will be exceptional."

"When will they be ready?" asked Claire.

"If Maddy and Nicky get them to Boston right away, I'd say early October."

Morrie's voice sounded from a short distance away, and they all turned to watch him approach.

"Nicky and Maddy just left for Boston to deliver the paintings to Mr. Cline, then they're heading home to Fort Kent," he reported breathlessly, clearly full to bursting with the news.

"That's good," said Guy. "The sooner the paintings are restored, the sooner the drama will be behind us."

"Nicky's anxious for that, too. Did you know she's only nineteen?"

Guy's brush paused over the canvas.

"If I hadn't seen her as Nicky, I'd never have believed it."

"Seems she took a dare from some friends to dress up and hit the bars in Portland with that phony name. She and her friends spent weeks developing a look and character before she tried it on for real down there. That's where she met Leroy. It started out as just a lark, but she was quickly taken by his attentions. He was older, good-looking, strong…"

"And she was stupid," declared Claire.

Morrie jumped. Meilin stared. Guy's brush hung again in midair.

"Sorry, but it's true. I was once just as stupid, just as ready to toss reason aside for an undeserving man."

"Naiveté can be really dangerous," Meilin agreed. "Spoken harshly, Claire, but what you say is true."

Claire took the hint and turned back to Morrie with improved composure.

"So, Nicky got caught up with Leroy and didn't know how to get out?"

"Exactly. It was exciting in the beginning. As Monique, she felt attractive and uninhibited. Over time, it became harder and harder to keep the character going, especially as he bled her wallet dry. She was afraid to tell him she was just a poor, small-town girl from up north. It didn't help that her friends hung on her every report and thought the whole affair was a real adventure."

"So, she followed Leroy to Mayenne Bay, where they got involved in the show," Meilin concluded.

"Yes."

"It had to be exhausting trying to sustain Monique," Claire reflected. "And then, Leroy got rough. No wonder she began to unravel."

"Nicky couldn't keep up the pretense any longer," Morrie told them. "She's relieved to be free of it and grateful for everyone's help. She deserves credit for taking the first step, though, escaping Leroy and appearing at the residence as she did." His voice was so earnest in his defense of the young woman, it cracked.

"Did she say where Leroy might be?" Claire asked.

"No. He didn't share much."

"Seems he shared selectively. Nicky knew enough about his cash dilemma to give up her inheritance," Meilin observed.

"Yes," Morrie agreed. "She took this for a temporary thing, just until the condo project took off. Leroy promised her repayment at a high rate of interest once his ship came in. She had portrayed herself as financially well-off, so the gig would have been up if she had refused." He saw the dejection on their faces. "Don't look so down. A wiser Nicky is returning home."

"That's the silver lining," Claire said. "Strange that everything about Nicky this summer—her Monique act, her relationship with Leroy, her inheritance, her paintings— is gone, except the lesson learned. What a bittersweet ending."

Ben Tripp, on duty and circling the park, approached.

"Hi, everyone," he said. "Sorry to intrude. I'm canvassing for missing garden gnomes. Seen anything?"

They all shook their heads. Claire broke into a giggle.

"How do you do it with a straight face, Ben? How absurd it must feel to launch your law enforcement career chasing an adolescent bandit and a bunch of garden ornaments."

"Someone has to do it," he shrugged philosophically. "Of the two, the gnomes have been the real thorn in my side. Jay accosts me everywhere and he keeps buying more. He even names them, like they're his children. And the saga has taken a dark turn in recent weeks."

"How can anything to do with garden gnomes be 'dark'?" Claire asked.

"The first few were found intact or bearing light damage—loss of a toe or the tip of the hat."

"Reparable," observed Guy.

"Yes, up to that point," agreed Ben. "The latest have

been seriously damaged— smashed faces, missing feet, hole in the belly—and stuffed in unseemly places like a compost pile and a bucket of fish bait." His listeners scrunched their noses in unison. "Another was spray-painted black and upside-down in the muck at low tide. I wasn't fussed at first, but with the increasing defacement..." He shook his head. "Jay still thinks it's the little bandit, but it's become too sinister to be a prank. I can't think of anything else to do except keep my eyes peeled on patrol."

He shrugged and went on his way.

Town gossips found perverse enjoyment in the creepy demise of Jay's gnomes, their only preoccupation these days aside from half-hearted guesses as to Leroy's whereabouts. Sally Eaton, whose antennae were always tuned to sidewalk chatter, relayed the latest grapevine rumblings to her boss. Sandra flat out ignored the gnome capers and she let the art show committee field the fallout over the phony paintings. As mayor, she had far bigger fish to fry.

In the several weeks' time since Leroy had been discovered absent from his cabin, her office had been deluged with calls and impromptu visits from constituents. Undesirous to reveal how little she actually knew, she answered evasively and even began to avoid the main streets of town. Today, she wandered the canning factory site as though, somehow, the answers would be found at the centerpiece of Leroy's scheme. The place was silent as the grave except for the gently lapping water and the crunch of her shoes on the sandy asphalt.

Over the past months, Sandra had learned something of Leroy and his deliberate nature. It was this, more than anything, that puzzled her. With the archeological inspection concluded, the project was on schedule and ready for its next phase. Leroy, its primary driver, in lockstep with every stage, knew this. Yet, he was nowhere to be found. As far as she knew, he had contacted no one. Over and over, Sandra had emailed and received no answer and dialed his cell phone only to find his voicemail was full. Yesterday afternoon, she had even driven out to the cabin and peered into its windows for a sign of life.

Could something bad have happened? An accident?

She'd speculated plenty on benign reasons for Leroy's absence from town. Vacation. Family. Sourcing. Investment meetings. Other deals. She doubted debts were the cause. As a seasoned entrepreneur, he would take weak cashflow in stride, not pack it in. Besides, Madeleine Littlefield had covered his and Nicky's accounts in town and relieved a great deal of local pressure. Nor did Sandra believe Leroy feared consequences over his treatment of Nicky. The man's temerity with women was deplorable, but he'd broken no law, and no formal complaints had been lodged. Perhaps a new tryst? Possible, but even if true, nothing explained his total silence.

Could Leroy have been spooked by the August 1st executive session? The timing of his absence was certainly suspicious; he'd left in the days just following the meeting. He hadn't been invited, despite his previously accorded insider status. But Sandra doubted the mere shroud of mystery over a confidential meeting would have shaken the unflappable Mr. Hood, so well ensconced among the town elite.

The executive session had been instigated by a visit from Juan and Maria Rodriguez to Chief Manning. On first hearing, Sandra had been skeptical of the couple's tale. It had seemed outlandish, even calculated. She'd been polite and professional in their presence but, afterward, unwilling to accept the story of these strangers at face value. So much of the town's future hung in the balance on its unsubstantiated veracity.

Mr. and Mrs. Rodriguez were avid art collectors

who'd spent their vacation winding along Maine's serpentine coast taking in shows and galleries. They'd spotted the *Central Maine Reporter*'s feature spread about the Mayenne Bay Art Show and decided to squeeze the awards exhibition into their itinerary before heading home.

And there had been another attraction.

In their meeting, Mrs. Rodriguez had stood up and spread *Central Maine Reporter* pages across the chief's desk. She focused his and Sandra's attention on a color photograph of Monique LaBelle, surrounded by admirers and standing in front of her paintings. A few feet from Monique's side smiled a confident-looking man: Leroy Hood.

"We hoped to satisfy ourselves about this man," Mrs. Rodriguez told them, tapping Leroy's image with a manicured fingernail. "From the interview he gave to the paper, we knew he had interest in the show, so there was a good chance he'd attend awards night. We had to see him for ourselves, in person, before coming to you, to be sure. Then, there he was," she exclaimed raising her hands in emphasis, "sidling up to Ms. LaBelle with some drinks. His hair is longer and darker than the last time we saw him, and he dresses differently, but his features and stature are the same. There's no mistaking the mouth, the chin and that deep dimple on his right cheek. I'll never forget that."

"We moved in closer to get within earshot of him," Mr. Rodriguez said. "Ms. LaBelle became irritated because a woman—the buyer, we think—removed her prize painting from the wall. The buyer rehung it at the artist's insistence but was clearly distressed at the public scolding from the artist. When the buyer stepped back, the dimpled man leaned in and told her, 'She's in a horn-tossing mood' and jerked his head toward Ms. LaBelle. That's when we knew for certain."

"Yes!" agreed Mrs. Rodriguez. "The voice was the

same. There was even a trace of accent. And he used that very expression when he inspected our house in Texas. There had been a lot of property damage in the region. He was referring to everyone's temperament after the hurricane blew through."

According to this couple, Leroy's most recent incarnation before Maine had been in Texas, not Florida. There, under the name of Gabriel "Gabe" Williams, Leroy allegedly represented himself as the owner of Blazing Star Roofing. He'd traveled across the Texas counties hardest hit by a ferocious storm posing as a roofing contractor and collecting deposits for repairs and replacements. None were ever performed. Gabe initially claimed the delays were due to the volume of work and the difficulty getting supplies into the storm area. In actuality, he planned to take the money and run, which he did. The Rodriguez couple themselves lost five thousand dollars to his scam.

The mayor and chief were stunned and sat in his office without speaking for some time after the couple departed.

"If that story is true, it's a rare stroke of luck the Rodríguezes discovered the art show," the chief said, breaking the silence.

As mayor, Sandra was forced to echo his sentiment, but her stomach churned in protest. If the accusation were true, the townspeople…the voters…would have a field day over Leroy's duplicity. Skeptics of the condo project and confidential deliberations would exult in their prescience. Little sympathy would be spared for property owners, politicians or a naive mayor. For the second time this summer, her stupidity would be the featured topic of the town grapevine.

"It's almost too coincidental that this particular couple vacationed in Maine just as Leroy got some press in Mayenne Bay, don't you think?" she answered the chief.

"They seem credible—it's clear they believe their own story—but they could be mistaken. We can't act without substantiation of their claim. And we need to tread carefully and keep this quiet until we're sure either way. I don't need to tell you how invested this town is in Leroy's project."

The chief shared Sandra's reservations and apprehended the stakes. He offered to investigate the case personally. He videotaped the Rodríguezes' statements before they departed for Portland International Airport, then discreetly began his research and inquiries. Meanwhile, Sandra paid a call to Attorney Bobby Tripp, who advised her to schedule the August 1st executive session of the town council. Regardless of Chief Manning's findings, the mayor was not empowered to charge or acquit; she would need to clear any action or inaction with the council. She complied, glad she wouldn't bear the burden alone.

Sandra had encouraged speculation about the executive session to spin around the legalities of the artifact exploratory instigated by Louis Rainwater. Tribal matters were always sensitive, so it was a good cover. Had Leroy, despite her secrecy and this decoy, guessed nonetheless? Sandra doubted it. Only a solid leak from a well-placed spy, she concluded grimly, would have been enough to trigger his abrupt departure, if, indeed, the session was the cause. It was a troubling thought. If he wasn't absent for the harmless reasons she'd invented, something else had compelled him to take a break.

She stepped over a fallen "A Better Idea for Mayenne Bay" sign as she reached down to pull two photos from her pocket. She studied the competing images, one of a confident, impeccably dressed Leroy Hood, the other, courtesy of the Texas police, of a cocky-faced Gabe Williams in jeans and cowboy boots. Leroy's dark hair was immaculately combed. Gabe's blond hair was short-clipped and matted from the cowboy hat he held in his hand. The men looked to be of similar stature with the same chin, piercing eyes and white teeth. And then, there was that telltale dimple on the right cheek. If Leroy didn't return soon to refute the Rodriquez's claim, she'd be forced to conclude from all the gathered evidence that Leroy and Gabe were one and the same person.

Sandra released a long breath and looked around at the unsuspecting town. Mayenne Bay was moving into the end of August with its usual energy. The park was full. The boatyard couldn't be busier. Sidewalks were flooded with shoppers, and restaurants with patrons. Like the frenzy of the honeybee before it tucks in for cold weather, the whole town buzzed with heightened activity, unaware its immediate prospects for improvement might be dashed. The town citizenry would be incensed at Leroy's deception, but its sense of injury would subside. Mainers were resilient that way. She only hoped they could forgive their mayor. Even if they didn't, no matter what the outcome with Leroy, she would find out how he got wind of the investigation if it was the last thing she did.

34

Bands by the Bay

To Claire, there was something arresting about Labor Day weekend, like a deep, exhilarating breath almost spent. Nature would hold just enough in reserve for its colorful leaf-intensive before it slipped into the gray slumber of winter. Already, the nights were cooler, and the days shorter. She could sense the lackadaisical pace of summer giving way to a general sharpness of purpose among Mayenne Bay's people. On Tuesday after Labor Day, the town would revert to off-season life.

She filled her lungs with the breeze flowing through her kitchen window and turned to Meilin and Guy, both up to their elbows in hors d'oeuvres preparations for the art club meeting.

"I'm hoping next summer will be far less theatrical with Monique gone and the painting mystery solved."

"Amen to that," agreed Meilin, "But the curtain hasn't dropped yet. The restored paintings are to come in early October."

"And don't forget the bandit is still at his game, and the gnome vandal is still at large," Guy said.

"They're being overshadowed right now by the big story of Jack Wayne, our not-so-trustworthy town manager.

301

He's under investigation for backdoor dealings with Leroy Hood," Meilin told them.

"What?" Guy and Claire responded in unison.

"Sandra disclosed the whole thing at this week's chamber meeting. Leroy has vanished as feared and has taken with him most of the project money. Jack is the lead suspect for tipping him off that he was under suspicion."

Guy and Claire gasped.

Ben and Rhonda knocked and entered, followed by the rest of the art club and Peggy, who would announce a formal unveiling of the restored paintings at the library on the first Sunday in October. Gloria, to the group's relief, was not present this evening. She'd taken recently to brooding in solitude at her B&B. It was just as well. They preferred to speculate openly about the restorations without fear of reprisal.

Guy had shifted Claire's living room furniture to allow room to display paintings against one wall. Next to his, Rhonda set her first study of a dog, and next to that, Christy placed an abstract work, for feedback from the group. A knot of artists congregated around the pieces to comment. Ben hung back with Claire to watch Rhonda, whose dark brown eyes widened as she listened.

"She's a good artist," Ben swelled proudly. "Self-taught except for high school classes. She's off to college this week to study art and marine biology. A double major."

Claire waited for the punchline.

"She may not want to date a small-town cop after meeting educated guys on campus with better prospects," Ben fretted, his face entreating contradiction. "I don't have a college degree."

There it was.

"Guy doesn't either, Ben. I graduated with a double major, yet we're together. The difference doesn't have to get in the way." Ben didn't look reassured, so Claire added.

"There's nothing inferior about being a cop in any town. If your relationship doesn't last, it won't be because of your profession or your wealth or a college degree. Not with Rhonda. She's made of better stuff."

Ben listened with eyes trained on Rhonda. Claire didn't miss the gratification on his face when the circle of artists broke up and Rhonda made her way directly to him.

The meeting ended early so everyone's attention could be turned to preparations for Mayenne Bay's annual Labor Day weekend Bands-by-the-Bay festival, scheduled to begin at ten o'clock the next morning at the waterfront park.

Ben had the unpopular dawn patrol on Saturday morning, an assignment that traditionally went to the town-force rookie. Starting at the first shard of sunlight, he began circling the festival grounds, inspecting exhibits and talking to volunteers and vendors as they prepared for the formal opening. He would have judged this a big undertaking for a lone cop had it not been that the festival was historically uneventful. He found nothing amiss among the food venues that lined the wharf. The Wharf Café's outdoor buffet. Mainsail Wine and Cheese's tasting table. The Grace family's grilled, grass-fed burger stand. The French Club's crêpes and espresso food truck. All was copacetic, too, at the small tent sponsored by the Mayenne Bay Historical Society to display the Wabanaki artifacts recently uncovered at the factory site.

It wasn't until Ben reached the Maine-made products canopy that trouble found him. Several vendors approached with complaints that products had disappeared from their exhibit tables. Just as he reached the tent entrance, he was flagged down by Sally Eaton.

"Officer Tripp!" she called and stopped, panting, having run over from the bandshell. "That masked kid just grabbed the mayor's speech off the podium. He bolted down the park path toward the wharf."

Ben's head jerked toward the stage where Mayor Edgecomb stood scribbling on a brown paper bag words enough to inaugurate the festival. The kid was gone. He looked at his watch and sighed. It was five minutes before ten.

"Sorry, Sally, but there's nothing I can do to help the mayor in time before the opening. She'll have to extemporize. Please apologize for me. I'm dealing here," he motioned to the tent as he spoke, "with missing merchandise. I'm the only one on duty right now. I guess they thought it would be a slow shift." He gave her an apologetic half smile and turned back to the tent.

"Several small baskets I hung on this rack are missing," claimed the purveyor of Wabanacki goods.

"I'm down two small bowls, Officer," complained the woodworker who stood up from searching a pile of boxes to be sure he hadn't overlooked them. "They're not here. I swear I placed them right there on the table corner."

"Someone took the name sign from my stall," the jewelry-maker at the next booth told him, "and I found this pot on my work table."

"Does this scarf belong to anyone?" called a vendor from the book exhibit featuring Maine authors.

To gain everyone's attention, Ben grabbed a stool, hopped onto it and whistled shrilly. He winced guiltily when he heard the mayor's stutter into the mic but was pleased he succeeded to quiet the general hum inside the tent.

"Everyone. Raise your hand if you have something missing or something that isn't yours."

Every hand went up. Ben dropped his head and chuckled. This kind of benign trickery had to be the work of the masked urchin.

"One at a time starting here," instructed Ben, eyeing them soberly and pointing to the first stall on his left, "tell me your situation."

One by one, items were named or held up, identified and returned to the proper owner. Within the span of ten minutes, everything was restored to its proper place, and the vendors were at peace again. Ben went on his way to resume his patrol, only to be accosted by a very agitated mayor.

"Officer Tripp!"

"Mayor, I'm really sorry about your speech." He gestured toward the tent. "I…"

"Forget the speech!" Sandra cut him off. "Look!" She pointed toward her waterfront property. "They're parking on my lawn! Why are they parking on my lawn? Get them off my lawn!"

Her shrill voice struck his ears more like a shriek than a command, but he interpreted her words as the latter. Ben broke into a run and headed toward Sandra's place on The Point at the far eastern end of the park. Like everyone else in town, he was acutely aware that the mayor's home was her pride and joy. The last thing he needed was to have her yard ravaged on his watch.

When he reached her driveway, he found, on the edge of the property, a store-bought "PARKING" sign with an arrow that pointed to the mayor's lawn. The word "FREE" was handwritten in thick, black letters across the top. Shaking his head, Ben quickly pulled up the sign and laid it face down on the ground, then ran over to intercept exiting visitors and exhort them to return to their cars and park elsewhere. He stayed until the last was gone, then surveyed the lawn. The ground was hard after the recent succession of hot, sunny days. The vehicles had done no lasting damage. He radioed the incident to dispatch to inform Chief Manning, hoping to beat the mayor to the punch. Ben's shoulders relaxed in the knowledge he'd arrived in time for his boss to save face. So much about keeping the peace involved politics.

Things remained quiet for the next hour, except for

the mounting chatter of festival-goers and the sometimes off-key, amateur music coming from the stage. The professional bands couldn't begin soon enough, in Ben's opinion, but he smiled and clapped at the underachievers nonetheless. He was soon joined by Rhonda, who patrolled with him for the brief interval before the face-painting table, sponsored by Creative Agenda, opened at noon.

Ben's radio buzzed. The dispatcher directed him to the home of Jack Wayne, town manager in disgrace, whose prominent house was located near the center of town.

"Strangers keep ringing his doorbell," the dispatcher reported.

Ben bade a reluctant good-bye to Rhonda and made his way up Main Street, working to shove the recent accusations against Jack aside. *Innocent until proven guilty*, he reminded himself as he chugged along. He arrived to find the chamber of commerce visitors' center sign planted at the end of the sidewalk leading to Jack's house, with its arrow pointed to the front door. Several tourists were even now walking away from his house with confused looks on their faces.

"It's probably that masked kid again, Ben. You've got to stop him," fumed Jack.

"I'm sure working on it, sir," Ben replied calmly.

He picked up the sign and started toward Main Street to return it to the chamber office veranda, his mind awhirl with what little he knew about the bandit after a full summer of his escapades. Business owners had borne gamely with the kid's antics without discerning any remarkable characteristics except stature and speed. Each time the rascal struck, Ben had followed up and attempted to get a description—a lock of hair, eye color, skin color—anything—but the reports were useless. There was consensus about the runner's remarkable agility and speed and his clothing, right down to his shoes. Other observations varied to such a degree to be of absolutely no use. Ben himself had discerned nothing more distinguishable than shoulders slightly broader than hips which, for an early adolescent, was close to universal. He had to hand it to the quick and clever bandit whose disguise was stumping them all.

He found the complaints more annoying than the pranks themselves and wondered if his complacency was due to his age, much closer to the youthful rebel than most in the business community. Would he, one day, forget what it was like to be a bored kid in the summertime? After all, no real harm had been done. And when school started in just a few more days, the kid would move on. Ben was savvy enough, however, to keep these musings private. At least no one had threatened to press charges if the kid was found.

No sooner had he restored the visitors' center sign to its rightful position than he was accosted by Vicky, owner of the lingerie store on the corner of Crest and Main.

"You've got to help me!" she shrieked, panting from the distance she had run. "They're swinging from the fire hydrants!"

She turned and immediately started jogging back to her store. Ben darted after her and kept pace.

"Who is?"

"Not who, what!" she yelled. "I was in the back room when that masked monster ran in and right out again. I only caught the back of him and all the colors." She paused to draw breath. "They're everywhere! On the hydrants!"

"What is?"

"BRAS!" she screeched in exasperation. "He grabbed a bunch from the rack— seven to be exact—the really expensive ones."

She stopped to point to the intersection of Main and Crest Streets, where a hot pink brassiere was flapping in the wind from a bright red hydrant on the corner. Ben looked down at the sidewalk to suppress the guffaw struggling to burst from his throat. He schooled his face into the most official expression he could muster before looking again into Vicky's.

"Right. I'll help you retrieve them."

"I need you to do it," she answered hotly. "I have no one else to watch the store."

Ben groaned and jogged over to the appointed hydrant with the bright pink bra. It was lace, no less, with huge underwires for very large, well…Ben thought it best not to focus on that just now. The color of his face almost matched the brassiere as he slid it off the hydrant before the mirthful looks of passers-by. Once he had the bra in hand, he tried to stuff it into his pants pocket. Between the padding and the underwires, it wouldn't fit. Swearing under his breath, he rolled it up, shoved it under his arm and kept moving up and down streets from hydrant to hydrant, trying to reach the end of this mortifying process in the quickest manner possible. Pink. Red. Yellow. There are yellow bras? Black. Tan. White.

By this time, Ben was unsure if the colorful lace bulging from his armpit didn't look worse than just giving the bras their own way in the wind. A pedestrian shaking with laughter directed him to the fire station itself where Ben retrieved the last of the seven. Lavender. Winded and overheated, he delivered all seven bras back to the lingerie store, hoping the masked trickster was done for the day. He'd been run ragged this morning and, despite his predisposition to laugh off the pranks, had enough.

Mercifully, his watch told him his patrol duty was over. He headed for the Main Street Coffee Shop where the station had pre-arranged for officers to meet for shift changes. From a block away, he could see his fellow officer leaning against the brick wall outside and leisurely sipping her coffee in expectation of his arrival and a pleasant afternoon ramble. He would quickly disabuse her of that notion. After relaying the events of the morning to his incredulous replacement, Ben formally passed the festival patrol baton, grabbed a large coffee for himself and headed off to Rhonda at the face-painting table.

While he walked, he mentally processed the events of the morning. In the course of seven hours on duty, he'd done no real policing. Instead, he'd rectified a succession of practical jokes. The vendors' tent. The parking debacle. The visitors' sign. And seven bras. He reviewed the sequence of events, and his pace slowed to a full stop. Was the bandit really so fast he could race from the podium to the mayor's lawn to the vendors' tent to the festival stage, then to the town manager's house and the lingerie store, not to mention six fire hydrants and the fire station? Was that string of capers humanly possible given the time span, even allowing for the kid's speed? Ben would ponder this when he was next on duty. For now, he set his sights on the lovely Rhonda.

He cut through the alley between the town office and the chamber of commerce where he caught a glimpse of someone behind the chamber building. He guessed it was the devilish sprinter with another trick to stump the afternoon watch—nothing major, but worth checking out. He reached for his radio and discreetly peered around the back corner of the brick wall. There he saw Ellie Brown, hair askew, eyes wild and face suffused with obscene satisfaction, heave two smashed garden gnomes into the chamber's dumpster.

35

The Unveiling

As it did every September after the Bands-by-the-Bay festival, Mayenne Bay settled down, aside from fall cleanup and autumn leaf-peepers. Prankster aside, the festival had been a resounding success. Even the mayor rallied enough, after her on-the-fly welcome speech and the parking fiasco, to declare it so.

No post-season event was more eagerly awaited than Peggy's October unveiling. It had taken practiced skills of persuasion to convince a disagreeable Gloria and, more easily, Nicky and Maddy, to allow her to receive delivery of the restored paintings directly at the library. She closed the library to regular patrons at two o'clock to get ready for the reception at three. While Aaron Cline unpacked the canvases, Peggy readied two table easels, loaned by Creative Agenda, on the checkout counter, each flanking a conspicuously colorful donation box. Aaron set the paintings on the easels, then covered each with a white sheet.

By the time Peggy swung the doors open again, a line had already formed. At just a few minutes past three, the library was filled with the curious—art club members, enthusiasts, town dignitaries, business owners and interested

311

citizens. A *Contemporary Maine* magazine reporter wound his way through the throng and stopped here and there to question guests and capture moments with his camera.

Maddy, Georgia and Nicky had brought lemonade, hot chocolate and an array of homemade confections and positioned themselves behind the food table to serve. From her color and radiant smile, it was clear Nicky was highly animated. Gone were the heavy lipstick, seductive dress and haughty attitude of Monique LaBelle. Gone were the sad face and defeated posture of Leroy's tormented companion. She bore none of the shame or embarrassment displayed when she had confessed her crimes all over town. Nicky looked genuinely happy and downright pretty in blue jeans and a simple, green sweater, her red hair French-braided down her back.

"Peggy's really outdone herself," Claire said to Guy, "orchestrating this." She waved her hands in a circle to indicate the whole arrangement. "From every possible angle, things will be brought to closure today. Nicky's comeback from Monique LaBelle and Gloria's acceptance of the restored painting will be witnessed…not by the entire public, but by enough, and especially by those more directly concerned." She turned to face the refreshment table. "Just look at Nicky, right in the thick of it. She and Maddy have gone through quite an ordeal to make things right. They both deserve a moment in the sun for the right reasons."

"They do," Guy agreed.

Claire felt a hand on her shoulder and swung around.

"Morrie!" She hugged him. "We haven't seen you for some time."

"Sorry about that. I've been busy with lesson plans and getting oriented. I've been hired full-time to teach math at the middle school." Claire hugged him again. Guy offered a handshake. While the two men pumped each other's arms,

Morrie continued, "The offer was so sudden and so late, I had to drop everything else. It's like I've been born again. And now this." He gestured toward the two easels. "An end to the whole sad saga. And Nicky has come so far. She's quite dear to me now, you know. I visited her and Maddy at their home place. That Maddy is a good woman."

Claire studied Morrie through this long speech. There was no residue of the wornout man who'd wandered the town like a vagabond. His health was restored. His face was alight with interest and vitality. He even sported another brand-new cardigan.

"Has Nicky decided what she's going to do now?" Claire asked.

"Yes. She's got two jobs, one in retail, the other waiting tables. After she pays her aunt and grandmother back, she wants to return to school for her college degree—a double major in art and mathematics. She's always been strong academically but suppressed all of that around Leroy. He wasn't interested in her intellect."

Morrie ended with a frown.

"No kidding," Guy snorted with a frown of his own.

"I imagine you played no small role in her choice of math," said Claire.

Morrie shrugged.

"I'm not sure I influenced her at all, except with a little forgiveness and support. What you see now is the Nicky that was always there, according to Maddy. She just needed to have her eyes opened. Her biggest asset is Aunt Maddy, hands down, and after that her grandmother, Georgia Wilson."

He politely excused himself and made his way over to the table to serve alongside the women.

John-Pierre, having skulked for a while in the new art section, now noiselessly appeared at Claire's side like a phantom, just as he'd done at the coffee bar. She caught his movement from the corner of her eye.

"So glad you made it, John."

His eyes flitted toward the covered easels, then over at Nicky. Claire perceived the pale pink of self-consciousness and understood the source, a mixture of guilt over his theft of the "Lupines" and vexation over the alteration in the woman he had once admired. She wondered what he made of the down-to-earth Nicky, after once being so smitten with her over-the-top alter-ego, but suppressed an itching compulsion to ask him.

At precisely four o'clock, the hum of conversation ended abruptly with the arrival of Gloria. Once a respected member of the business and art communities, her recent hypersensitivity and demanding nature had conspired to diminish her standing. She hadn't a single sympathizer in the room. She planted herself in silence in front of the unveiled paintings, arms folded across her chest, eyes staring straight ahead.

"She's positively a wet blanket," Guy growled in a low tone only Claire could hear. "That stare reminds me of Caroline Bristolwaite."

"I do see the resemblance. Let's hope she returns to herself when all this is over."

Guy grunted his doubt.

Peggy appeared at Gloria's side and called for everyone's attention.

"Welcome, everyone," she called. "I'm going to start with a history for those who don't have the whole story as to why we're here."

All eyes in the room automatically turned to Nicky, who now faced a Mayenne Bay crowd for the first time since her deceit had come publicly to light. She stood her ground unflinchingly, back straight and chin up. Maddy, Georgia and Morrie inched closer to her in support.

"As you know," Peggy continued, "these two paintings, the 'Lupines' and the 'Beach Roses', were presented by Monique LaBelle, whom we now know affectionately as Nicky Littlefield, for exhibition at the Mayenne Bay Art Show this summer." Peggy related the entire narrative blow by blow, putting the rehabilitated Nicky in as favorable a light as possible. "That brings us to the present day. Any questions?"

"Peggy is remarkable," Claire whispered into Guy's ear. "First, she recasts Nicky. And now, Gloria will have to declare her judgment in front of everyone."

"Even under public pressure, Gloria's a wild card," Guy whispered back.

"As there are no questions," Peggy began afresh, "let me introduce to you our special guest, Aaron Cline, the professional art conservator who restored these two canvases."

There was a smattering of applause, and necks craned for a glimpse of the person whose rare skills had been sought to set things right. Aaron, a short, balding man with thick glasses, dressed in tan slacks, a blue sweater and well-worn Docker loafers, stepped forward and uttered his thanks to Peggy. He then proceeded to give an overview of the art restoration process, a detailed description of the methods he used and the results of his examination of the two canvases. There were no surprises. Aaron had removed Monique LaBelle's alterations and cleaned the effects of aging, as Guy had predicted. When Aaron finished, he sidestepped to allow Peggy to take over again.

She planted herself next to the first easel.

"Louis! Robert!" she called to the Rainwater men. "I need persons far taller than me to lift the covers without knocking the easels down."

They moved in to assist.

"First, the 'Lupines'," Peggy announced, and the

two men lifted the cover. The audience gasped audibly and began to chatter. If the colors had been striking before, they paled next to the brilliance of the restored canvas.

"Wow," Guy and Claire exclaimed together.

"Yeah," John-Pierre agreed, eyes wide.

"It's not at all the same," Gloria exclaimed loudly, palms rising to her cheeks.

A strained silence choked all conversation as Gloria moved in to study the painting up close, palms now pressed together against her lips. Maddy's nerves, Claire judged from her flexing jaw, were on high alert at this moment of truth. Nicky looked down and gripped the table.

"No, ma'am," Aaron quickly stepped toward Gloria to explain, his voice incredulous and almost defensive. "There was no way it could be…"

"It's better!" Gloria declared, cutting him off and clapping her hands.

So it had already appeared to the general crowd, but they'd held their collective breath for Gloria's response. At the sight of the delight on her face, a wave of relief rolled over the room. Maddy's posture relaxed. Nicky smiled. Georgia looked heavenward. The primary mission had been accomplished.

"And now, the 'Beach Roses'," Peggy announced and signaled to Louis and Robert to undrape the second canvas. This time, Nicky and Morrie made their way to the front of the room with Maddy and Georgia close behind.

"Wow!" Guy and Claire said again, louder this time.

John-Pierre just stared.

"Aaron, you are a magician," Meilin congratulated him as the other viewers, who felt it safe to step in more closely now that Gloria had been mollified, moved toward the easels.

"If you want to compliment anyone," Aaron answered, "compliment the original artist. These are two fine pieces by the same person, it turns out."

He backed away to allow the crowd to appreciate them. Everyone fell silent at his last words.

"Who was it?" ask Morrie and Nicky at the same time, each leaning in to read the script barely visible on the canvases.

"Constance Cochrane," answered Aaron.

"Constance Cochrane!" echoed Morrie. "I don't believe it!" He was so excited, his body shook. "This is the artist who befriended my grandfather in the Navy and introduced him to art. My grandfather followed her throughout his lifetime and had a few of her paintings."

While Morrie caught his breath, Aaron stepped in.

"This gentleman is correct. Once I discovered her name on the canvas, I did a little research. Constance Cochrane was in the Navy employed to do design work. Later, she was a member of The Philadelphia Ten, a group of female impressionist painters from Pennsylvania who exhibited all over the country. It's hard to find images online or exhibits of her original work. I'd wager much of it is in private collections. She painted still-lifes and, in Maine, land and seascapes, especially on Monhegan Island. Look at the confidence of her broad brushstrokes and bold colors."

"An early female impressionist on Monhegan Island," Rhonda repeated and approached the paintings in wonder, Ben in her wake.

"Painters came from all over the world to paint on Monhegan, men and women alike," sounded the voice of Georgia Wilson from behind. "They still do. And they often attended gatherings at the Port Clyde House. It's mine now, and I plan to resurrect that tradition. What a wonderful discovery you've made, Mr. Cline."

As the crowd mulled over this new information, Georgia approached Claire.

"How lovely to see you again." She gestured to Guy.

"And this is the artist who sketched us throughout breakfast that morning, if I'm not mistaken."

Guy colored. Claire made introductions.

"I'm Nicky's grandmother. My mother was the art enthusiast who hosted artists at Port Clyde. Who knows? Maybe these two Cochrane paintings were among them. I've seen your work, Guy. It's wonderful. I hoped, once I've got the house resettled, you'd agree to an early exhibit."

Guy stammered words of acceptance and thanks.

The shrill voice of Gloria pierced the room and again shut down all conversation.

"Am I to understand that this artist…Cochrane…is famous? So, this painting may be worth more than I paid for it?" she stopped and waited expectantly for a reply from Aaron.

"Yes, ma'am, I would venture it's worth significantly more now that it's been cleaned and identified. You have, as well, what appears to be the original frame. The initials 'ELC' hand-carved on the back, stand for 'Elizabeth Lull Cochrane', the artist's mother, who made and gilded frames for her."

"Gilded, not just painted gold?" she asked and leaned in with greater interest.

"Yes," confirmed Aaron, speaking to Gloria as well as Nicky, Maddy and Georgia. "Hang onto the frames. They add value."

Gloria's eyes flicked to Guy, who shrugged his shoulders and flashed back an "I tried to tell you" face.

Roxie moved in to inspect them.

"Good thing you held off on the frame replacement, Gloria."

"Oh, my, yes," agreed Aaron. "The value is enhanced when the painting is in an original frame of such distinction."

Gloria said nothing more.

ARTIFICE

"Finally, something has left Gloria bereft of speech," Meilin said discreetly from behind Claire and Guy. The three looked down and sniggered.

36

We Have Time

"Great Grandma Catherine would be so pleased to see the paintings now," Nicky said, drawing closer to her aunt and grandmother. Tears filled her eyes and theirs.

Morrie stood with them as transfixed by the two Cochrane paintings as he had been when in their former state.

"My grandfather was a real collector," he gushed. "He had works by a number of impressionists. The 'Blueberry Blossoms' painting I so loved—the one I played in front of in grandfather's living room—was painted by Constance. I was drawn to these two paintings at the art show but never guessed that, underneath, they were actually the work of the same artist."

"It's too bad," sympathized Nicky, "that you couldn't have the blueberry painting when he passed away."

Morrie shook his head.

"I've had a lot of time to think about that, Nicky. I would have lost it in the later bankruptcy, which would have made me even sadder. I'm truly sorry you've lost the 'Lupines'."

Everyone pitched in to help Peggy clean up.

"You did a good thing here, Peggy," Claire told her

321

as they folded the sheets together. "Thoughtful on so many levels."

"Nice someone noticed. Mayenne Bay needs a lot of things. Infighting isn't one of them."

While the others worked, Gloria buttonholed Aaron and pulled him deep into the new art section to confer privately. When the two re-emerged, Gloria was full of her own plans and the revaluation of the painting. She overlooked that she had paid so little to gain possession of this treasure and disregarded the fact that its removal would constitute a final and unwanted farewell for Nicky and her family. Aaron was far more sympathetic and excused himself to the restroom to allow them a few minutes more to come to grips with their loss and to snap some photos of the refinished work.

"It's depressing seeing the 'Lupines' go to someone outside the family," Nicky whispered to her aunt and grandmother. "I'm so very sorry."

Maddy, eyes wet, pulled Nicky to her and kissed her on the cheek. Georgia gently rubbed the young woman's back.

"We're just so glad we have our own Nicky back," Georgia said. "That's far more important."

When Aaron returned, they watched impotently as the painting was prepared for removal.

"Aaron," Gloria offered loudly, "I'll give you a free room tonight at the B&B if you'll stay and go over this with me in detail." She cast him a winning look. "Supper included."

"So, she can be charming when she wants to," Claire observed in Guy's ear.

But Gloria's charm didn't extend beyond the art restorer. Without another word, she loaded her prize into her car. Nicky watched them pull away, bent her head and cried.

Morrie moved over to comfort her.

"Pretty out of character for Gloria to offer a free room and meal," observed Meilin.

"Her world just changed," said Guy. "In the span of a month, she's gone from owning a doctored, old canvas in a crappy frame to a famous work in the original frame valued far greater than she can believe."

"But to leave without a word to Nicky, Maddy or Georgia about their loss or even a nod to you, Guy, Meilin or me who made the discovery possible…" Claire's voice drifted off.

"I overheard part of her conversation with Aaron," Guy told them. "It was all about the painting's value and how to preserve and insure it. If you're waiting for Gloria to think about others, you could wait a long time."

No one disputed this statement.

They all turned again to the transformed "Beach Roses" painting where Morrie stood in awe, his eyes wistful. Nicky pulled her aunt and grandmother aside for a private consultation, then stepped forward to address Peggy.

"Peggy, would you accept a loan of the 'Beach Roses' painting for the library? You've done so much for me. The whole town has. You could keep it until I finish college and have a place of my own to display it."

"I second that offer," Maddy said, beaming at her niece. "Mayenne Bay has been so generous in its forgiveness. This is a wonderful gesture of gratitude, Nicky."

Georgia's face also lit with approval.

"I was especially thinking of Morrie," Nicky explained tenderly. "He'll be able to visit the painting here whenever he wants. And I'll have two reasons, Morrie—you and the 'Beach Roses'—to visit Mayenne Bay."

"Thank you," choked the little man.

Everyone hung around for the next twenty minutes while Roxie helped Peggy hang the painting behind the checkout counter. Meilin snapped a shot of Nicky and Peggy next to this new addition and shared it to Peggy's phone.

"For the *Contemporary Maine* reporter," she explained.

The scandal of the town's first art show, after generating so much consternation, was finally put to rest. Between Peggy's open report at the unveiling and the *Contemporary Maine* article, even the most determined critics were finally stifled. In place of the old scuttlebutt rose a newfound buzz about art—Maine art, in general, and Mayenne Bay's embrace of it, in particular. Only Gloria persisted in keeping the old story alive, complaining about Nicky's deception and the additional cost of insurance and security measures at the B&B. She found few listeners.

After the unveiling, on Sunday morning, October asserted itself with a chill that called for long pants and hooded sweatshirts. Guy and Claire walked, hand in hand, toward the wharf. Damp leaves blew across their path and stuck to their shoes. Goldenrod and asters drooped, but stalwart and colorful mums dotted front yards and flower boxes.

"Mind going to the Fish House for breakfast?" Guy had asked Claire when they had awakened at her place. His voice had cracked with the question.

"Let's try for our favorite booth."

Celeste was instantly at their side with tea and coffee, perky as ever, filling their ears with pleasant chatter. They ordered, and as they sipped their hot drinks, spied Ben and Rhonda eating quietly at a corner table in the back.

"Rhonda came back from school for the weekend again," Claire observed. "Ben looks happy to see her, don't you think?"

Guy looked over distractedly.

"Yeah, I guess," he answered vaguely.

When his blue eyes returned to Claire, they burned with such intensity, it startled her. She swallowed.

"Can we set other people aside this morning and have one of those private breaks we talked about?" Guy requested gently.

She nodded her consent, unsure where this was going.

"How do you think things are going between us?"

She shifted in her seat. Guy's question was uncharacteristically forthright, and his regard was uncomfortably penetrating.

"You see your influence," he joked at her unease. "Under your tutelage, the slug has been through boot camp, and my tongue has become painfully direct."

They were interrupted at this poignant moment by Meilin and Roxie, who entered the Fish House arm in arm. They stopped at Guy and Claire's booth before heading for a back table. Claire waited until they were out of earshot before returning to Guy's question.

"I'm happy," she answered, then sucked in her breath. "Why are you asking? Aren't you?"

She sat stiffly awaiting the verdict.

"Extremely."

Claire didn't fully exhale. She was waiting for the other shoe.

"We spend a lot of time together—outings, meals, overnights," Guy said, "but I can't help wishing for more."

He watched her face while she processed his meaning.

"You mean...move in together?"

"Exactly," he said, reaching for her hand. "You set the thought in motion, you know, when you said you couldn't live with my sloppiness. 'Live with', you said. I wasn't sure what made you choose those words, but they spurred me to change my habits, if it meant winning you.

There isn't anyone else for me, Claire, but you. Will you consider it?"

"I…yes…well, maybe," she faltered and squirmed. "But, Guy, there are things you don't know about me."

"I knew you'd say that," he told her, squeezing her hand.

"I mean…" She withdrew her hand so she could gesture when she spoke. "I wouldn't be easy to live with. I'm über-clean, very fussy—even obsessed about some things. Sometimes I change my clothes four times before deciding."

"Only four?" he laughed. "Claire, these aren't deal breakers for me. If you're willing to chance it, so am I."

She exhaled a long breath and gripped the table as she forced the next morsel of honesty from her mouth.

"Not until you meet my mother, plus whoever else is living in her house at the moment, and my father."

He watched the waves of emotion pass across her face. Nothing seemed to distress her more than mention of the Munro family and, especially, her mother. He had anticipated this hesitation. He understood Claire's need to be impeccably honest about her past and her relations before she could consider a long-term commitment.

"We'll start with your family, then."

He covered her hands in his.

"That's easy for you to say. Your family is like family-style dining, you know, 'please pass the peas', 'may I have the salt?'. Mine is more like a middle-school cafeteria food fight. My mother alone is an emotional cyclone."

Guy leaned forward.

"Claire, you can't change where you came from. Anyway, nothing I learn will make one bit of difference as far as my wish to be with you, so we might as well get cracking."

She looked doubtful, but, to Guy's surprise, didn't raise further argument.

After breakfast, they walked along the waterside, hoods up against the cool sea air, sipping their takeout drinks, then sat down on a sunny park bench overlooking the blue-gray water. Guy said no more about his proposal, nor would he. He would wait until Claire raised the subject again, however long that took.

Behind them, a group of adolescents in hoodies and sweatpants chatted noisily around a picnic table. Two boys rose and began to dribble a soccer ball. The rest of the group jumped up to join in. A skinny blonde girl held back momentarily to scratch her knee, then hopped up and flew past the other players like a brisk wind.

Claire drew a sharp breath.

"That blond girl. I wonder if…"

She stopped short when she saw Ben, in full uniform, making his way toward the soccer practice.

"Hey, kids," he called out, "Can I have a minute?"

They stopped playing and pulled into a tight, wide-eyed group. Ben ran his eyes over each and every one. Guy and Claire did the same.

"Guy!" Claire said under her breath. "Most of those kids are wearing the same running shoes as the masked bandit. And remember that day the bandit fell onto his right knee? That's the knee the blonde girl keeps scratching. Look at their faces. They all know something."

"Have a seat," they heard Ben say with a gesture toward the picnic table.

"Looks like Ben has nailed the bandit," Guy said.

"Bandits, plural, you mean," whispered Claire.

They didn't need to hear Ben's words. The guilty stillness that overcame the youngsters told them all they needed to know. None made eye contact as Ben spoke. Some nervously squeezed and popped their empty water bottles. The gig was clearly up. There would be no more masked bandit escapades in Mayenne Bay.

Claire sat back after this small-town-style resolution to a pesky problem. She looked all around her at the harbor, the park and the town, so perfectly imperfect. She had entrusted her future to this place. Guy was now asking for the same trust. That was the decision that lay before her.

Her attention was drawn by a small figure walking down the pathway and heading directly toward their bench.

"Here comes Meilin," Claire said, "by herself. I wonder what happened to Roxie."

She twisted around but didn't see the framemaker anywhere. Claire had a premonition of what was coming. When Meilin finally reached them, unmistakably upset, Claire cast Guy a questioning look.

He stood up.

"Sorry to run, Meilin, but I've got to get started painting." He pecked Claire's cheek and moved away with a wave. "I'll be back a little later with my gear."

There was a time when Guy would have resented this interruption. Not now. From behind Meilin, his blue eyes spoke to Claire. *Take care of our friend. It's who you are. We have time.* And turning away, he left Claire to do what she did best.

Epilogue:

Asher Dunleavy

Behind door number 14 of a seedy New Hampshire motel, Asher Dunleavy stretched across the lumpy, double bed binge-watching reruns of The Waltons TV series on his tablet. Internet, it seemed, was the one upgrade the motel manager had deemed worthy of his limited dollars. He certainly hadn't pumped them into the furnishings.

Asher's overgrown red hair clung to his head thanks to his West Virginia University ball cap, which now hung from the back of the only chair in the room. He had kicked off his muddy boots at the door and lounged in his flannel shirt and faded jeans. They were comfortable enough as he sipped coffee and picked at the take-out breakfast from the diner just down the road.

He zeroed in on "Daddy", John Walton, Sr., one of TV's all-time greatest fathers, played in the series by Ralph Waite. Industrious, good-natured and wise, Daddy told it straight. He could be brash but he would do anything to protect his family. Hour after hour, Asher minutely observed

Daddy, his morality, accent, expressions and body language. Occasionally, Asher would pause the show and position himself in front of the motel mirror to mimic what he'd seen.

Over a year ago, Asher had read Earl Hamner Jr.'s book, *Spencer's Mountain* and watched the 1963 film of the same name. Then, he'd turned to the TV series based on Hamner's tale and taken careful notes. He'd studied Appalachia from online sources, books and documentaries. At the time, "Daddy" had been only a fallback, a backdoor plan…just in case, but Asher's bags had been prepped against the off chance he would need them in a hurry. Clothes, hair color, IDs, cash, plan of escape—all of it had been stashed away as insurance.

And the moment for Asher Dunleavy to take his place in the world had come sooner than he'd expected. Damn that Rodriguez couple. That had been a rare stroke of bad luck. Asher Dunleavy, formerly Leroy Hood and Gabe Williams before that, had slipped out of Mayenne Bay just in time. If it hadn't been for Sally Eaton's blind puppy love, so assiduously cultivated by him in secret all summer, he wouldn't have received warning of the threat in time.

Asher paused *The Waltons* episode and clicked on a country music station for a bit of variety in his immersion program. He stood up, stretched and paced the room. After a few advertisements, Gary Allan came on singing "No Regrets". Asher chuckled. He had no regrets over Mayenne Bay. Leroy Hood had been a splendid character, confident and commanding—his best so far. His take from the scam was copious: all the project proceeds—the investment money, the deposits on future condos and even some early incentive payments toward the future marina. He'd left a little money behind in his hasty retreat. Nothing for faithful Sally or the greedy Jack Wayne. Asher reached over to pull a wad of cash from under his pillow. He flipped through the bills like a deck of cards, inhaling their aroma while he hummed to the song.

Among the perks of playing the dashing Leroy had been the surfeit of female attention. Scaring up women had been a cinch—too easy, in fact—and he had had to discipline himself not to partake of every single opportunity. He'd enjoyed the convenience of that little piece, Monique, until her artful little masquerade had started to unravel and she'd become more trouble than she was worth. He grunted his satisfaction. Even she had contributed a little cash to his take.

Asher disciplined himself to analyze his work with a ruthlessly critical eye. He placed a premium on not getting sloppy. In the case of Leroy, he was more fastidious in his study than usual. It irked him that he didn't know how or when the Rodríguezes had identified him. Leroy and the Maine condo complex had been a far enough cry from Gabe Williams and Texas roofing, and he'd allowed ample time between the two. Day after day since he'd arrived at this motel, Asher had worked a timeline from memory, photos and news clips to discern what the couple had seen, when and how. He had to know.

His success and his escape equally thrilled Asher to the bone. Hadn't he pegged Mayenne Bay as provincial from the get-go? The hungry, gullible town council. The weak and greedy town manager. The scrawny, hard-up mayor. The self-serving property owners. The malleable Sally, his insurance policy. He laughed to himself. The game had been as exhilarating then as the transformation was now, in his book. God, he was good. His agility, getting in, then getting out unscathed, his rapid change of character—all of it. Not everyone could play the game.

Asher allowed himself a few more minutes to bask in the power and sheer arousal he felt over Leroy's success, then bid a final farewell to Leroy Hood. He had to be careful not to get lost in celebration in the periods between schemes. He shifted back to the newly minted Asher Dunleavy, who needed a foolproof path to acceptance in country society. In Texas, football had been Gabe's ticket in. He'd learned the game well and memorized the teams and stats. In Maine, it had been his promise of economic salvation. In Appalachia, music would afford him entry into the world of the rustic clod he was working to emulate.

Asher Dunleavy would be a gentle hayseed, not a typical, rough-and-tumble red neck. The distinction would require greater concentration, more patience and an aura of humility, but this was the kind of challenge that excited Asher. He would be Daddy—the nice guy with the soft drawl, the sweetheart, the diamond in the rough, the pillar. Women loved that crap. And who was to say he couldn't nail as much skirt being a country bumpkin as a real estate developer?

Asher laughed under his breath. His adaptability was his strength. He could just as easily roar into town in a beat-up Ford pickup as roll in elegantly behind the wheel of a Mercedes. Somewhere in Appalachia—he hadn't decided exactly where he would land yet—lay another unsuspecting town where he would blend in. Then he would devise his plan. From what he was hearing on this country station, there was plenty of money in music and even in saving souls, if it came to it.

Afterward

Constance Cochrane

Constance Cochrane (1888-1962) was a Pennsylvania impressionist painter who exhibited nationally as a member of the Philadelphia 10. She painted on Monhegan Island, Maine. Her old house is still there. As of this writing, the Monhegan Museum of Art and History is in possession of two Cochrane seascapes.

Constance's mother, Elizabeth Lull Cochrane, took up the art of frame making exclusively to frame Ms. Cochrane's paintings. She carved her monogram, ELC, onto the back of each frame she created and also gilded the frames. Her gilding technique was perfected under the tutelage of James Fitzgerald, artist, famed gilder, and their close friend on Monhegan.

The "Beach Roses", "Lupines" and "Blueberry Blossoms" paintings mentioned in this book are fictitious, though Ms. Cochrane was known to paint brilliant flowers. She also painted landscapes. She used broad, bold brush strokes and colors. She did not sign all her work.

A great deal of Ms. Cochrane's work may be in private collections.

Port Clyde House

The Port Clyde House is an invention of the author for this book. Port Clyde itself is a real place, well known as a departure point for visitors headed to and from Monhegan Island. It is also a popular place to paint for artists.

Acknowledgments

Nothing happens in my life without the support of my husband, Peter. He stokes my imagination, critiques my ideas with brutal honesty and serves as my first reader. He is seconded by our daughter, Charity, also a reader and a creative sounding board, who designed this book and cover. Our son, Justin, too, a natural critic and extensive reader, contributed materially to this book.

Thanks to Mitch and Katherine whose candid and sound advice did much to improve this novel.

I am especially grateful to all of the colorful characters who have touched my life and helped me realize how extraordinary people truly are, even those deemed the most ordinary among us.

About the Author

      KIM YESIS is a former business manager with a bachelor's degree in French and a master's degree in Counseling. As a lifelong student of human nature, her mission in writing is to highlight that bit of extra in ordinary people that makes them fascinating and extraordinary. She is the author of **Side by Side Tales from Behind the Canva**s, a memoir and a Maine Literary Award and Indie Book Award finalist, and **Artist in the Allagash**, a wilderness journal. Kim writes from her home in Mid Coast Maine where she lives with her husband and creative partner, fine artist Peter Yesis.